"For what is seen is temporary, but what is unseen is eternal."

2 Corinthians 4:18

"The true mystery of the world is the visible, not the invisible."

The Picture of Dorian Gray by Oscar Wilde

Robert [illegible]

[illegible]

kat heckenbach

SEEKING UNSEEN

Seeking Unseen

Cover design by Newsome Creative

Editors: Diane M. Graham, Robynn Tolbert, Grace Bridges

ISBN: 978-1-927154-29-8

Published by Splashdown Books, New Zealand

http://www.splashdownbooks.com

Prologue

An emaciated figure hovered in the corner of a cold, damp, stone room. His eyes shifted nervously, and a tattered coat clung limply to his bony frame. He concentrated, and prickly heat surged through his veins as a field formed around him. He knew it wasn't necessary to exercise his power in this way, in the solitude of his dark cell.

It was supposed to be impossible.

Empowereds used electricity only for their jail. Current flooded the walls, floors, and ceilings of each and every cell, running just below the surface. The barrier it created drained the prisoners of their powers, including their Talents. It cancelled out their magic.

Not in this case.

The man rubbed his gnarled hands together eagerly, rejoicing in this anomalous fact. He had found the way to tap into knowledge unwanted by everyone around him. He welcomed the power they so shunned. They were afraid.

He would make them more afraid.

Whispered promises filled his ears. Fame and glory would belong to him when he finished his work. The idea of it all made him quiver. He shifted his weight and something crunched under his shoe. He raised his foot, smiled at the glob of guts and exoskeleton, and smeared the remains across the craggy floor.

Life extinguished to make room for the new.

His heart pounded and he sucked a breath through clenched teeth, the acrid air burning his lungs. Nevermore would others scoff at his ideas. No longer would they question his true position. Everyone would see him for who he really was.

And they would cower.

The man paced back and forth, hands trembling. From corner to corner he strode, and then changed rhythm and circled the perimeter of the room. The internal heat intensified, bubbling under his skin, beckoning him to try more. He focused on the field he had created around himself; and a smile of self-satisfaction crept across his face.

The field had fluctuated in a way he'd never experienced before.

In the adjacent cell, a young man slept peacefully, impervious to the dank chill. He had been transformed by knowledge and newfound power as well. Hardened and molded by new experiences. But something separated this man from the other. Something stronger than thick walls and bars of steel.

Tomorrow, he would be set free.

Chapter One

Bookstore Visitors

"Here you are, Mrs. Charleston." Angel handed the leather-bound gardening book to a petite woman, who smiled beneath her purple bonnet. Rosy cheeks poked out, and crinkles appeared around her sparkling green eyes.

Angel had worked at *The Professor's Roost* for six months and had memorized the location of almost every book on every shelf in the bookstore. She didn't *need* to memorize them, of course; her Talent allowed her to locate any book in the world if she chose.

Mrs. Charleston waved to Angel as she stepped through the arched wooden door and merged into the crowd of shoppers. Her bonnet caught the spring breeze, and she threw her hand on top of it to keep it from flying away.

"Angel, can you come help me, please?" Sir Benjamin's muffled voice reached Angel's ears and she turned to find him rifling through a box in the back of the bookshop. His salt-and-pepper hair stuck out in the back as if he'd forgotten to comb it.

"What do you need, Sir B?"

He stood and huffed a sigh. "I need you to Find Niles's hedgehog again. I've searched everywhere." Sir Benjamin brushed some dust from his goatee.

"Why didn't you just ask me in the first place?"

"Sometimes you have to try these things on your own, I suppose. I give up. Besides, it's time for tea."

Sir Benjamin waved his hand, and the silver tea tray lifted from the far table and began its journey toward him. It followed him to his desk and landed on the wooden desktop. Sir Benjamin pushed up the sleeves of his plaid shirt and grabbed a mug from the tray.

Angel concentrated on the little leather hedgehog.

"It's under your desk."

Sir Benjamin bent over and peered between the desk's ornately carved feet. "Oh, of all things!" He summoned the hedgehog out from under the desk and sent it over to Niles, who was batting at Spike's wing with a furry paw. Niles's tabby fur bristled and his undersized wings spread as he pounced on the hedgehog.

The older dragon glared at Niles but did nothing to stop him.

Angel laughed. "He's getting so big, isn't he?"

"I wouldn't have expected him to grow quite so fast, being half cat. The dragon side must be dominant. He certainly acts the way Spike did when he was that age. I guess there was no way to predict with a new species like this. Dr. Damian knew that as well, though, didn't he?"

Angel didn't answer. She'd never had a chance to get to know Dr. Damian, the geneticist who'd rescued Niles as a baby and dubbed the cat-dragon hybrid a Cagon. Dr. Damian was also the man who'd given his life to save both Angel and her cousin, Gregor, even though they had doubted him and accused him of heinous crimes. Angel wished she could thank him for his sacrifice…

The *ding* of the doorbell snapped Angel out of her thoughts. The door swung open and a man in solid navy blue walked stiffly into the bookstore, his perfectly shined shoes squeaking against the floor. His crisp shirt bore the white shoulder stripes of a police officer and a gleaming silver octagon adorned his front shirt pocket.

"Dr. Benjamin Punnet?" He gripped his navy hat in one hand and held something Angel couldn't see in the other.

"Yes, that's me. What can I do ya for?"

Angel stifled a giggle. That phrase always sounded odd coming out of Sir B. Her former foster father used it all the time, but he was country-boy to the bone. The only things country about Sir Benjamin were his cowboy boots and that one phrase.

"Well, sir..." The officer cleared his throat, and his Adam's apple rose and fell, accentuating the long neck that reminded Angel of a turtle. "It seems one of the notebooks you requested fell behind a desk when we gave you the others, and we've only recently found it. Chief Graham asked me to drop it by on my way home." He held out a leather-bound notebook.

Angel's eyes widened. She remembered seeing notebooks like that at the University. The scientists used them for logging their research. Which meant, if it was being brought by an officer, this one had to have belonged to either Dr. Randall or Dr. Damian.

Sir Benjamin took the notebook and flipped it open. "Thank you. I thought the notes stopped rather abruptly."

"I apologize for the oversight," the officer said.

Sir Benjamin lifted his head. "Please tell Grandmaster Graham I said thank you as well. And that after our next match he'll be taking dictation for me again." He chuckled and turned to Angel. "Grandmaster Graham—I could call him Graham-master. How's that for clever?" He winked and turned back to the officer.

The officer cleared his throat, face stoic. "Will do, sir. Good luck in your continuing research." He turned and strode out of the bookshop.

Angel followed Sir Benjamin to his desk, where he sank into his high-back leather chair. She chewed her lip as she peeked over his shoulder at the scratchy writing. Definitely Dr. Randall.

"You never told me you were looking through *his* research notes." The words came out hard, angry, and Angel felt her hand ball into a fist. *If it wasn't for Dr. Randall and his research, Siophra and Gregor would both be here.* She took a step back. "How long have you had them?"

Sir Benjamin turned around in his chair and peered over his glasses at her, then stood. He sighed. "I've had the notes for a couple of months now. I gave thought to getting them right after the investigation closed, but just thinking about what that man did made me so angry. However, watching Niles develop, I realized I need to know more about him. Being a hybrid may have...implications down the road. I thought Dr. Randall's notes may have clues about what to expect."

Angel glanced down at the little tabby-striped Cagon, who was curled up on his green pillow next to the metallic-green Spike on his purple one, the little hedgehog gone missing again.

"So he really is part of that monster's experiments like we thought?"

Sir Benjamin shook his head. "Actually, I didn't find anything to *prove* that Niles is, but I've learned an awful lot about what Dr. Randall was up to. Hybridizing animals in an attempt to fuse different magic together, from what I can see. But I haven't figured out *why*. Much of it makes no sense."

"I don't know how any of it could make sense," Angel said. "He's crazy."

Sir Benjamin nodded. "He's definitely unbalanced. But I want to learn what I can from this." He reached out and touched her forearm, and then returned to his desk.

Angel walked across the room to the overstuffed couch in the front of the store and grabbed a book from the glass coffee table. The pages blurred in front of her eyes, and she set the book down.

Dr. Randall's research wasn't even the worst of it. He'd killed Siophra. And with Siophra gone, Gregor had willingly given his life in order to defeat the madman Dr. Randall had chosen to work with.

She wiped away a tear that made its way to her cheek, hating the anger that lingered. Two years hadn't dulled the loss. Two years without Gregor, who had become not only her best friend but also her family. The only one closer to her before Gregor found her and brought her home was her little foster brother, Zack.

Angel's heart still ached. Would she ever see his strawberry blonde curls again? Feel his small hand in hers?

She breathed deeply and slowly, and fiddled with the locket on her charm bracelet, then carefully opened it. The tiny chip of wood remained in place. Such a small thing to hold so much power—the ability to fulfill any single wish. A wish she had yet to use.

Its silvery grain reminded Angel of the specks in Gregor's eyes. *I know I can't wish him back. He's happier now than ever. He's got both his parents alive and well, and Siophra at his side.* But she would wish it if she could. Maybe even more than having Zack back in her life. Was that why she'd held back on using the magic of the wood?

The chime announced the entrance of another customer, and Angel glanced at the reflective surface of the glass tabletop in front of her. The sight of her tear-streaked face and red eyes made her turn quickly away instead of greeting the customer. Fortunately, she heard Sir Benjamin striding across the room.

"How can I help you, young man?" he said.

Young man?

Angel rubbed her cheeks to even out the flush and inhaled quietly to calm her nerves. After pretending to replace a book on the shelf, she turned to greet the customer—and tensed her jaw to keep it from dropping.

Whoa.

Heat returned to her cheeks all over again.

The "young man" looked a little older than her. Maybe seventeen or eighteen? One forearm rippled as he tapped his fingers against his thigh, and the other was hidden behind his back. He stood at attention, accentuating the broadness of his shoulders beneath a gray t-shirt. A perfect Roman nose and square jaw jutted out from under the brim of a red baseball cap, which obscured Angel's view of his eyes until he glanced at her.

A gasp caught in her throat. She had seen eyes that intensely blue only once before—on Dr. Damian.

He spoke with a voice that relaxed every muscle in Angel's tense shoulders as he looked back at Sir B. "Are you Sir Benjamin?"

Sir Benjamin nodded.

"I was told you're an expert on arachnids. I've got a strange…inhabitant in my yard. A spider I've never seen. I was hoping you'd help me identify it." He had no trace of a local accent. Actually, no accent at all.

Where's he from? Angel bit her lip.

"Certainly." Sir Benjamin motioned him further into the room. "Do you have a picture?"

"No, sir. But I don't live far from here. Maybe this evening when you've closed up shop…"

Angel stood, speechless, overly aware of her arms that seemed unable to find a comfortable position, and the fact that she was staring. She couldn't help it. *Those eyes. That voice. He's got to be a Tamer. But what are the chances? I've never seen him before, and if he were a Tamer the whole town would know.*

She let herself sink into the couch.

"I'd be glad to," said Sir Benjamin. "I don't believe I've seen you in town before, and I feel a disadvantage. You know who I am…"

"I'm Ayden. Ayden Reese. My family just moved here from America."

A squeak escaped Angel's throat and Ayden and Sir Benjamin turned toward her simultaneously.

"Angel, I nearly forgot you were here." Sir Benjamin winked at her and flashed a devilish grin. "Come, be sociable. Meet Ayden. I guess you heard, he's from America, too."

"You too, huh? Where are you from?" Ayden's ice-blue eyes twinkled in the combination of sunlight from the windows and lantern lights inside the room.

Angel cleared her throat and found her voice, although it sounded as if it were coming out of someone else as she spoke. "Florida, for a few years anyway. It's a long story."

His amazing eyes widened, and then his lips tilted into a sly grin. "Red hair, dark eyes, from Florida. You're the Finder."

"How did…how did you know about that?" She pushed herself up on her knees.

"Oh, I met a friend of yours. The one who told me to come to Sir Benjamin about the spider. Skinny guy, long hair. Tattoos…" His eyes brightened and the corner of his mouth turned up even more.

Angel sighed. "Kalek. It figures."

"Yeah, he's an interesting guy."

Ayden's gaze fell on Niles, and he watched the Cagon chase the found-again toy hedgehog around the room. "Um, is that a dragon?"

"Yes, sir," said Sir Benjamin. "Sort of, at least. He's part cat as well. A fortunate result of a very unfortunate situation."

"You mean that little guy was part of Dr. Randall's research?" Ayden's eyes brightened and he knelt down and took a closer look at Niles.

The Cagon sniffed him curiously. He tentatively licked one of Ayden's outstretched fingers and then rubbed his cheek against Ayden's knee.

"You know about the research?" Angel asked.

"I moved here to attend the University." He scratched behind Niles' ears. "My mom is the new genetics professor."

Angel replayed some of her more recent conversations with Dr. Watson, the University's botany teacher, but Dr. Watson hadn't mentioned a permanent genetics teacher. *I am so giving her a hard time about not telling me…*

"Well, you picked the perfect time to move here," said Sir Benjamin. "You'll have the whole summer to get settled before starting your studies. Maybe Angel can be your guide for the summer."

Angel shot him a look that said *mind your own business*, and Sir Benjamin flashed his sweet Santa smile at her.

"Maybe he'd rather have Kalek show him around, Sir B."

Ayden smiled in a way that made Angel's heart skip. "No, I think I'd rather have the prettier tour guide."

Chapter Two

Neighbors

Sir Benjamin conveniently had "something come up" that prevented him from following Ayden home to check out the spider.

"You go on home, Angel." He practically shoved her and Ayden out the front door. "I'll finish closing up. I'll come by another day and help you with that spider, Ayden. Actually, you ought to have Angel take a look at it. She's read enough of my research that she could probably identify it for you. Take care. Good night." He closed the door before Angel and Ayden could say goodbye.

They stared awkwardly at each other for a moment as people bustled by. The air had cooled a bit, but sunset was still a good couple of hours away. Angel pulled her gaze down. Shadows were just edging the town square so that the cobbled walkway reminded Angel of Niles' markings.

"If you think you could identify the spider," Ayden said, "I'd really appreciate it. It's probably something completely harmless, but I've never seen anything like it before. Of course, I didn't have much opportunity to see anything but ordinary animals growing up."

Angel looked up and found him smiling. A dimple showed in one cheek. He adjusted his cap as his eyes moved to the side and then back toward her, locking her breath in her lungs.

She cleared her throat and forced herself to speak. "I know exactly what you mean." She nodded toward the cobbled path leading out of the town square. "I'll come take a look."

Ayden motioned for her to lead the way, and they crossed the courtyard, passing the swinging wooden signs in front of the stores.

Angel waved goodnight to a flour-spotted Miss Elsie as she locked up the bakery, and continued along the path. When they reached Old Man Brady's, Angel stopped walking and grabbed Ayden's arm.

"How far is your place?" She cocked her head toward the barn on the other side of the fence. "My horses are in there. Should we ride?"

"I live right down this road." He pointed straight ahead of them. "Just a couple of miles, but we can ride if you want. Is this where you live?"

"No, but Old Man Brady keeps my horses for me. Our property's not big enough. He sends one of them to me in the morning so I can ride to work, and then I send 'em back after I ride home."

"Send them?"

Angel laughed as she opened the gate, then waved at Ayden to follow as she stepped through and headed toward the barn.

"My dad…he made bridles for the horses that guide them automatically. He Transformed a strip of bark from a Columb tree into leather strapping, so if they're not given other instructions it will pull them either here or to my house depending on where they start off."

Angel readied the horses, then handed one set of reins to Ayden. "Here, you take Romeo." She tugged gently on Juliet's reins, and together they led the horses outside.

Ayden rubbed the reins between his fingers. "These were really tree bark at one time? Cool Talent. What's your mom's?"

"She's an Artist. Her paintings become real objects."

"That's awesome…" Ayden kept his eyes aimed straight ahead as they walked toward the gate, but he had the same expression Gregor used to get when he was planning his day—deep concentration and a half-smile crinkling one corner of his mouth.

Then something shifted in his expression. His eyes narrowed and he stared at the reins in his hand the way someone studies a machine to see how it works. He glanced at her suddenly and his eyes shifted nervously back to the road.

What was that about?

Once Angel had the gate closed and locked, she and Ayden mounted the horses. A slight chill ran down Angel's spine seeing him seated on the Palomino. It was the first time Romeo had been ridden by anyone but her or Kalek since Gregor...

The horses started walking in the direction Ayden had indicated. There was only one neighborhood down that way—Angel's.

"So, how did you meet Kalek?" Angel asked as they passed the end of Old Man Brady's property and moved toward the neighborhood ahead. Trees lined both sides of the road, their upper branches stretching above like an archway. Brightly colored flowers footed the trees here and there, adding a hint of sweetness to the air.

"My mom and I checked into that abandoned farm up the road," Ayden said "Or, I should say, the one we *thought* was abandoned. We found out it belonged to Kalek's family. We would've bought it in a heartbeat, but he said it's not for sale. Something about a contract that's not up for another two years." He turned and looked at her with that smile again.

Angel's cheeks heated, but not just because of the smile.

"The farm doesn't belong to Kalek's family," she said. "Not exactly. It belongs to Kalek…and to me." Angel peered at him out the corner of her eye.

His face was like stone—no visible reaction.

"You own it with Kalek?" His jaw twitched. "You're not, like, betrothed or something…"

She smiled and her cheeks heated all over again.

"No…nothing like that. Actually, we're sort of cousins. Really distant cousins. It's a long story. But his father gave us the land to run together until my eighteenth birthday, and then it becomes mine. That's the two-year thing he was talking about. We're not allowed to sell it at all until then."

Ayden visibly relaxed, and the smile returned to his eyes. They reminded Angel of the sky in the eye of a hurricane, a strange combination of calm and impending storm.

"We're here," Ayden said with a slight crack in his voice. He pulled on Romeo's reins and turned his head toward the house.

Angel tapped Juliet's neck and she stopped next to Romeo. Two lots away from Angel. She hadn't even noticed someone had moved in. The property had been for sale for ages, and she'd quit paying attention to it. *Now I know why Dad was giving me a hard time the other day about being "unobservant."*

"Well, then," Angel said as they dismounted. "Spider time." She grabbed Romeo's reins out of Ayden's hands before he could tie up the horse. "No need for that." She nuzzled each horse in turn, scratching Juliet's cheek and stroking Romeo's neck. "Okay, you two, off to Brady's." She clicked her tongue twice, and the horses were trotting down the road.

"How are you going to get home?" Ayden asked.

"Walk, silly. It would be ridiculous to ride a horse from here to there." She flashed a smile at him as she pointed to her house, and then motioned for him to lead the way.

Chapter Three

Home

Angel's hand slid over the familiar bump on the railing as she climbed the wooden steps to her front porch. No matter how she tried to tone it down, the smile would not leave her face. Those intense blue eyes and the look of relief on Ayden's face when she told him the spider was harmless played over and over in her mind.

"You're sure?" he'd said. "Those bright red stripes look awful threatening."

"Mimicry. It's a harmless garden spider, I promise. It just uses those stripes to throw off predators. It will keep away some nasty critters for you if you just leave it there. And tonight at sunset, go out and look at the web."

"Why?"

"You'll see."

Thinking about the way he'd tilted his head curiously made her smile push even broader. She tried shoving her cheeks back in place, and realized how ridiculous she must look. That did it—her embarrassment dropped the smile instantly, and she slipped through the front door.

Before she'd taken two steps, something whizzed past her head, chittering wildly. It flew in circles around her, and landed on her shoulder.

"Horatio! You act like you haven't seen me in days. What's your issue?"

The chittering turned to chirping, but the beetle's wings continued fluttering nervously. Angel giggled.

"I already know about the spider, and it's not what you think. I promise. It just copies the vampire spider's stripes to scare animals away. Apparently, it does a good job of it."

Horatio twittered angrily, but snuggled against Angel's neck.

"I can't believe you'd doubt me," she teased.

The beetle chirped an apology, and Angel put her hand to her shoulder. Horatio crawled across her knuckles and onto her palm as she slowly flipped her hand over, and finally calmed his fluttering wings. The bright silver specks picked up even the dim light of the hallway and sparkled against the beetle's midnight black exoskeleton.

Zoe pounded into the foyer from the kitchen, her wagging tail pulling the entire back half of her body from side to side. She pounced, and slammed her paws into Angel's stomach. Horatio darted away.

"Easy, girl." Angel scratched the Boxer's forehead. "I missed you, too." Zoe licked Angel's fingers, dropped down on all fours, and dashed back into the kitchen. A second later, the doggie door slammed shut.

Angel headed toward her room, but halted in the middle of the hallway at the sight of her parents. Her mother rushed forward and grabbed Angel's elbows, looking up into her eyes. "Where have you been? I called Sir Benjamin when you didn't show up here, and he said he'd let you go early. We were just about to go looking for you!"

Before Angel had a chance to reply, her mother was squeezing her in a hug.

Her father stood a step away, hand cupped around the back of his neck. "Tell me where you've been," he said sternly.

"I'm sorry…Sir Benjamin let me go without helping him close up because…well, because…"

Her mother stepped back, but still held Angel's elbow.

Horatio fluttered to her shoulder again and wedged himself into the crook of her neck.

"I—I was just at the new neighbor's house. I—" Her stomach twisted.

"What new neighbor? Which one?" her father asked as her mom's grip tightened. Her red hair was pulled back in a sleek braid, but it did nothing to stop the worry lines from forming on her forehead.

"Ayden," Angel said. "His mom's the new genetics professor. They just moved into the house on the other side of Marcy and Doug."

Angel's mother let out a deep sigh, and her father's arm lowered. They both smiled as relief washed over them.

"What's going on?" Angel asked.

"Let's go into the kitchen," her mom said. "We'll tell you while I get dinner started."

Angel nodded and led the way into the kitchen. She took a seat on one of the barstools as her mom rounded the island where half-chopped vegetables covered the butcher-block counter top. Her mom picked up a knife and grabbed a carrot.

"Do you know that house around the corner?" her father said as he sat on the barstool next to her. He touched the edge of his glasses to straighten them, but managed to just tip them the other way. "The one at the end of Dark Elm?"

"Yeah." Angel's stomach untwisted. *They're not mad about Ayden.*

"The owner is back. He was released today."

"Oh…"

That house was owned by a man who went to prison while Angel was missing from the island. He was barely fifteen at the time. He'd gotten caught stealing, and probably would have been sentenced to no more than community service if he hadn't beaten the arresting officer to a pulp. While he was in jail, both his parents died.

"Wasn't he supposed to be in longer?" Angel asked. "Was he released for good behavior or something?"

Her father frowned and shook his head. "I don't know all the details, but it wasn't good behavior. Actually, Mr. Samson's nephew works at the prison and said his behavior has gotten very *odd* recently. I don't know what to expect, but I don't feel at all comfortable knowing he's so close to us."

He leaned toward her and put a hand gently on her shoulder. "I feel particularly uncomfortable with the idea of him being so close to *you.* He's all of nineteen and has had no contact with anyone for four years." His eyes narrowed. "Do you understand what I'm saying?"

Angel nodded as a sour taste rose from her stomach.

Her parents glanced at each other, and her mother tipped her head, telling him to continue.

"We can't watch over you every second," he said. "But we expect you to be more careful. You're going to have to let us know your plans, and call right away if you're going to be late. Let us know when you arrive at work."

"And take Horatio with you from now on," her mother added. "He can always come get us if you're in trouble."

Horatio chirped proudly.

"I will. I'm sorry I didn't call."

Her mother smiled and rounded the island, then wrapped her arm around Angel's shoulders. She brushed Angel's hair behind her ear with the other hand.

"You know we trust you. But we don't trust *him*. There's nothing we can do about Doran Ashe living in the neighborhood, but we can do everything in our power to keep you safe. You understand, don't you?"

"Yes, Mom. I promise I'll be careful. I should tell Ayden and his mom, too. They probably don't know anything about it."

"Good idea," her father said.

Her mother released her shoulders and moved back to the other side of the kitchen island to resume her chopping. "Dinner will be ready in about half an hour, now that I can concentrate on cooking again." She winked at Angel as she picked up the knife.

"I'm going to go read, then." Angel rose from the barstool.

"Love you, Anna," her mother and father said together as she walked out of the room.

The name still rang in her ears every time her parents said it, even after two years. Hearing them call her Anna helped bring back the memories that had been stolen from her when she'd disappeared from the island so long ago. Bit by bit, she regained her early childhood with their help.

She'd thought about switching back to her old name completely, but disregarded the idea. Angel was much more than a nickname. It was the person she had become. She was both Anna and Angel now, and would not, *could* not, discard one name for the other.

That evening, she climbed the steps to her mother's loft. She stumbled over the drop cloth under her mother's easel, and wove her way through the piles of canvases and small tables that held a multitude of art supplies.

A gray and white face peeked at her from behind a stack of canvases leaning in the corner. A paw poked out after a moment, toes flared, and then a pink tongue curled from an open mouth. The paw retracted and two gold eyes blinked open.

"Shakespeare, you missed dinner."

The cat looked at her reproachfully.

"I know you're mad, but Mom made stew. It's not like there were scraps or something. Your food's still in the bowl, but she's not going to leave it out all night. I suggest you get moving now."

He blinked again and closed his eyes.

"Fine, but you're the one who's going to suffer, ya know."

As if to prove to her he would not be coerced, he stretched from head to tail, ruffling his fur inch by inch, ending with a pronounced flick of his long, skinny tail. He stepped gracefully from his hiding spot and wound his way past art supplies and lumps of drop cloth, avoiding Angel. She stood in front of the window with her arms crossed, and when Shakespeare looked over his shoulder at her, she stuck out her tongue.

"Little snot you've become," she said. "Remember this when you want to sleep in my bed tonight. It's not me who won't let you have leftovers."

Shakespeare released a meow that sounded very much like a harrumph and marched out the door, his long tail held high.

Angel turned to the window. *He's more spoiled here than he was at Gregor's.* She lifted the sash and leaned through the opening.

The sun had almost completed its descent, and darkness crept out of the forest to cover the neighboring houses. A faint tinge of orange highlighted the leaves of the trees behind her house, but soon even that succumbed to black. Stars twinkled above her, dancing to the sounds of the forest. Kalek would say they were singing the wonders of Creation. She remembered vividly, still, the first day he'd played for her at the Temple and she'd experienced the wonder of his music that drew its power from the same stars she watched at that moment.

She leaned over a bit farther, craning her neck until she caught sight of the back corner of Ayden's yard. As if on cue, the spider web lit up with every color of the rainbow. It reminded Angel of the fiber optics she'd seen during her life in America, when she didn't know her true identity. Ordinary science amazed her back then, but now it seemed just a cheap imitation of nature. The rainbow colors trailed along the spider web, putting on a show that no man-made display could ever replicate. Man could set lights to music, but they could not transform music into light the way the spider web did.

A shadow suddenly blocked Angel's view. Ayden. She smiled. *He listened to me.*

He turned around and held his hand above his eyes like someone searching. She hoped the light coming from the room would be enough to illuminate her in the window, and she waved. The silhouette waved back, and then disappeared. A few seconds later, the quiet sound of crunching leaves reached the window.

Ayden's voice followed in hushed tones from the edge of the yard. "It's beautiful, Angel. Thank you." Angel could just make out the edge of his silhouette again.

"You're welcome. There's just no way to describe it, is there?"

"No, I admit that now, but all evening I've been thinking you were teasing me."

Angel laughed. "I wouldn't do that to you. I know too well what it's like to be the newbie."

"Well," he said, moving back toward the forest, "I better go. I don't want your parents thinking I'm a stalker or something. See you later."

With that, he disappeared into the forest. Angel watched the corner of his yard until she saw his shadow pass in front of the spider web again, and then she pulled her head back inside and closed the window.

Chapter Four

Talents, Knights and Criminals

Ayden tilted his head at her as they rode to town. "So, why *is* Sir Benjamin called Sir Benjamin and not Dr. Punnet?"

The sun painted his hair with blonde highlights. The faded blue t-shirt he wore made his eyes look even more intense, although they hadn't been the blue of a Tamer since the day Angel met him. They were blue, yes, but paler, softer now. Had she imagined it that day?

Regardless, she felt the weight of his gaze every time he looked at her, even after spending nearly every day together for three weeks. He'd visited her in the bookstore, eaten dinner with her and her parents several times, and helped her and Kalek with chores around the farm. They'd spent hour upon hour with his mother, Sarah, at the University while she set up her lab and prepared for the coming school year.

"I'm surprised it's taken you this long to ask," she said with a sly grin.

Horatio hovered behind her, following like a shadow. Every now and then he buzzed ahead or fluttered around her head, and then pulled behind again. Angel hadn't seen any sign of Doran Ashe since her parents had told her of his release. She and Ayden had discussed the situation at length in the beginning. Over the past three weeks, the subject had lost its intrigue, but Horatio took it as seriously as ever.

"Are you calling me nosy?" Ayden asked, one eyebrow cocked.

"You said it, not me." Her tone carried a harshness she hadn't intended, and she cringed as Ayden's eyebrow lowered and his smile dropped.

He remained silent.

In three weeks, Ayden had asked more questions than Angel could remember asking in her entire life. Not an issue, but he probed more deeply than most people when it came to the subject of Talents. It wouldn't have bothered her except that *not once* had he even hinted about his own.

Angel peeked playfully at him from the corner of her eye. "You have to let Sir B tell you himself," she said. "He tells it better than I do."

Ayden looked at her solemnly again. "I didn't mean to pry. I didn't think it'd be a big deal."

"It's not. I just—the name's not a big deal, but just don't ask about his Talent. Even I don't know what it is, and the way you've been…I mean…" The words caught in her throat. *How do I say this without seeming like I don't trust him?*

"Oh…I get it." His gaze wandered forward, and he stared ahead for a moment without speaking. His next words were hesitant. "Listen, I need to tell you something. I—"

The horses stopped, and Angel pulled her gaze from Ayden. They'd reached Old Man Brady's. Ayden dismounted and began the walk to the barn without her.

What's up with him? He's the one who said he needed to tell me something! She climbed down from Juliet's back and followed, her gut stirring.

When the horses were settled in the barn, Angel turned to leave.

Ayden grabbed her arm.

"I'm sorry," he said.

His eyes reflected the sunlight streaming through the open door, and Angel stared into them, nearly breathless. The expression on his face made her feel the way she did when a storm was coming—cold and nervous because she had no way of gauging the force of what was about to hit. The blackest of clouds could mean anything from a steady, cooling rain to a hurricane. She tensed and swallowed hard.

Ayden looked at his hand holding her arm, then released his grip and pulled his hand away. He took a step back.

"There's a reason I've been asking about everyone's Talents."

His voice relaxed her the way it always did, but she braced to hear something awful. He crossed his arms in front of him, suddenly looking like a child who was fighting the memory of a bad dream.

"It's because of my own…It's kind of rare, and I…don't normally tell people. My mom knows, of course, but she can't explain it. It's one of the reasons she decided to specialize in genetics."

So, it wasn't going to be a hurricane, but it wasn't a gentle rain either. Angel sat down on a bale of hay and motioned for Ayden to join her. "But magic isn't controlled by genes," she said. "Why would she go into genetics because of your Talent?"

"It's not that simple." He took her hand.

Her palm tingled where their skin touched and her heart *thmp-thmped* out of sync for a few beats. He'd never held her hand before. Never anything more than brotherly jabs in the shoulder or getting close enough to help her lift something while doing chores on the farm. There were times when she thought she was misreading his signals because he'd held his distance, but now…

She forced herself from the distracting thoughts, the thrum of her too-quick heartbeat in her ear, and the electricity buzzing along the skin of her hand in his.

"What do you mean?"

He ran his thumb along the edge of her index finger. "Our genes limit the expression of magic, to an extent. Your brain is wired to send a directive, and your Talent obeys, right?"

She swallowed, nodded.

"But the Talent isn't created by your brain. You don't get to pick which one you get." He looked at her and waited.

"Right. I understand."

He exhaled and looked down at his knees where his hand was wrapped around hers. "Well, I do."

"You do what?"

"I pick my Talent." He squeezed her hand and looked up again. "I can shift from one Talent to another at will. It's not easy. I can't be a Finder one second and a Fire-starter the next, but with concentration and time, I can change my Talent."

The thump of her heartbeat intensified. *Why did he have to say Fire-starter? He knows about Dawric…*

A dull ache invaded her temples where sharp pains once plagued her when her thoughts turned to that night. She closed her eyes.

"This is what I was afraid of," he said suddenly. "I'm sorry, I—"

"No, Ayden, it's not that." She opened her eyes.

He met her gaze and exhaled. "Oh, yeah. I shouldn't have mentioned…man, I'm stupid."

"Don't say that." She leaned her head against his shoulder. "And your Talent is a gift. You should be glad."

She felt him relax.

"Not everyone thinks that. When I was younger, people thought there was something wrong with me. It's why we moved to America. My mom couldn't find anyone who could help explain it, and she decided to start studying everything she could about genetics and its role in the expression of magic. Not easy information to come by, I can tell you."

"I'm not surprised."

His cheek brushed against the top of her head as he continued. "My mom found a great university that incorporated information from ordinary scientific studies. It helped her look at things from both an Empowered perspective and unempowered, and focus on the differences between the two views. She thought that gap might offer some clues."

"Did it?"

"It helped her see where our genes come into play, but it certainly didn't get her much closer to figuring out what's going on with me. The only thing she thinks she knows for sure is that it won't last. She thinks I'll eventually have to pick a Talent and keep it."

So Ayden's questions weren't fueled by idle curiosity—he was doing research. If he had to pick the Talent he'd be stuck with, he wanted to know his choices. All of them.

"I bet that's going to be a hard decision to make. Sometimes I wish I could choose something other than Finding, but then when I really need it, I'm so glad it's the gift I have. But I'd like to have my mom's Talent, even for a little while. My drawings never look nearly as realistic as hers do."

Ayden's cheek pressed against the top of her head. "Your drawings are great. I love that one of Shakespeare looking out the window that's hanging in your room."

Angel sat up and slipped a stray tendril of hair in place behind her ear. "I guess we better go. I'm starting to itch from this hay."

Sir Benjamin didn't look up as they stepped into the bookshop, despite the loud clang of the door. He was behind his big wooden desk, scribbling madly as a long wood shaving spiraled off his pencil and flopped onto the desktop. He paused for a moment, brushed the shaving aside, and continued scribbling.

"It's Saturday," he said, staring at his work. "You should be out doing something fun."

"Visiting you *is* fun, Your Eminence," Angel said.

Sir Benjamin's pencil ceased its movement, and his glasses glinted as he tilted his head to peer over them.

"You came all the way over here just to be smart with me, did you now?"

Angel giggled, and pulled Ayden by the hand over to Sir Benjamin's desk.

"'Course not. I can do that any time." She grinned at Ayden and winked.

Sir Benjamin lifted an eyebrow at her, his eyes fixed on their joined hands. A satisfied smile pushed his cheeks out, and his Santa face appeared.

"Well, then, what did bring you out here? Or were you just intent on interrupting my work today?"

"Actually," she let go of Ayden's hand to pet Niles, who had appeared at her feet with his hedgehog dangling from the side of his mouth, "we're here to hear a story."

Ayden joined her in scratching the Cagon behind his tabby-striped wings. Niles purred and dropped the hedgehog. Spike stirred on his pillow, huffing hot air that sent the tassels on his pillow into a momentary frenzy. He blinked his amber eyes and pulled his wing up over his face.

Horatio landed on Angel's shoulder, twittering something she couldn't make out. She listened more carefully, and laughed.

"What?" asked Sir Benjamin.

"He's scolding Spike. Says he needs to be more careful where he snorts, and that he's got dragon-breath."

"Well, I should think so." Sir Benjamin took his glasses off and set them on the corner of his desk. "Now what's this about a story?"

Ayden looked at Angel as if to say, *I'm not asking*, and moved over to pet the offended Spike.

"A story about the famous Dr. Punnet's knightship."

"Oh, good grief! Why that?"

"C'mon! Ayden wants to hear it."

"Fine, fine. But let me make some tea first."

Angel curled up on the couch, watching Ayden stare at Sir Benjamin, who knelt on an oval area rug.

"So there I was," said Sir Benjamin with his hands clasped on his knee, "wearing an ancient Elven suit of armor. Dr. Stetson stood over me with a sword nearly as long as he was tall—about toppled him over when he lifted it—and he says, 'I dub thee Sir Benjamin, knight of the mighty Kingdom Animalia, Phylum Chordata, Class Mammalia…' Then the crazy bugger loses his grip on the sword because he's laughing so hard. I managed to duck just in time."

Sir Benjamin demonstrated by ducking his head, lost his balance, and almost squashed Niles as he landed with a thump on the floor. The Cagon tore off across the room, with Horatio zooming behind.

Ayden and Angel burst out laughing, and Sir Benjamin pulled himself up onto his backside, looking disgruntled but smiling brightly.

"All that," said Ayden when he'd calmed down, "just because you didn't want to be called *doctor* anymore."

"I'd spent forty years teaching college. I'd had enough of formal titles, but they insisted I could never be 'just Ben.' The only person who's ever called me that is my dear friend, Kate, other than my wife, anyway."

"How long have you been married?" Ayden asked before Angel could motion to him to stop.

Sir Benjamin's eyes darkened and he gave a weak smile. "Would have been forty-two years this July."

Ayden opened his mouth, but Angel shot him a meaningful look and he snapped it shut again. She shook her head as inconspicuously as she could and when Sir Benjamin stood and walked back to his desk, she whispered to Ayden, "I'll tell you later."

The bell on the front door jingled, and Angel turned her head to see who had arrived.

A man stepped in, hands stuffed in his jeans pockets, eyeing the room nervously. His brown hair hung to just below his shoulders, brushing the back of his denim jacket. He looked young, maybe twenty at the most, but moved like a stiff-jointed old man.

He glanced in Angel's direction. Deep, forest green irises locked on her, and their color began to fade. His pupils dilated and then shrank back, and the green was completely gone, replaced by near-black flecked with silver.

Angel's breath caught, and she pushed into the back of her seat.

Sir Benjamin strode over to him with a wide, welcoming smile. "How can I help you, sir?"

The stranger turned and smiled, a crooked smile, as if he were trying to determine whether or not to answer. He cleared his throat and spoke in a strained voice, "Just here to browse."

"Well, let me know if you need anything."

The stranger nodded and walked toward the nearest bookshelf.

Sir Benjamin rejoined Angel and Ayden on the couch. He squinted as he watched the stranger nose through book after book, and absentmindedly scratched his beard.

He leaned toward Angel after a few minutes. "I need to check something in the back. Stay here with Ayden and keep an eye on that one for me."

She nodded, and he rose and walked to the back of the store. She heard the storeroom door swing open, and scooted closer to Ayden. He wrapped his arm around her shoulder.

Ayden's breath tickled her ear. "I think I saw him stuff a book in his jacket."

She looked closely and noticed a strange bulge under the guy's arm.

"What do we do?" she whispered.

Ayden didn't answer. Instead he smiled mischievously and held out his hand. A second later a book sat in his palm.

The stranger's hair swung as he spun his head around. When he spied the book in Ayden's hand, panic flashed across his face and he dashed out of the store.

Sir Benjamin walked through the back door with a newspaper in his hand. He eyed the front door, then looked curiously at the book in Ayden's open hand, but didn't question. Instead, he brought the newspaper over and held it out for Angel and Ayden to see.

"I thought there was something familiar about him," he said.

Angel gazed at the picture and read the name in the caption below.

Doran Ashe.

Chapter Five

Prisoners and Plans

Horatio chirped mournfully in her ear.

"It's okay. Honestly." Angel tilted her head so he could nuzzle into the crook of her neck. She sat on the couch in the bookstore while Sir Benjamin made tea and Ayden paced. "If Niles needed you to sing him to sleep, then that's what you should have been doing. Ayden was right there. And so was Sir Benjamin. Doran couldn't have tried anything."

The beetle settled down, but released one last chirp of apology.

"Don't worry. It's not like you were far away. Your job is only to get to Mom and Dad if I'm in trouble, and you could have done that easily."

"What was he doing here?" Ayden said for the third time as he passed by. He still clutched the nearly stolen novel.

"Like I said," Angel answered again, "He was probably just stealing because he doesn't have any money anymore."

"But a book?" He stopped pacing. "Food, I could see. Clothes, maybe. And he didn't exactly look destitute. I think he was seeing if he could get away with it in here. Checking out how secure this place is."

Angel smirked. "Casing the joint, eh? And if he got away with the novel, he'd move on to the really valuable books hidden in the safe, right?"

"What?" Ayden said, and then glared at her.

Sir Benjamin *tsked* at them as he brought over their tea.

Angel smiled an apology for teasing. Her emotions were whacked out at the moment and for some strange reason it was surfacing as sarcasm. The way Doran's eyes had changed to dark brown, with silver flecks just like Gregor's was too much. Besides, she wasn't even sure she hadn't imagined it.

She returned her focus to the picture in the newspaper. It was definitely the guy who'd come into the store, but there was something different about him and Angel was determined to put her finger on it. The Doran in the picture was nervous looking. The picture had to have been taken early on in his prison days because he still had the look of a teenager. He would have been frightened about going to jail.

The Doran who'd entered the bookstore was nervous, too—no big surprise for someone just released from prison. And if he was still a thief at heart, he'd be nervous about being caught again.

But that wasn't the difference she detected. She gnawed on her bottom lip. *It's like he doesn't have the haunted prisoner look anymore. Does that just go away after a while?* Maybe he was actually used to jail now, and was more scared of being in the open than he'd been of being locked up.

Satisfied that she was on the right track, she folded the paper and set it on the coffee table. The men's voices carried over, and she turned her attention to them.

"—not going to do anything about this?" Ayden was saying while Sir Benjamin shook his head.

"The man needs a chance to redeem himself. Even the best of us do things we regret, but we're not all given a chance to change it. I won't take that away from him." The dark, melancholy look had returned to Sir Benjamin's face, the same look that had come over him at the mention of his wife.

Angel walked over and grabbed Ayden's arm, then slid her hand down into his and their fingers entwined.

"We should go," she said. "I don't want to be late for dinner."

Ayden nodded and they bade their goodbyes. Angel ached at leaving Sir Benjamin looking so heartbroken, but she had the feeling he needed time alone.

Angel's parents asked Ayden to stay for dinner, and as always, he accepted. Afterward, she and Ayden sat in matching lounge chairs in the back yard. The forest sounds filled the air as Zoe chased butterflies and the sun inched toward the tops of the trees. Angel's mom cleaned up the kitchen, and her father had gone into his workshop to tinker with his latest invention.

"She's watching us through the window," Angel said. "I can feel it. That's why she insisted we come out here, you know. It's a test."

"Are we passing?"

"I am. You better be." She smiled, and then turned and waved at her mom through the window.

Her mother's silhouette put its hands on its hips and shook its head.

She turned back to Ayden. "Yeah, you're passing. I could tell they were really glad you were with me today."

"You have a great family," he said. "It amazes me how close you are after spending all those years apart. Don't they ever worry you'll want to go back?"

"I don't think so. They know how much they mean to me, and how much this whole place means to me. I miss the Masons and Zack, but I wouldn't trade this in for anything."

"How did they take it, your foster parents?"

"They were happy to know I was back with my real parents. I talked to them after Mom and Dad took care of all the legal stuff. They wanted to make sure I was okay, and they said they'd miss me. We all cried. They actually did want me to come see them again, but…" She inhaled, cooling the ache. "It's hard, though. I don't know…I'd talk to Mom about planning a trip, and stuff would just happen. It was so easy to make excuses." The ache burned again, and tears pushed their way out. "I couldn't…I couldn't say goodbye to Zack *again*…"

She felt Ayden's fingers brush her forearm and let him grab her hand.

"What about Finding them? Did you ever…"

Wiping her eyes, she shook her head.

Ayden's chair scraped across the wooden deck as he moved closer. His hand tightened around hers, gently, comforting. He hadn't condemned her for ignoring the little brother, the *family*, she claimed to love so much—the way she had condemned herself for so long. She'd done so much damage by leaving, and justified not visiting them by telling herself she didn't want to add more.

But Mr. and Mrs. Mason had *asked* her to come. Had even called and sent letters in the beginning. So had Zack, and Angel wrote them back—a few times. Then the calls stopped because…well, *because*. There was always a *because*. Before long *because* stopped her from writing, too.

Angel twisted the charm bracelet around her wrist again, thinking of the tiny but powerful wood chip inside the locket. Maybe she could have fixed it all with her wish, but was dragging Zack away from his family *less* damaging?

And there was Gregor.

You couldn't bring people back from the dead. She knew that.

But Gregor hadn't technically *died.*

There was that chance. That tiny chance. But he had a family, too. And Siophra.

No matter what Angel chose she would be pulling someone from happiness.

She felt the pressure of Ayden's hand again.

And with that she knew. Ayden had shared his deepest secrets with her. Her parents and Sir Benjamin adored him. *Gregor* would have approved of him.

Gregor. *He'd* chosen his family. He'd chosen Siophra. He would tell Angel to choose the same way.

And so she would.

She wouldn't pull Zack from his life, but she was *going* to visit her little brother.

Unable to sleep, Angel stood at the window of her mother's loft, staring out at the twinkling midnight stars. *Zack's never seen stars like this before. I wish I could bring all this with me when I go see him.* She leaned forward and looked at the spider web in Ayden's back yard. The colors were different again, all blue and green instead of the whole rainbow. Angel wondered what the colors meant. Even Sir Benjamin had never figured it out.

A shadow moved in front of the spider web, and Angel shifted to get a better view. *Ayden?* Maybe. It turned. The shoulders weren't broad enough, but it was definitely male. Was someone in his back yard? Could it be…Doran? No, even as shadow, the lines were distinct enough for Angel to tell the hair was thick, probably wavy. The way he moved was familiar. His arm reached up, his hand raking the hair, and he turned. He faced her dead on, and his eyes shone like a cat's in the dark, flickered, and then he walked toward her.

Angel pulled back from the loft window and stepped behind the wall. She was suddenly aware of her heart pounding erratically, and she breathed deeply to calm herself. Her hands trembled. *Oh, God, who is that? Please don't let him come over here…*

Time gripped her like a vice as she waited for a sound, a footstep in the leaves below, but nothing came. She pressed herself against the wall and inched her head toward the window again, stopping the second she could see beyond the border of her yard. The shadow stood at the edge of the trees, outlined by moonlight. The arm rose again and raked through curly bangs.

The movement….*Just like Gregor.*

A bright beam of moonlight hit his face.

It can't be…

Then the shadow darted off into the forest.

Angel couldn't breathe. Her ribs refused to expand and her lungs burned. Her legs shook, and her hand clamped around the window frame was the only thing keeping her from falling over. She slid to the floor, and dropped her head between her knees. *Breathe…breathe…*

She swallowed a lump of air and her ribs finally released their grip, allowing her lungs to fill. *I'm imagining this. Gregor's gone, and I don't believe in ghosts.*

The chime of the grandfather clock downstairs traveled softly to her ears, bringing her back to her surroundings. Two o'clock in the morning. *It's late, and I'm just overtired. I'm imagining things, feeling guilty about choosing Zack over Gregor. Yes that's it. It's just guilt.*

Relief swept over her, and her breathing eased. It was probably one of the Elves, maybe one of Kalek's friends, lurking in the forest. He must have stopped at Ayden's yard to see the spider web and heard her at the window.

She pushed herself to her feet and peeked out the loft window. Nothing menacing peeked back. She laughed at herself. *Honestly, Angel. Ghosts. Get real.* But a tremor in her hand betrayed her composure.

Shakespeare appeared at the edge of a painting leaning against the wall. Angel knelt down and held out her hand. He rubbed against her knuckles, purring. She gathered him into her arms and adjusted herself until she was sitting on the floor with her back against the wall.

As she stroked Shakespeare's fur, thoughts of Zack pressed their way back into her head, leaving no room for ghosts or Elves. She longed to see the image of his little-boy face and sweet curls. She concentrated, relaxing and allowing her Talent to push forward. She'd learned a long time ago that she couldn't force it, that her Talent was designed to work only when she relinquished control of her will. An image formed in her mind, foggy at first, and then gradually sharpened into a crisp, clear vision.

The image hit her harder than she expected. Seeing him, even just in her mind…that strawberry blond hair she wanted so badly to muss. The soft cheek she kissed goodnight so many times…

The image faltered, and she shoved the emotion down to keep her focus. It cleared again and she searched the details.

Zack was sitting in the dark, leaning against a headboard Angel had never seen before, hugging a pillow. Angel could only see the objects immediately surrounding him, but the room was definitely not in the Mason's house. They would never have—could never have—decorated with such rich, stuffy furniture. Where was he? Why wasn't he at home?

Could they be on vacation? No, Zack would be busily playing, not sitting solemnly on a bed. Unless he was ill…

She tried to place the location on a mental map. East of the Masons. At the beach? No, not that far. It didn't make sense.

She couldn't control the angle at which she saw these images, and Zack sat facing sideways. She willed him to turn around, and was stunned when his head moved. Just enough to catch a glimpse of his face before her emotions surged and the image burst in her mind. Zack's expression terrified her.

Angel ran downstairs, charged into her room, tripping over a sleeping Zoe in the doorway, and banged her shin on the edge of the bookshelf just inside her bedroom door. Her pain triggered a burst of anger, and a tiny glass figurine on the bookshelf shattered with a quiet *tink-shishhh.* She huffed at herself. *Angel, get a grip!*

She spotted the newspaper on her nightstand, and dove across the bed to reach it, mentally igniting the lantern on her wall at the same time. Doran Ashe stared out from the front page with gray, newsprint eyes. The lack of color was not enough to mask the desperate look on his angular face. It still dug into Angel that Doran was practically a kid in the picture, but his face already reflected more hardship and pain than most people experience in a lifetime. That look matched the look she'd just seen on Zack's face exactly.

A tear hit the newspaper. *He looks like a prisoner. Where is he? What's happened to my little man?*

Chapter Six

Petitions

Ayden and Kalek sat across from Angel at the kitchen table of the farm, their empty lunch plates stacked by the sink. Both guys looked at her as if they thought she'd gone crazy—Ayden perched forward in his chair and Kalek leaned back, arms crossed, Horatio clinging to his shoulder.

"You can't just show up, Angel," Ayden said.

"Why not? He needs me. You didn't see his face—he's a prisoner there!"

"You don't even know exactly where *there* is. And maybe he just had a bad day, or he's sick, or—"

"No!" She slammed her fist on the table.

Kalek, who hadn't said a word since Angel brought up the topic, smirked. His onyx eyes glimmered in the lantern light. The sky, visible through the window behind him, churned with black and gray clouds.

A chill ran down Angel's spine. The incoming storm had the same feel to it as the one that had trapped her and Gregor inside for three days, when they discovered the Prophecy.

She lowered her voice and continued, shaking off the chill. "It's more than that. You *have* to trust me on this. I'm not asking you to go with me, or anything. I just want you to help me think of a way to get him here."

Ayden peered out the window, as if he'd just noticed the storm. "Good thing we got everything done already. Let's go before that hits. We can talk about this later."

Kalek nodded casually, still silent. The storm had to be a good while from hitting, or he'd be more enthusiastic about leaving. His Elven instincts were more effective for gauging the weather than the most advanced radar system in existence. And he never went home unless it was absolutely necessary.

"Fine," Angel said, "we'll talk about it on the way home." She stood and waited for Ayden to follow. Horatio stayed put on Kalek's shoulder.

Ayden reached out to shake Kalek's hand.

The Elven musician slipped his hand out from under his crossed arms obligingly. "Thanks for the help with the shelter," he said. "Of course, it wouldn't *need* to be rebuilt if Angel would agree to sell the rest of the goats." Kalek glanced at her, and back to Ayden.

Angel ignored him. She was not going to argue about it again. She turned on her heel and headed out the front door, Horatio buzzing right behind her.

Ayden insisted they run the horses all the way home to make sure there was time to send them on to Old Man Brady's before the storm hit. Angel agreed, but turned on him the moment they walked in the front door of her house.

"Ayden please, I've got to have a plan or my parents will never let me go."

He reached down and grabbed her hand as he turned his head from side to side, examining the living room. "Where are they, anyway? And Zoe?"

"They must have gone out. There's probably a note in the kitchen."

He turned back to face her. "Then I should go home."

"This can't wait."

His gaze dropped and he bit his lip before speaking. "My mom could use my help. She still hasn't finished unpacking."

"My parents trust us—you don't have to go."

He avoided her eyes as he brushed her hair behind her ear and ran his knuckle along her cheek. "I know. And I want them to keep trusting us."

Angel's heart thumped and her thoughts nearly derailed. She blinked to make herself refocus. "I have to get this figured out."

Ayden nodded. "Then let's go talk outside."

They moved to the front porch and stood on the top step. Thunder cracked in the distance and the first drops of rain splashed on the ground around the porch.

"This means that much to you?" he asked as he traced the edge of her fingernail with his thumb.

"More than everything. As far as I'm concerned, Zack is my real brother. I only left him behind because he loves Mr. and Mrs. Mason so much. But if he's not there anymore…" She choked on a sob.

Ayden's hand moved to her shoulder. His arm slipped around her and she leaned her head against his chest.

"I have to make sure he's okay," she said. "I wouldn't even think of bringing him here if I didn't know for sure he was in real trouble."

"Then what can I do to help?"

She sniffled, and her voice came out creaky. "I need a plan for a way to get there. Something that will convince my parents to let me go. I don't want to sneak behind their backs, but I will if I have to."

"There will be no need for that."

Angel's head popped up at the sound of her father's voice.

"Daddy!"

Her parents walked toward her with Zoe tugging at the leash. Her mother held an umbrella and winced as a bolt of lightning hit close by, followed immediately by a tremendous boom.

"That was too close," her mother said. "Inside. Now. Everyone."

Angel and Ayden sat next to each other on the couch, which faced the fireplace. Her father sat on the loveseat, which was angled toward the couch with its back to the hallway. Her mom sank onto the thick area rug, cross-legged, her back against his knees.

"So…where were you guys?" Angel asked.

"Actually," her father said, looking straight at Ayden, "we were visiting with your mom."

Ayden sat stiffly, looking remorseful.

She frowned and fiddled with her charm bracelet. *He feels bad and he didn't even do anything wrong.*

"We took her some of those brownies," her mother said.

Her father smiled reassuringly at Ayden.

Angel felt the couch move and noticed Ayden had released some of the tension in his posture. She touched his arm, and he relaxed even more.

"Mr. and Mrs. Kleidon," he said.

Her dad waved his hand and grimaced. "C'mon, Ayden. It's William, please. We know full-well Angel is the one plotting to visit Zack. We've known since we told her about the woodchip that she'd use it for Zack somehow. Either that, or try the impossible and bring Gregor back."

Angel gasped. "How did—"

"We're your parents," they said together, and looked at each other with surprise.

Her mother smiled sweetly as she turned back toward Angel.

"We wanted you to figure out what you wanted on your own," she said. "We thought you'd come to us, though. I can't believe you thought of sneaking off behind our backs. Don't you know that we care about the people you care about?"

Tears pushed against Angel's eyelids. Her thumb ran back and forth over the engraved beetle on her locket. Inside was the magic woodchip that would grant her wish. But it was already being granted, in a way. Was that how it worked? She thought she'd have to close her eyes and say the wish out loud or something, but it seemed to be happening on its own, without any kind of ritual.

Angel's mom continued. "Anna, the first thing we need to do is find out the real situation with Zack. We'll start by calling Mr. and Mrs. Mason, okay?"

"But I saw—"

"I know. But that was *one* vision."

"Right," her father added. "One phone call, got it?"

"Fine."

Angel stood and followed her mom into the kitchen. She crossed her arms and tapped her foot as her mother picked up the phone and dialed. *They're not going to be there…*

Her mother held the phone to her ear for several moments. Her bottom lip tucked between her teeth, and she hung up the receiver.

"The number's been disconnected."

Angel pulled her arms down to her sides and balled her hands. "See!"

"Now hang on…." Her mother opened a drawer and rifled through some papers. She pulled out a business card and held it up for Angel to see. "This is the case worker we spoke with for you. Let me make some calls and see if I can find out what's going on." She glanced at the kitchen clock.

"Two o'clock here…nine-ish in the morning there? The office should be open."

Her mom shooed her from the kitchen and she returned to her spot on the couch. Ayden was talking with her dad, but she didn't hear a word they were saying over the rushing of her pulse in her ear. Why was the Mason's number disconnected? Where could they be and was Zack with them?

Why didn't her parents believe her? She *knew* Zack, and that image was nothing like her vibrant little brother.

She felt pressure on her hand, and looked down to find Ayden's wrapped around it.

"Angel? You okay?"

She blinked at him, and her lip quivered. She couldn't answer.

Her mom walked back into the living room and sat on the loveseat, scowling. She released a sigh.

"Well, all I can say is every person in that office now has a voice mail from me. Only one person actually answered, and all she did was repeat a bunch of mumbo jumbo about privacy. I say we wait a couple of days, but I doubt we'll get anywhere."

Angel sat forward. "Then let me go *now*! I can find his exact location, and I can get there right away, before anything worse happens. Please!"

Her parents looked at each other.

"I suppose we could go," her mom said, returning her gaze to Angel, "but you'd need to Find him again a couple of times. And it will take a day or so to make the travel arrangements, so we might as well wait a little while for someone to call back."

Angel shook her head and turned to Ayden. "No. *No.* I can get there immediately. With Ayden's help." She lowered her voice and looked more deeply at Ayden. "We need to tell them about you."

His eyes crinkled as he considered her words. A look of vague understanding appeared on his face, but there was still a hint of confusion in his eyes.

She whispered, "You can become a Gate-maker, like Gregor."

He nodded, and they turned toward her parents.

After explaining about Ayden's Talent, and her plan to use it to reach Zack, Angel moved over to the couch where her parents sat, snuggling in between them. "We'll take Horatio, of course, and we won't stay long enough for it to affect the expression of our powers. It will be safe, I'm sure."

"You say 'we' as if you mean only you and Ayden," her father said.

"Well, yeah. Why would we all have to go? I just want to *see* Zack with my own eyes. Just check on him. I can Find his *exact* location, and Ayden could Gate me *right there*."

Her mom's eyes welled with tears. "Are you forgetting what happened last time you Gated away from here?"

"Mom, really? That was nothing like this. Gregor was *ten*, and *terrified*. He and I Gated hundreds of times after that!"

"On the island!" her mother said. "And Gregor had been a Gate-maker his whole life. Ayden has never even done it before and you're asking him to Gate you halfway across the world!"

Her father remained quiet.

Angel stood up and faced them.

"Dad, you trust us don't you?"

She stepped back and sat beside Ayden again.

Her father stared at her a moment. Her mom clung to his arm and began to sob. He tilted his head, pressing his cheek against the top of her mom's head and closed his eyes. "We'll discuss it."

Her mom sat up and glared at him through her tears. She opened her mouth to speak, but stopped short when he faced her.

He kept his gaze on her mom, but spoke to Angel. "Give us time to talk about it, and you think long and hard about why you're doing this. Got it?"

She squeezed Ayden's hand as hard as she could, clinging to the hope that her dad hadn't said *no* outright.

"Yeah," she said.

Her parents got up and headed to their room.

She sat silently, straining to hear their discussion. Their muffled voices carried through the wall, but not well enough for Angel to hear their words. Her mom's tone was panicked, though, and Angel could hear her crying. But her dad's voice was deep and even.

Ayden put his arm around her, and stroked her hair. He stayed quiet, but she couldn't tell if it was from nervousness or that he was trying to listen, too. Both, probably. Either way, she was grateful he didn't talk and just held her.

When her parents finally emerged from their room, her mom's eyes were red but she was no longer crying. Her father sat down across from her again and leaned forward with his elbows on his knees.

"I'm not entirely sure why you are so set on doing this alone, but I trust you that it's not for reasons that should worry me. He's your little brother. I can understand that."

Angel nodded. She hadn't really thought about *why*, but the idea of her parents being there the very first time with Zack felt…invasive. Her father's understanding made her heart swell with love for him. She sat still, waiting for him to continue.

"Nothing in your vision convinces me that Zack is in physical danger. And I trust you and Ayden to be careful and assess the situation before rushing in." He glanced at her mother and then looked back at Angel. "Your mom is still very worried about your safety. But I've convinced her that if we take the proper precautions we should let you go."

"Oh, Daddy! Thank—"

He held up his hand.

"Ayden will leave the Gate open while you're there. Horatio will go with you, as you suggested. But I'd like to add Kalek to that as well. Not to go with you, but to stand guard at the Gate on this end. That way if none of you come through after a given time, he can follow or come get us."

"And what if it takes longer? I might have to wait for him or something. What if—"

"Then you check in with Kalek," her mother said, voice hoarse but insistent.

They continued discussing the plans until her parents seemed satisfied. Or as satisfied as they *could* be. Angel still couldn't see why they were being so paranoid and making it so complicated with all their conditions. But at least they said yes.

Angel lay in bed that night, staring out her bedroom window into the darkness of the forest behind her yard. She didn't see dark, though. In her mind, the forest was bright, and full of sparkling leaves, rustling in the summer breeze. She imagined a strawberry-blond mop of curls bouncing through the foliage as Zack chased down orange and purple lizards, and buzzing wonder bugs.

Her parents had made her promise that if Zack was really fine, and in a family that he was happy with, she would not tell him anything to make him want to leave with her. The promise was easy enough to make. She'd done that once already and she knew she was right about his situation anyway.

She and Ayden would leave the next day. Ayden needed a few hours to change his Talent to Gate-making, and rest afterward because the change drained him of energy. He hadn't told Angel what his present Talent was, only that it was something he'd tried out of curiosity and never found much use for.

Angel's thoughts traveled to Gregor. Would he be okay with Ayden mimicking his Talent? It was something he'd been so proud of. But he'd want Zack rescued, too. She picked up the picture on her nightstand, the one she'd taken from the mantle at the farm. She leaned against her headboard, her legs pulled up, the picture tilted against her thighs. Gregor's silver-flecked eyes sparkled behind the framed glass as he sat astride Romeo. He couldn't have been more than nine years old, so close to the way he looked the first time he'd saved Angel's life. She owed him so much, and never had a chance to repay him for anything.

A deep whisper startled her out of her daydreams.

"It's impossible, you know." Her dad stood in the doorway, a melancholy smile on his face.

"What is?" She pulled a pillow onto her lap.

"Bringing Gregor back."

"I know." She hugged her pillow to her chest, fighting the urge to protest. *But he didn't actually die.* It didn't matter. The decision was made. "I just keep wondering what it will be like when I see him again. Someday."

"Well, for my sake, I hope you don't find out for a long time." He flashed a sly smile, but his eyes were soft and brimming with love, and then he disappeared into the hallway.

Angel put the picture back on the nightstand, and snuggled under her covers. She had finally relaxed, a blanket of sleep just beginning to overtake her, when music drifted into her consciousness. A soulful tune that filtered through the sounds of crickets and frogs, calling her as if by name. Her lids lifted slowly and she turned to see a mass of tangled curls reflecting the moonlight, and two onyx eyes peering into her bedroom.

Angel got out of bed and opened the window. "Kalek, what are you doing here?"

Horatio fluttered wildly around her head, admonishing Kalek in a way that made her stifle a laugh and choose not to translate for Kalek's benefit.

"I was worried about you," he said.

"You? Worried about me? C'mon, Kalek, for real. What's up?"

"*For real,* I'm worried. I just talked to Ayden. You shouldn't do this, Angel. Or at least, you must wait. With Doran Ashe on the loose again, this is no time to be bringing your little brother here."

"Do you really think Doran is that dangerous?"

"Yes." The tone in his voice sent chills up her spine. His polished-stone eyes looked even blacker than usual, deep and scared.

"And you couldn't have said something earlier, when I asked about it? Why are you sneaking around here now?" Angel glared at him through the open window. She should have known this would turn out to be difficult. Her parents had actually agreed to her plans, and she had the perfect person available to take her to Zack quickly and safely. There had to be a snag, and now she'd found it.

"I wasn't sure, until tonight, after you left the farm." Kalek pulled away from the window and cocked his head as if he'd heard something. He waited a moment, and then leaned forward again. "I don't know exactly what he's up to, but I intend to find out. I don't want anyone getting hurt before I do."

"What are you saying? You think he's planning on hurting me? Or Zack? He doesn't even know us."

"No, but he knew Gregor. He *hated* Gregor for taking the one thing he wanted for himself: my sister." Kalek shifted his weight, leaves cracking under his feet. "I hoped he'd gotten past that, but he obviously hasn't. What if he decides to take things out on you?"

"He's been locked up for four years. You really think he's still hung up after all this time? Gregor and Siophra aren't even *here.*"

"I've been watching him, and there's something going on. I need to learn more. Promise me you'll be careful. Visit Zack, but don't bring him back yet."

She sighed, and waved Horatio away from her ear. "I *can't* promise. He may be in more danger there than he would be here."

"I highly doubt that." Kalek turned his head slightly, and his eyes captured the moonlight again, reminding Angel of her visitor the night before.

"Wait, you said you'd been watching. Were you here last night? Was that you?"

"Last night? I don't—" He spun away from the window. Angel could tell from the way he held his shoulders that his hand was probably resting on his dagger. After a moment, he turned back to the window. "I've got to go." He spun again and dashed away toward the forest, swallowed by the darkness as if he'd never been there at all.

Angel had to stop herself from slamming the window shut.

"I hate it when he does that! Why does he always have to be so dramatic, all full of Elvish mystery, like it makes him cooler to leave that way. Urgh." She plopped onto the bed, and Zoe blinked a sleepy eye at her from her spot on the floor.

"And you, lady! Not much of a watchdog, now, are you? He was at my window, you big lump, and you didn't even notice."

Horatio buzzed over to her ear again.

"Yes, I know, you really told him what-for. Of course, he can't understand you."

The beetle zipped across the room, landed deftly on Angel's dresser and rustled his wings indignantly.

"Oh, don't pout. I'm sorry." She looked back and forth between Horatio and Zoe. "Both of you. I'm just irritated. The important stuff never goes smoothly. I shouldn't have gotten my hopes up."

Chapter Seven

Old Friends

Angel clung to Ayden's hand as they walked into the forest behind her house. His fingers were cold even though it was late-afternoon and warm. It made her shiver. The dark circles around his eyes worried her as well. His breath came hard despite the fact they were walking downhill. He stumbled and Angel grabbed his arm.

"What's wrong?" Her voice cracked.

He swayed ever so slightly. "I'm fine. Just tired. This change took more out of me than it's done before."

Angel took his other hand, searching his face in the dappled light. His cheeks looked hollow, and his skin was paler than normal, even though he'd had all day to rest. They had to wait until afternoon or it would be too early in Florida. Angel assumed Zack wasn't being homeschooled anymore and wanted to try and catch him as he came home from school.

"Maybe we should wait," she said.

His face hardened. "No. I can do this. Any tree will do, right? Let's just go from here."

Angel ignored his protest. She wanted to use a magical tree for the Gate, to boost his powers. She knew of a Silver Spruce nearby—where had she seen it?

"Right there," she said as it came into view. As they moved closer, Angel saw Kalek leaning against a tree nearby. She exhaled, relieved. After his little show the night before she'd been afraid he'd bail on them.

Kalek nodded as they stepped up next to him.

"This better be quick," he said.

Angel rolled her eyes, but led Ayden to the Silver Spruce. He kept his grip on her hand, and placed his other hand against the tree trunk, closing his eyes. Angel felt a slight shift in the air, only detectable to her because of all the times she'd Gated with Gregor.

Then, before she had a chance to step toward the Gate, Ayden's hand tightened around hers. He swayed. She slid her arm around his waist, faltering under his weight as he lost his balance. But Kalek pulled him up and in seconds had him sitting on the ground, back against a broad oak. Angel knelt by his side.

"Give me just a minute," he said. "I just need to—"

She moved her finger to his lips. "No. If you go through and are too weak, the Gate may close and we'd be stuck. I can do this myself. No one there knows me anymore. And anyone who might would never recognize me." She instinctively twined her finger through a tendril of hair. Magically changing it to brown had been her mom's idea, knowing that their bright red was an attention-getter.

"Then let's go tomorrow. I'll be totally fine by then."

Angel glanced at the Spruce. The Gate was made. Zack was right there on the other side. *Right there.*

"It will only be a little while. I just want to *see* him."

"You promised your parents."

"I know I did. But he's my baby brother!" The sting of tears made her rub her eyes. "I'll have Horatio with me. He can be here in seconds to get both of you."

Ayden's jaw twitched and he leaned forward, hands pressing against the ground. One hand slipped before he could push himself all the way up, and he groaned as his back thudded against the tree. He huffed.

"Kalek, are you going to step in, or what?" he said.

Angel looked up at Kalek and narrowed her eyes.

He shook his head. "No way, dude. I know better than to mess with her when she's like this." His gaze hardened, boring into her.

Chills tingled her spine. Kalek had warned her not to go, and now he was taking her side. What had happened last night to change his mind? She'd promised not to bring Zack back with this visit, sure. But if he was in danger, this would not be the end of it and Kalek had to know that.

He pulled his gaze away and crossed his arms. "Just hurry."

She ran her fingers along Ayden's pale cheek and then threw her arms around his neck. "I'll hurry," she said, then let go and turned to the tree.

Horatio burrowed under her hair at the back of her neck.

She stepped through.

On the other side, she scanned the area around the trunk of the huge oak from which she had just emerged. She was on a side street, with six-foot brick fencing along either side. The sidewalk and grass lining it were pristine. Not a single piece of cardboard or fallen branch she could prop against the tree to block the Gate. She shrugged.

With a deep breath, she walked briskly toward the main road, which ran through the grand neighborhood where she had pinpointed Zack. Heat beat up from the pavement, and she had to squint against the midday sun at the huge houses sitting on small, perfectly manicured lots. The road was lined with ornate, wrought iron light posts and matching mailboxes.

She rounded the corner and walked along the sidewalk, looking side to side at the row of mini-mansions. A clomping noise—footsteps?—came from behind her, and she spun around. She sucked her lip between her teeth and brushed her bangs out of her face.

Nothing there. She turned and kept going.

A few paces more and a familiar voice made her stop in her tracks

"Angel? Is that you?"

Angel spun around and regretted it the second she did so. *Melinda.* She tried to hide the surprise on her face, but felt like one of those cartoon characters with bugged out eyes and chin crashing to the floor. Melinda was *here*? Wasn't she living in Germany?

"What are you doing here? What happened to your hair?" Melinda looked pretty much as Angel remembered her. Long, black hair that blended in with her all-black outfit. Combat boots with massive buckles on the ankles. Some kind of leather strap wound around her arm. But her eyes were what caught Angel's attention. They weren't sad and searching like they used to be. They were angry. Bitter. Even the smile on Melinda's face and her quasi-friendly tone of voice couldn't hide the harshness in her eyes.

"Oh, yeah," said Angel nervously as she touched the chocolate-colored strands of hair that fell in front of her shoulder. Horatio moved against the back of her neck, but stayed quiet. Angel smiled. "I colored it." *To hide. Lotta good that did…*

"But the red was so cool..."

"It's temporary."

Melinda curled her lip as she looked Angel over. "Good. Is the funny accent temporary, too?"

Angel ignored the question. Here stood the girl she'd tried so desperately to reach when they were young, the girl whose father turned out to be a killer. Whose father had tried to be *Angel's* killer. Her stomach quivered, twisted, churned.

Melinda crossed her arms in front of her. "Fine, don't answer. But what are you doing here? I heard you took off like two years ago. Did you really run away? Does Angel the brain really have a rebellious streak?"

Angel tried not to return Melinda's smirk. *Why does she always have to be so snarky?*

"It wasn't like that. It's kind of a long story."

"So? I've got time. I ditched school today, but Toby got busted and couldn't make it." Melinda picked at her chipped black nail polish. "I've got all day."

"Toby Evans? You're skipping school with *him*? Melinda, seriously, even you…I mean, come on!" Toby Evans was the biggest loser in their class when they were in junior high. He spent more time in the principal's office than he did in class the whole time Angel knew him. She could only imagine what he'd gotten into since starting high school. And if Melinda lived here, which was a good hour from their old town, how had she even met up with him again?

Melinda's lip curled up farther, and she snarled, "I haven't seen you in years and the first thing you do is start lecturing me. Now I know why we quit hanging out."

"We quit hanging out because you *moved to Germany*, Melinda. And I'm not lecturing you. I just know you've been through a lot and hanging out with Toby Evans is not going to help." Angel reached out to touch Melinda's arm.

"What do you know about what *I've* been going through?" Melinda growled through clenched teeth and ripped her arm away as if Angel's touch had burned her.

"Your dad. I'm so sorry…"

"How did *you* know about my dad?" Melinda glared and a muscle in her jaw twitched.

Angel, you dork! Think before you speak! Angel's brain spun as she searched for something to say that wouldn't make Melinda question her again. But before she could blunder out another stupid reply, Melinda spoke.

"Duh. The papers." Melinda's narrowed eyes lost a touch of their harshness. "I guess even *runaways* would have seen those headlines. 'Renowned Scientist Disappears' and 'Dr. Watkins Still Missing, Presumed Dead.' Well, at least he finally got what he wanted. He made the front page of every paper. He's *famous* now! Not that it does him any good if he's dead. What good is fame to a pile of dust?"

Angel's stomach turned again. What would have happened if Melinda hadn't moved away? Would they be friends? If her dad were still alive would she still hate him?

"Don't look at me like that, Angel. My life's better without him around. I can do anything I want and Mom doesn't have a clue. Want to come over to my house for a while? It'll be like old times." Melinda pointed to a house two lots down.

"You live in this neighborhood? Do you see Zack?" Angel couldn't hide her excitement.

"Ahhh, that's why you're here. Duh. Yeah, I see him now and then, when his *parents* let him off the leash." She said *parents* with such venom it sent a chill down Angel's spine.

"What does that mean?"

Melinda started walking toward her house and Angel followed.

"They treat him like a show dog. You know, because he's so smart. I knew he was a brain, but he makes even you look dumb."

"Gee, thanks."

"Come on, you know what I mean. He's a genius. So they show him off at every science fair and spelling bee they can get him into. They're making him go to some ritzy private school where he has to wear a goofy uniform and everything. He does look cute in it, but I don't think he likes it very much."

They stopped in front of a house that nearly knocked the breath out of Angel. It towered over her, with columns that reached to a third-story balcony. The ornate front doors had to be a good eight or nine feet tall, made of rich, dark wood. Angel followed Melinda up the brick steps leading to Melinda's front door and waited while Melinda dug out her house key.

Inside the entryway, a twenty-foot cathedral ceiling supported a massive crystal chandelier. Gleaming tile floors spread out for as far as Angel could see, and the furniture that decorated the enormous entry hall looked like it was straight out of a magazine.

"Your house is beautiful," Angel said.

"If you like this kind of stuff, yeah."

Melinda led the way through the living area, which was more richly decorated than the entry hall, and stopped in the kitchen. Her boots clomped across the tile as she walked past an expanse of polished granite countertop. Then she opened the refrigerator door, which matched the cherry wood of the miles of cabinets, and pulled out a soda.

"Want one?"

"No thanks. Water's fine."

"Oh, right," Melinda said with a laugh. "I forgot. Not organic."

She grabbed the drinks and they continued on to Melinda's room. What once must have been a beautiful canopy bed was painted matte black and stuck out from the corner of the room at an angle. The rest of the furniture was covered in clothes and other stuff Angel could barely identify. Speckles of black nail polish dotted the plush carpet, and junk overflowed the open closet. Melinda shoved a pile of clothes over and sat against the headboard.

Angel crinkled her nose and slid onto the edge of the bed. "So which hurricane did this?" She pushed at a large spot of hardened nail polish with her toe. "How can you stand this?"

Melinda flashes a sarcastic smile. "Sorry I don't have your OCD tendencies. Deal with it. Now are you gonna tell me where you've been all this time, or what?" Melinda looked greedily at Angel.

Angel took a deep breath, twisting her hair around her fingertip. "I found my real parents. I've moved back with them. I...I'm just back to check on Zack."

"Just Zack?"

"I…don't really want a family reunion. Please don't tell anyone else I'm here."

"Don't worry. I'm not tracking them down in Chicago just to nark on you. I'm not even sure where in Chicago they live now."

"They *moved* there? I just assumed they were visiting Aunt Mary."

Melinda cocked her eyebrow. "What?"

Right, like that makes sense.

"Um…I tried the old house first, but no one was home."

"But you must have known about Zack. Isn't that why you're in this neighborhood?"

Ugh.

"Listen, I only have pieces of information, not the whole story. I couldn't find out everything from where I live now." Angel hoped that would satisfy Melinda, but no luck.

"Where *do* you live now? Why are you being so evasive?"

"Evasive? When did you start using words like that? I thought you'd burned your dictionary in some ritual."

"Ooooh, that reminds me. Guess what? My mom says she's gonna help me start a fortune-telling website. It's gonna be so cool." Melinda's eyes glimmered.

"You still believe in all that stuff?" Angel spied a stack of Tarot cards on what she assumed was a desk, but other than that there were no signs of Melinda's old "toys."

Melinda shifted nervously on the bed and shook her head.

"'Course not. I know it's a bunch of hocus-pocus, but it makes money. And that's what it's all about, ain't it? Just look around here. Mom's got gobs of money these days, thanks to her latest. *Hank*." She rolled her eyes. "Combs his hair all the way over like it's really gonna make people think he's not bald. But he's loaded, so I guess he can do what he wants. At least I get to do anything I want, with him dragging my mom to banquets and cruises, and whatever." Melinda reached over and flipped open a magazine.

"Here," she said, "Look at this. Mom and Hank at a movie premiere." The picture was of Melinda's mother dressed in a full-length gown with her arms wrapped around the neck of a man in a tuxedo. Her mother was grinning from ear to ear and held onto the man as if she needed his assistance to stand. He was busy gaping at another woman passing by.

"Looks like a real catch."

"Yeah, whatever." Melinda's eyes darkened even more.

Angel reached over to put the magazine back on the nightstand and noticed a folded newspaper with a black and white picture of a very familiar face.

"This is Josh!" She grabbed the paper and opened it.

Josh was pictured with one fist held triumphantly in the air and a grin lighting his face as he gripped a huge trophy.

"Yeah, I never would have believed it if I hadn't seen it myself. Check this out." Melinda pointed to a paragraph halfway down.

Angel could barely believe what she read. Josh made quarterback in his second year at a major university. Straight-A student, too.

"No way!!"

"Yep! Can ya believe it? Old Joshie. I always thought he was dumb, but I guess he was just playing along to fit in with his football buds." Melinda's face brightened with a genuine smile. There was almost a twinkle in those deep, forlorn eyes.

"I always thought Josh and Jacob were so different from each other," Angel said. "I knew Jacob was smart and just used his brain for all the wrong things, but I thought Josh was the opposite—lacking in brain capacity and at least a little serious about things. Serious about football anyway." Angel continued staring at the picture and found herself welling up with pride for her foster brother.

"Well, something got up his rear and changed his mind." Melinda leaned back against the headboard. "When we moved, I remember him being the big dumb jock, but when mom and I came back, he was changed. And I never saw him and Jacob together anymore. He was even nice to me. Really freaky."

"What about Jacob? How is he?" Angel had never even thought to Find either of them. She had assumed they'd be living together in some frat house or something. She really had no desire to see either of them in the same way that she wanted to see Zack.

"Well, he's not homeless or anything. Of course, that's only because he's got a roommate that's not quite as much of a loser as him." Melinda said this so casually that Angel jerked her head up from the paper.

"Jacob's that bad off? How do you know?"

"His roommate is Toby's brother."

"Charlie?"

Melinda nodded.

"But, what…what happened?"

"Well," Melinda said, absentmindedly filing her chipped black nails, "Toby said Jacob's been partying with Charlie for a long time. Josh used to hang out with them, too, until one night when they got busted by your dad. Scared Joshie straight, I guess. Kinda funny though, 'cos Charlie's the one who nearly bit it when he ran his truck off the road that night, and he ain't changed a bit."

Angel remembered that night all too well. She could still see clear as day the vision of the headlights speeding straight toward her and Gregor. A shiver ran down her spine, and she folded the newspaper and set in on the bed.

"I gotta pee," said Melinda. "I'll be right back." She flung the nail file at the nightstand, rose from the bed, and headed out to the hallway without so much as a glance in Angel's direction.

Angel surveyed the room again. *How can she live like this? The clutter in here would give Gregor a stroke.* She smiled to herself and gazed out the window.

The street had been quiet, but a few cars rolled past. Angel glanced at the clock on Melinda's nightstand. Two-thirty. Wouldn't kids be getting out of school about now?

She turned back to the window and caught sight of a Mercedes cruising slowly by. A mop of unruly strawberry curls were just visible through the open back window. Angel jumped up and pressed her face against the window.

Zack!

The muffled sound of a toilet flushing told her Melinda would be right back, but she had no time to wait. She spun on her heel and nearly fell as her sneaker gripped the carpet. She caught herself by stepping forward onto a particularly large nail polish stain. *Ugh, what a slob.* She waved her hand, and ran out of the bedroom.

"Melinda, gotta go!" she yelled over her shoulder as she opened the front door and dashed outside.

Chapter Eight

Melinda

Melinda watched Angel's head disappear around the big oak tree down the street and then closed the front door. *Weird.*

She walked down the hallway to her room, her foot dragging along the carpet as she passed her bed. Something was different, but it took her a moment to pinpoint it.

The nail polish spots were gone.

Really gone. Not just faded, but disappeared. She dropped to her knees and dug her fingertips into the carpet. It wasn't like she'd ever really tried to get the stains out, but she knew there was no way nail polish would come out like that. She crawled around the floor. The nail polish was *gone.* It was like someone had replaced the carpet. *Impossible.*

She scanned the rest of the room. Nothing else was different. Although, the mess did seem worse than she remembered. *Maybe I should clean up.*

What's the point?

She kicked at the trashcan next to her desk, knocking it over. Tiny black flecks littered the carpet in front of the open end of the trashcan. Melinda bent down to inspect them. They were flakes of dried nail polish. She scooped them up into her palm and let them rain down onto the carpet. She thought of Angel's expression when she'd toed the dried nail polish.

Could Angel have…?

No.

Melinda dropped the last bit of nail polish and curled up against her headboard. She wasn't at all surprised at being stood up by Toby. It was typical of him. It was typical of all her friends. Well, maybe "friends" wasn't the right word, but she didn't know what was.

Ever since her father's disappearance she hadn't made a single *real* friend. She'd had a few in Germany, where she was happier than she'd ever been in Florida. Her father had actually spent time at home. Granted, most of it was alone, holed up in his office, but when he came out, he seemed to really notice her. Then, one day he started traveling again, and before long, he'd just disappeared without a trace.

A voice from the hallway pulled her out of her daydreams. It took a moment for the words to register.

"Melinda, I'm home. 'Night, dear. I'll see you tomorrow." Her mom sounded drunker than usual. *And it's hardly night.* Another voice followed, but Melinda didn't hear the words. She covered her ears and scrunched her eyes. *I wish that loser would stay away from my mom. Maybe I'll cut off that stupid comb-over while he sleeps…*

Her mother's bedroom door slammed. Melinda lowered her hands and scooted off the bed. She stuffed her feet into her boots and left her room, not bothering to sneak as she plodded down the hallway toward the front door.

As Melinda rounded a corner a block from her house, she heard what sounded like someone sniffling, and then a half-sob. A quick scan revealed two sneaker-clad feet sticking out from behind a tree in front of Zack's house. She walked toward them and knelt down in front of Angel.

"They won't let me see him." Angel didn't lift her head. Her brown hair hung like a curtain in front of her face, then spread into tendrils that clung to her arm-enclosed knees.

"Let me guess," Melinda said. "You told them you were Zack's sister." Angel nodded. Melinda dropped her knees to the ground. "What'd'ya expect? Girl, I thought you were the smart one."

Angel lifted her head and peered at Melinda through her mess of brown hair. Melinda shook her head. *Pathetic.*

"Look," she said. "You can't be honest with people like that. They know Zack's not happy. You think they care? He's just something to brag to their friends about."

Angel's lip trembled. "I asked them if they love him. They said...they said they were good for him, that he was lucky to have them. But they wouldn't answer my question. They don't love him at all." Her voice cracked.

"I snuck around and peeked in his window. He was sitting on the bed, rocking back and forth, crying. There's nothing in there—none of his science stuff, not a single toy. Trophies were everywhere, and ribbons." Angel sniffed, as her eyes glistened with tears.

Melinda's stomach tightened.

"He's not Zack anymore! He looks haunted, Melinda. Like a prisoner."

Melinda sighed. "He *is* a prisoner. And if you wanna see him, you're gonna have to be sneaky. I'll help if you want."

Tears ran down Angel's cheeks as she looked helplessly at Melinda. It was heart-wrenching, but Melinda pushed back the pity she held for Angel. She'd offered to help only because she'd enjoy seeing those ratty snobs get what they deserved for being so rotten to a little kid. She couldn't afford to get caught up in whatever Angel was really into, whatever gave her the ability to make all that nail polish disappear. She'd given up on stuff like that. Hocus-pocus, illusions, deceptions. Her dad was right—there was no such thing as real magic.

Angel seemed to pull herself together, but her voice wavered when she spoke again. "I have to see him, but I don't want to lie. There have been too many lies..."

Melinda tried reading the girl's eyes. *There's something there I've never seen before. She's got secrets, I can feel it.*

"Listen, goody-two-shoes, there's no other way. Mr. and Mrs. High and Mighty are never going to let you near him. Trust me, I know. My mom told me all about it. She was dating their lawyer."

The look that appeared on Angel's face made Melinda avert her eyes. She sniffed. *I don't need this freak to feel sorry for me. I'm outta here.*

She stood to leave, but Angel grabbed her arm. The pity was gone, replaced by an imploring look.

"Please," Angel said. "Don't go. I need you to help me. I don't want to lie to them, though. You have to tell me how I can get him alone."

"You're the smart one, remember. Why are you asking me?" That look didn't fool her for a minute. Melinda knew Angel felt sorry for her. Poor Melinda with the jerk of a father, poor Melinda with no friends, poor Melinda with the drunk mother…

"It's been two years! I have to see him. This may be my only chance. Please. Can you think of something by tomorrow?"

"I don't need 'till tomorrow. We'll get his attention while he's at recess."

"You know his school schedule?" asked Angel.

"Toby and I ditch and hang out right outside the fence all the time. Nothing like hanging out at school to keep from getting caught ditching. Besides, there's…no, never mind."

"What? Tell me." Angel grabbed her arm, but this time Melinda didn't pull away.

"There's a bully, okay. I caught him picking on Zack a few times. I make sure he sees me now and then so he leaves Zack alone. He's not too keen on getting another bloody nose, so all I gotta do is show my face enough that he knows I haven't forgot."

Angel gave her a quizzical look, and then smiled through her tears. "You're amazing, Melinda." She straightened up and brushed her hair out of her face. "Okay, I'll meet you tomorrow at your house? What time?"

"Ten o'clock."

"Thanks," Angel said as she stood.

Melinda rose as well, eyeing Angel curiously. *Maybe I can find out what she's up to. She's changed. I gotta know what's giving her that look.*

Angel smiled one more time and turned away. Melinda watched her walk down the shadowy sidewalk heading toward town. After a few moments she decided to follow, but as she rounded the corner Angel had just taken, she lost sight of her. Nothing was there. Not even a stray cat.

Chapter Nine

Zack

"You're not going without me this time." Ayden's jaw was set firm, his feet planted on the leaf-strewn ground of the small clearing. Angel shot an imploring look at Kalek, who leaned against a nearby tree turning his forearm back and forth as he admired his latest tattoo. He glanced up, gave her a hint of a shrug, and resumed his examination.

Thanks, you're a big help.

"But, Ayden…"

"No, I feel much better today. I just won't close the Gate, and Kalek can stand guard here."

Kalek glanced up again and said in a monotone. "It's my call to serve." He looked back down and immediately grimaced. "Gah! Gunther messed this up. I asked for red here."

Angel rolled her eyes. She turned to Ayden, and reached up to brush his bangs out of his eyes, letting her hand linger at his ear. "Please, I'm worried about you."

Ayden wrapped his hand around her arm and tugged gently, snaking his other arm around her back. "No. You had me terrified yesterday. Your parents were completely freaked out. I can't believe they're letting you go again."

"I was only gone a couple of hours, and Horatio was with me the whole time."

"But *I* was supposed to be with you, too! I should have gone anyway." His hands clenched the back of her shirt.

"And, what, collapsed on the other side of the Gate? Maybe closing it or something? Think my parents would have been happy about that?"

"Quit rationalizing."

"I'm not. It's the truth. Mom and Dad saw that—why can't you?"

"What your mom and dad saw was that you're intent on doing this with or without their cooperation. *What they saw* is you being stubborn." Ayden's words came out hard, but his eyes glistened.

Angel couldn't control the smile on her face and the pounding of her heart. "I'm not the only stubborn one, though, am I?"

Ayden smirked.

Before Angel could register what was happening, Ayden's lips pressed against hers.

"Okay…" The word slipped out of Angel's mouth on a breath.

Ayden smiled and Angel's heart did a somersault.

"Dude!" Kalek's tangled curls hung over one eye, but the other onyx orb peeked between coiled tendrils. "Don't do that. She's like my sister. I don't need that visual. Now go through the Gate already, I want to get to the Temple before sundown."

"It's only three o'clock, Kalek," Angel said.

"Not the point. Go."

Angel clung to Ayden's hand as they watched Melinda at the fence. She completely understood why Melinda and Toby chose this spot to hang out. The overdone landscaping around the grand campus of Zack's elite private school offered perfect camouflage from the road. The classroom windows were too high to afford a view of the spot from inside the building. The only place from which they could be seen was an isolated corner of the courtyard used during recess. And only one kid seemed interested in spending time there.

"Pssst, Zack," Melinda hissed with her face pressed between the wrought iron bars that spanned the gap between huge brick columns. "Zackie, I've got a surprise for you."

Angel's heart pounded as Zack seemed to move in slow motion. His curls caught fire under the midmorning sun, the varying red hues dancing as he lifted his head. He clutched a scuffed and battered game system in his hand. His eyes widened. "Angel?"

She smiled and nodded, joy welling inside her. She nearly slammed into the fence. The emotion had to come out or she'd burst.

"You still use that old thing?" Tears streamed down her face. She'd bought it with her own money. It represented months of babysitting the Anderson brats, and Zack still used it even though it was obsolete, and his adoptive parents could afford the newest and most expensive one on the market.

Instantly, his expression changed. The sweet-little-boy face she'd known and loved twisted into a vicious snarl, eyes squinting, as he screamed, "Go away! I don't want to see you!"

He turned to run away, but before Angel could blink, Melinda had jumped the fence and grabbed him by the arm.

"Zack, you little snot, march over there, *now*, or I'll never do another thing to stop Eddie from kicking your—" Melinda glanced over her shoulder. "Butt."

His eyes remained slits.

Angel's heart felt as if Zack had personally smashed it with a sledgehammer. She eyed the end of the fence where Melinda must have used the crossbars to climb over, but her feet wouldn't move.

Melinda tugged his arm, and he dragged his feet toward the fence. Just as they stepped up to the bars, a kid with buzzed hair, wearing a uniform like Zack's, appeared at the corner of the building. He stood at least six inches taller than Zack, and twice as thick.

"Well, well. What do we have here? Zackie's got a whole group of freaks with him today. Good thing I brought back-up this time." Two more thugs appeared, both of them tall, though not quite as thick as the leader.

"*Edward*," Melinda said in a sickeningly sweet voice, "thanks so much. Now I have lunch to share with my friends." She curled her upper lip like a dog revealing its teeth. Angel scrunched her eyes and blinked.

Fangs?

The three boys backed up, and all reached into their pockets at the same time. Then they each pulled out a wooden dowel with one end hewn into a rough point. Melinda laughed. "You're kidding me, right?"

One boy nudged Eddie, and, with eyes bulging, pointed at Angel and Ayden. Angel turned her head ever so slightly and caught sight of Ayden. He held his mouth open in the same manner as Melinda, and Angel distinctly saw long, sharp fangs.

Seriously?

She glanced back and forth between Melinda and Ayden, then finally smiled. *Okay….*

Angel concentrated, using what little magic she could access, and forced her teeth into points. The boys were waving the pointed sticks in front of Melinda, and she reached out to snatch Eddie's from his hand. As Angel bared her teeth, the boys spun on their heels and ran headlong across the field.

Melinda burst out laughing, dropping the plastic fangs into her palm. Angel quickly returned her teeth to normal, but not before Zack noticed. He stared at her, mouth open, a tear coursing down his cheek. Awe, fear, and anger seemed to be struggling for footing on his face.

"M-Melinda's are fake," he finally said in a whisper, "but you…what are you, Angel?"

"Zack, please. Oh, I'm so sorry…" She choked on the sobs that erupted, and gripped the fence with iron fists. "Please, Zack, you have to let me explain."

"No! It's your fault I'm here. They took me from Mom and Dad because of you. The papers were almost signed, but you ruined it all, and now I have to live with Aunt Ivy and Uncle Clarence. I hate you!"

Everything clicked into place. The couple had never given Angel their names, but now it all made sense. The people who had taken Zack were his aunt and uncle. They'd never wanted him while his mom was alive. They said they didn't claim "trailer trash," and Zack ended up in foster care while his mom tried to straighten out her life. She kept blowing it, though, but not enough to lose her rights entirely. She must have finally bombed out, and Zack's aunt and uncle must have gotten wind of how smart he was.

"Zack, please, if I had known, I would've never gone. But I had to. If you let me explain, you'll understand. Please…"

He clicked a button on his watch and crossed his arms. "You have two minutes."

Angel felt Ayden's arm wrap around her shoulder and the reminder of his presence energized her. She rambled as she told Zack the story of meeting Gregor and discovering the truth about her real parents and her mysterious past. Tears streamed down his cheeks, and soon Zack's arms dropped. He ignored the beeping of his watch and let her continue. Melinda stood to the side, mouth gaping. Angel felt a twinge of fear. She hadn't planned to reveal the truth to Melinda, not yet. Not this way. But she had to tell Zack, and this might be her only chance.

Her tale complete, her energy drained, she let go of the fence and put her arm around Ayden for support. Zack stood still, tears drying on his cheeks. Angel wanted nothing more than to put her hands on those cheeks and inhale the scent of his hair.

His lip quivered. "Take me with you."

Ayden stepped forward. "Zack, that's not what—"

Zack's little hands balled into fists. "Take me with you! I hate them! I hate it here!" He ran to the fence and grabbed the bars.

Angel reached out and touched his hand.

"Please..." He stared into her eyes. The same blue eyes that had peeked over the sheets at her every night when she tucked him into bed. The same eyes that had shadowed with ghosts of understanding the night she'd left even though he'd been only six years old.

He was still a child, but he'd never been like other children.

"Yes," she said. "We'll take you."

Ayden grabbed her shoulder. "Angel, he's—"

"No, he's not. Zack understands. Trust me. He may be eight, but he gets it."

Ayden turned to Zack.

Zack returned his gaze, one eyebrow raised. "You better be taking good care of my sister."

Ayden smiled. "You bet. I'm Ayden, by the way."

A voice creaked from off to the side, but Angel couldn't make out the words. She turned and saw Melinda staring at her with greedy eyes.

"What?" Angel asked.

Melinda cleared her throat. "Take me, too."

"I...don't think that'd be a good idea. What about your mom? And school? You can't just leave like that."

Melinda's eyes narrowed and she shifted her stance as if getting ready for a fight. "Why not? I'm failing everything and I already skipped half my exams. Besides, you ran away. What's the difference?" She huffed. "You're practically kidnapping Zackie and you're gonna lecture *me* about ditching a mom who probably won't even notice? No way. I'm going. You can't stop me." Her nostrils flared and her fists tightened.

Melinda's words hit Angel like a freight train. Until that moment, she had justified everything, claiming she was rescuing Zack. But, despite his rotten situation, legally he belonged with his aunt and uncle. She stumbled backward from the fence, woozy. The ground lurched under her feet. "I've made a mistake…I'm sorry…Ayden, let's go."

"No!" Zack and Melinda's voices hit Angel's ears in stereo. Melinda lunged forward. "You're not backing out on me now, Witchie-poo. I hate my life here. My mom would rather have me gone. She tells me every time she's not drunk. And Zack's aunt and uncle treat him like their little pet. He's a kid—he deserves to be treated like a human being!"

Angel cringed at the anger in Melinda's voice. But she found her footing and ran her gaze over Melinda's face. The anger was a mask, and pain seeped through.

"Fine," she said, "but we're gonna figure out how to do this without kidnapping him. And, Melinda, you have to tell your mom. Tell her you're coming to stay with me for a while, but you make sure she understands this is your choice."

Melinda relaxed her fisted hands and smiled. "You got it."

Angel and Ayden headed home to work out a plan with Angel's parents, sending Melinda off to talk to her mom. Angel had hugged Zack fiercely before leaving, and promised that nothing would stop her from returning. The love that had appeared in his eyes before she turned to leave was all the motivation she needed to set things right for him.

Two days later, Angel stood on the front stoop with her parents. A horse-drawn carriage waited in the road in front of their house, its back end loaded with her parents' suitcases. Ayden had offered to Gate them over, but with all their luggage, a permanent portal made more sense. Located on the outskirts of town, it would take them to a small Empowered area a few hours from Zack, where they'd arranged for a room. Angel had been amazed when she found out there were other Empowered so close to where she'd lived in Florida, a whole town she never knew existed on an island in the Keys.

"Thanks so much for this," Angel said, throwing her arms around her father's chest. "I promise we'll be careful while you're gone. We'll get Melinda and come right back. And Kalek promised to keep an eye on us. And Ayden and Sarah are right—"

"Yes, I know," her dad said, hugging her more tightly. "You've already presented your case."

Angel squeezed him again, then turned to her mom. None of them had seen or heard anything about Doran Ashe since the day at Sir Benjamin's, yet her mom's unspoken fears were written clearly in her expression.

Her mom cupped Angel's cheek with her palm. "I know you said you're staying here for Melinda, that there's no use dragging her along through all that's likely to happen with Zack. But I know you, sweetie. Are you sure you don't want one last chance to spend time with Zack if this falls through?"

"It won't fall through," Angel said. "Remember how easy it went with me?"

"That was different." Her mom's eyes shadowed. "You're *our* child. We may not be able to create a case for custody of Zack."

Angel shook her head, and her mom dropped her hand. "It's not different. He's meant to be here. I can feel it. It's just like when Mr. and Mrs. Mason tried to adopt me—nothing happened the way it was supposed to, like something was stopping it because I was meant to come back here. Only, this time the opposite will happen. Look how quickly you got a court date! It could have been set for months away, but next week?"

There was even more than that. How coincidental had it been that she'd run into Melinda, the one person who knew about Zack's situation and could help her. Who had the article about Josh on her nightstand. Who hung around with the brother of Jacob's roommate. No, it was more than coincidence. This was all meant to be.

Her mom's expression softened, and after a moment she nodded. "It does seem pretty strange."

"Right," Angel said. "Zack's coming back with you because he's *supposed* to."

Her mother sighed, and then wrapped her arms around Angel. Angel pressed her cheek against her mom's hair.

"I love you," her mom said.

Angel nodded, unable to repeat the words because they balled up in her throat as tears pushed against her eyelids.

She let go of her mom, and watched her parents walk away. They waved as they climbed into the carriage. Angel wiped the tears from her cheeks.

Ayden appeared at the edge of the yard and caught her gaze.

"Spying on me?" she asked as he approached.

"I'm not the only one." He nodded in the direction of Kalek, who stood on the other side of the yard.

"He wasn't spying. We knew he was here the whole time, otherwise my parents wouldn't have left. He just doesn't do good-byes." She turned to Kalek. "Either come over here, or get off to whatever skulking you have planned for today." The words came out sarcastically despite her attempt to make them playful.

Kalek scowled. "What time must I come back to play tree-guard?"

"Same as before," she said.

He gave a single nod and stalked down the side of the yard toward the forest behind the house.

"How about we kill time helping Mom for a while?"

Angel nodded, locked the front door, and followed Ayden to his house.

When they returned to Angel's house a few hours later, they checked on Zoe, then walked to the Silver Spruce behind her house. Kalek was waiting, scowling just as he had that morning. He didn't say a word as they approached, just crossed his arms and nodded toward the Spruce.

"Good afternoon to you, too, sunshine," Angel said.

"Just be quick. I promised your parents I'd look after you, but I have better things to do than be the welcoming committee for your little friend."

Angel sighed. "Whatever. It should only be a minute."

Ayden stayed quiet, but turned to the Spruce and raised his hand. Then he stepped through the Gate. Angel followed.

They emerged from the same huge oak tree as before, and walked to Melinda's house. Ayden kept his gaze straight ahead, but Angel couldn't help looking at the grand houses as they passed by. It still didn't gel in her mind that Melinda wanted to leave, no matter how awful her mom was.

Angel and Ayden stopped in the street in front of Melinda's house. Melinda stood on the front porch, a piece of paper clutched in her hand. She waved it at them as she ran down the porch steps. A huge backpack hung on one shoulder, tugging at her tight, long-sleeve black t-shirt, and her cell phone was clipped to the pocket of her baggy black jeans.

"Here, this good enough for you?" She stuck the paper under Angel's nose and continued in a singsong voice, "A note from my *mommy*. She was so glad to have me out of her hair for the summer, she nearly busted. Well," she sighed, "at least I finally did something to make her happy."

Angel mused over the mixture of pain and joy in Melinda's eyes. *This may actually be the best thing for her. I hope so, anyway.* "Okay, then," she said. "Let's go."

Ayden led the way to the tree. Angel stood to the side so he could step through first. When his boot disappeared, Melinda's eyes bulged. She twisted her gaze toward Angel, a catlike grin curling her lips.

"Wicked cool, girlie," she said, and stepped through.

Chapter Ten

New Friends?

"Where are we?" Melinda spun slowly, her gaze landing on tree after tree. Was this what she was supposed to be seeing? Angel had told her they'd be traveling across the globe, to someplace magical. This was just a forest.

"Toch Island," Angel said. "It's kind of near Ireland. Hidden, though, so you could never have heard of it."

Melinda snuffed, and started walking around. "A hidden island. Wicked. But where's the magical stuff. All I see are trees."

She felt Angel's hand on her forearm, and turned toward her friend from what seemed like ages ago. Little goodie-two-shoes. Couldn't keep her nose out of a book, except when she was sticking it in Melinda's business.

"Some of the trees are magical." Angel guided Melinda back to the tree they'd just stepped out of.

The thought hung in her mind. *We just stepped into one tree and out of another.* She blinked at the tree.

"It's a Christmas tree."

"No, a Silver Spruce. Look closely."

Melinda ran her hand across the silver-green needles. Their softness surprised her. They were the color of Toby's car, pearly and metallic. If she hadn't seen the thing growing out of the ground with her own eyes, she would have thought the tree was fake, spray-painted. But when the needles caught the sunlight, they glimmered with life.

She plucked a cluster of long needles from a branch and laid it across her palm.

Something crunched and she sensed the presence of someone behind her. The voice that came over her shoulder sent chills racing up and down her spine.

"She hasn't been here two minutes and she's already vandalizing the forest. I told you it wasn't a good idea to bring her here." The voice was smooth as steel, honed to a razor-sharp edge.

Melinda spun, feeling like a bull who'd just spied a red flag. But the words she'd intended to sling dropped like bricks, pinning her tongue down.

Long hair, all tangled and wild, tattoos on his crossed arms that pulsed with the lean muscles flexing underneath. Was that a dagger strapped to his leg? *Wicked.* And those eyes. Dark. Deep. Soulful. Pissed off.

He glared at her through the curtain of hair. "Those trees are rare. Don't take what you're not going to actually use."

Melinda's nostrils flared. This guy may be hot, but he had no right harping on her. "It's one needle. What's it gonna hurt? And who are you—the tree police?"

"Kalek." Angel stepped in front of him, her back to Melinda. "Give her a break. She didn't know. It's no big deal."

Melinda huffed, and squeezed the needles in her palm. Kalek's jaw twitched, but he backed off.

Angel turned and faced Melinda. "Sorry. He's protective, but he won't give you a hard time again." She shot a glance at him that made Melinda smile. *Ooh, girlie finally grew a spine.*

Ayden stepped over, and put his arm around Angel. Melinda stuffed the needle into her pocket and hooked her fingers onto her backpack straps. The silence dragged to the point of discomfort until Ayden spoke.

"Let's get to the farm and get something to eat. I'm starving."

Melinda's eyes popped. "Farm? You're kidding, right?" That was too much. First she's plopped into the middle of a boring forest—okay, the one tree was pretty cool—but the rest of it looked just like the woods by Angel's old neighborhood. The first person she meets is a jerk. Hot, but totally rude. And now, they gotta go hang out on a *farm*? Maybe this wasn't such a great idea.

"Why the farm?" Angel asked. "We're right here by the house."

House? Where? Melinda stepped away from the group, searching between trees. The trio's voices lilted past her ears, but she only caught words and phrases. Something about goats and checking the new shelter. No way. If there was a house that didn't involve farm animals, Melinda was going to find it first.

She spied a cluster of homes beyond the edge of the forest. She picked up her pace, but stopped dead in her tracks when she reached a white picket fence.

This wasn't a neighborhood. Neighborhoods had paved roads, street lamps, wrought iron mailbox posts, and deed restrictions. This was too cute, and *rustic,* to be a real neighborhood.

Great. I followed Witchie-poo to the magical land of Po-dunk.

"Melinda!"

Angel's voice sounded almost panicky. Good grief. The girl needed to chill out.

"Over here!" Melinda waved her hand, and laughed at the sight of Angel and Ayden running toward her. Mr. Long-hair trailed behind, slinking along like a cat. Kalek? Yeah. He really was gorgeous. And cool. Too bad he was a jerk. He stepped up beside Angel, who was now glaring at Melinda, and shook his mass of curls.

What was that? His ears looked pointed. Melinda stepped back, trying not to look shocked.

"What?" Kalek's eyes flickered with malice.

Melinda slipped a glance at Angel, and then back at Kalek.

"Nothing," she said, letting her gaze drop. "Thought I saw something."

Angel grabbed Melinda's arm. "Well, no point in going to the farm now. Let's just go to my house."

Melinda sat on a barstool while Angel, now a redhead again, cleaned off the dishes from lunch. The kitchen had wood everywhere, and a deep, white sink with a curtain-framed window above it overlooking the back yard. A glass-paned door opened up to a small patio in the back. The floor was a stone tile. Not at all the country-blue and floral cluttered room she'd expected.

She took another sip of water. No soda, of course. Not that Angel would have that even if she wasn't living in some backward, hillbilly magic town. The house, at least, wasn't completely primitive. The living room furniture had looked pretty modern when she walked through it. Sleek couch, loveseat and chair all in matching tan with bright red pillows. Glossy wood floors and a brick fireplace.

Angel waved her hand over another plate and the food scraps all swooshed into the trashcan. Just like the nail polish from the carpet. Melinda stared, watching until Angel was done.

The guys had left the second they finished eating. They went to the farm Angel had mentioned, to go feed goats. Whatever. At least the long-haired forest ranger had stayed off her back during lunch.

"He's really an Elf?" Melinda asked.

"He's *Elven*," Angel said as she flicked her finger toward a cabinet door and it flew open. "He's not like one of Santa's little helpers or something."

"So, what's his damage?" Melinda asked. "Why's he so OCD about pine needles?"

Angel laughed, and floated the clean dishes into the cabinet. Melinda gulped hard on her water. She was *not* going to choke and let Angel know she was impressed. The girl was doing real magic. Not the hocus-pocus stuff. She was making dishes *fly*.

"Kalek's a good guy. Really." The last dish flew into the cabinet and Angel waved her hand. The door swung shut. She sat on the stool next to Melinda. "His sister died two years ago. Someone poisoned her. Then his best friend in the world disappeared. And then his dad had a stroke. He's been through a lot."

Angel looked at Melinda, and Melinda tensed. She hated that expression. The *I'm so sorry about your dad* look everyone had been giving her for the last two years.

"Hm," Melinda said, "two years. That's a long time. Shouldn't he kinda be over it by now?"

Angel's face got all scrunched up like it used to do when they were kids and she was mad about something. "No. Seriously, Melinda. It's okay to miss someone, you know."

"Don't look at me that way. You have no idea how much I *don't* miss my dad. He sure didn't miss me when he was flying all over the friggin' globe, lecturing people about adaptations and cross breeding species. The only thing he cared about was his work. So, no, I don't miss him. Not one bit."

Melinda stood and walked over to the kitchen window. Angel's dog was running around like an idiot in the back yard, chasing some big flying bug. Angel had actually talked to—no, not *to*—she'd talked *with* that thing when they got to the house. She'd had what looked like an actual conversation with it. That was probably the strangest thing Melinda had seen so far.

Okay, maybe not. She'd had lunch with an Elven rock star.

She turned and said, "So what's out here besides trees and Elves?"

"Do you want to go see the town?" Angel's eyes sparkled like they had gold swirled into the brown. Melinda had never noticed that before.

"Sure."

They headed out of Angel's yard and down a road with dirt packed so hard and smooth it seemed paved. A lot of the yards were pretty densely treed, and the lawns were patched with colorful flowers. Most of the houses in the neighborhood had little fences and wood siding like Angel's, and looked like they'd been built before the invention of the telephone. At least they *had* telephones. The no electricity thing, though—completely weird.

The big black bug whipped past Melinda's head every few minutes, chirping like a mutant chick. Angel told her he was guarding them from some criminal. *So, this place ain't all sunshine and daisies. We might find something truly interesting after all.*

The walk seemed to go on forever once they left the neighborhood and followed a long, lonely road lined with log fencing and—big surprise—more trees.

Angel rambled on about some guy named Gregor who disappeared into a magic Temple. Angel told her all about how she was homeschooled, which explained why she'd been lurking around on a school day. Then there was her job at the book store, and her drawing…

Melinda's head hurt trying to keep up with Angel's chatter. The words drifted through her brain like wisps, only bits of them catching hold.

Her attention snapped back to Angel when she heard the word "convict." What? Hadn't Angel just been babbling about *The Picture of Dorian Gray?*

Before Melinda could ask about it, they rounded a bend in the road and Angel said, "Here it is."

Melinda found herself staring at a town center that couldn't make up its mind what it wanted to be. The red brick buildings and wooden signs looked historic, but the freak show on the sidewalk was a different story. Some kid with a green mohawk was talking to a guy with overalls and cowboy boots. Mohawk Boy grabbed the arm of an old lady as she walked by. Melinda cringed, but the old lady reached up and wrapped her arms around the kid's neck in a hug.

Angel zipped between people and Melinda tried to keep up as her gaze jumped from person to person. There was no rhyme or reason to this place. It was like people from every culture and time period had crash-landed together and built a town. And somehow it just…worked.

Melinda found herself dragged into a little building and a bell rang in her ears. She looked around—books filled every square inch of the place.

"You brought me to the library?" She snatched her arm out of Angel's grasp.

Angel laughed. "This is the bookstore I work at. Haven't you heard a word I've said?"

Something like a grunt pushed its way out of Melinda's mouth, and she stepped further into the room. She stopped when she saw two Elven guys standing in front of a big wooden desk. An old man in a checkered shirt had his head down on the desktop, moaning.

Angel flew past, and skidded to a halt in front of the desk. "Sir B, are you okay?"

Neither of the guys was Kalek, and Melinda breathed a sigh of relief as she walked over and stood next to Angel.

The old man lifted his head. "Oh, dear. I'm feeling awful. These gentleman had to help me to my chair." His hair and beard were salt and pepper, and his cheeks round and flushed under his glasses.

Melinda sides flinched as she stifled a giggle. Angel had said the *Elven* weren't *Santa's little helpers…*

Angel turned to Melinda and cocked one eyebrow. Melinda had to cover her mouth to keep from laughing. The two Elven guys swung their heads around and glared. Her laughing suddenly seemed completely controllable. *Man, what's with these guys? It's like having pointy ears takes away your sense of humor.*

"Sir B," Angel said as she moved closer to him. She put her hand on his forehead. "Do you need me to call the doctor? What happened?"

The old Santa pulled her hand away, clasping it between his own, and gave a weak smile. "Just a dizzy spell. No need to call the doctor."

Angel's mouth scrunched to one side.

"I appreciate the concern," he said, "but I'm sure with a little rest I'll be fine."

"At least let us walk you home," one of the Elven guys said.

Sir Benjamin nodded. "Not a bad idea."

Melinda watched all the men leave, Sir Benjamin not quite steady on his feet. She turned to ask Angel a question, but the thought shot from her brain the second her gaze reached the desk. Angel was kneeling next to—

Melinda stumbled back.

"That's a dragon!"

Angel laughed and pushed her hair behind her ear. "His name is Spike."

No sooner had Angel said the words, another dragon head popped up from behind Spike. The furry face stretched into a yawn, and golden eyes blinked before closing again. The head dropped back out of sight.

"That's…I mean…that's really…" Melinda dug her hands into her hair and held them there. She scrunched her eyes. *Dragons.* Her brain felt like it was going to pop. This was too much for one day.

She opened her eyes.

Angel said, "Do you want to pet him?"

Melinda's head shook as if it had a will of its own. "No, I…you know what, I think I need to take a walk. I'll be right back." She spun on her heel and dashed out the door.

Melinda plunged through the warm air, turning down a road that led away from the town square. Angel's voice hung in the background, calling her name.

"I'll be right back!" Melinda shouted over her shoulder, and ducked behind a building. She leaned against the wall and gulped in several breaths. Reality slammed the breath back out of her. She'd left home, and she was in a town where people were magic, and Elves lived here, and Santa Claus wore cowboy boots and had pet dragons…and…

And she was going crazy.

She realized tears were streaming down her cheeks, and smeared them away with her sleeves. She closed her eyes and let her head tip back and smack the wall, letting the pain that blossomed across the back of her skull soothe her with its reality.

"What am I doing here?" she said.

"It looks like you're having a fit."

She jumped and released a half-scream. A guy with longish, stringy hair stood in front of her, a sneaky grin plastered on his face.

"Where did you come from?" Melinda pressed her back into the wall.

"Ah, that is an interesting question. To know the answer to that would change the world. Simply put, I'd say the same place we all come from." His head tilted back ever so slightly, but it was enough to make him look like he was peering down his nose at her.

She mimicked his posture. "You know what I meant."

"That I did." His grin widened, reminding Melinda of the Cheshire cat. She'd always hated *Alice in Wonderland*, and now she felt like she was trapped in it.

"The name is Doran Ashe." He tilted his head in a mock-bow.

"M-Melinda."

His left eyebrow rose with a twitch. "Nice to meet you."

Something about him felt oddly familiar to Melinda. The name…Doran Ashe.

Angel hadn't been talking about *Dorian Gray*—and she *had* said *convict.* Was this him? What had he done? What kinds of crimes did magic people commit?

Replacing the Cheshire Cat, an image of the Mad Hatter shoved its way into Melinda's head. Nothing about it matched the guy in front of her, except the eyes.

His eyes swirled with color, but Melinda couldn't pinpoint it. Green? Gray? It was impossible to tell, and it made her stomach lurch.

"Um, I gotta go." she said, and began to scoot along the wall.

"Oh, too bad." His eyes dropped, and the sneer left his face. He looked genuinely sad now. "Honestly, I didn't mean to scare you. I guess it's just been a while since I've…oh, never mind." He turned and took a step away.

This was getting weirder and weirder.

"Dude, don't be like that. I really do have to go…but I'll come back."

Why did I just say that?

He spun around and his face lit up. The smile he wore was completely different now. He was actually kind of cute. And if this really was the guy Angel said was a convict it could make things…interesting.

"Tomorrow?" he said, stepping closer again.

"I don't know. I'll have to see, but probably."

He reached up and tugged at his ear. His entire demeanor had changed. He looked at Melinda with soft eyes. "I should tell you, um, I'm—"

"I know," Melinda said. "Don't worry, it's cool."

His face paled, and his hand dropped from his ear, but his expression didn't change. His voice came out deeper, reluctant. "You're not scared of me?"

Melinda swallowed.

"Should I be?" She pushed back against the wall. "I mean, if they let you go…"

He tilted one half of his mouth in a smile. "Yes…they let me go."

"Then I'm not going to judge you. Um. At least, if you promise not to judge me."

"What do you mean?"

Melinda clenched her fist as her throat tightened. She was supposed to be playing it cool, trying to not draw attention to her lack of magic. So why did she feel compelled to tell him?

"Nothing. Just, I'm not quite like everyone here."

"Me either," he said. "And not just because I've been, well, you know." He sucked in a breath and blew it out hard. "Not just because I've been in jail. That's part of it. But I'm different now for other reasons. So, maybe tomorrow I can tell you my story and you can tell me yours."

He really was cute. His left eyebrow seemed to always stay just a bit higher than his right, and when he smiled for real like that he almost had a dimple. Pretty eyes, too. They were now the same green as the pine needles she'd snagged. Melinda's mouth curled into a smile.

"See you tomorrow," she said, and then turned.

She felt his gaze follow her as she walked away. Not like Kalek. Who needed someone so uptight anyway?

Chapter Eleven

Light

Angel stopped. Had she heard right? She and Melinda were on their way back to Angel's house—walking, because Melinda hated the smell of horses—and Melinda had just said something.

"You spoke to who?" Angel asked.

Melinda bit her lip and started picking at her nail polish. "Um, Jordan. Some guy named Jordan. I ran into him down the street from the bookstore."

Angel scowled. "I thought you said Doran."

Melinda snorted out a half-laugh. "No way. Would I do that?" She started down the road again, and Angel reluctantly followed.

I know she said Doran. She's lying.

Angel wanted to kick herself for not following Melinda when she'd run out of the bookstore. But Angel hadn't wanted to leave the store unmanned. And all her memories of Melinda told her that pressure of any kind tended to backfire.

She jogged and caught up with Melinda. They walked in silence the rest of the way home.

Ayden came over later that evening, and the three of them hung out in the back yard. The sun glittered through the tops of the trees, shades of red and pink that reminded Angel of Florida sunsets at the beach. Ayden tossed a ball across the yard and Zoe dashed after it.

"When do you think your parents will be back?" he asked. Zoe skidded to a halt, grabbed the ball and dropped it at his feet. He tossed it again, and then sat in the lounge chair next to Angel. Melinda was stretched out in her chair on the other side.

"I don't know." Angel leaned back in her chair and crossed her ankles. "We never had to do any of this with me. Mom and Dad are my real parents, and it was mostly sending papers and stuff. Honestly, I didn't pay attention. But Zack's aunt and uncle have legal rights to him."

"Well...." Melinda said like she was about to dish some serious gossip, "if they were rich enough they could just buy Zack the way his aunt and uncle did."

Angel pushed her elbows into the chair arms and sat up straight. "What's that supposed to mean?"

Melinda peeked at her from the corner of her eye, then sat up and pulled her knees up under her chin. "Remember I said my mom dated their lawyer? I heard the whole story. Zack's *auntie* is his mom's sister. She wouldn't take him before because she thought Zack's mom was a loser. When she found out Zack's got a super brain, she dove in like a vulture on road kill. Her rich hubby's got connections and basically bought Zack."

Angel chewed on her lip as she squeezed the chair arms.

"Anyway," Melinda said, turning her head, "*Thomas* told Mom he'd never seen a case like that settled faster. It was like Zack's uncle went to the pet store and walked out with a puppy."

Heat buzzed under Angel's skin. Her jaw clenched. "Well, Mom and Dad are going to do everything they can to prove those people shouldn't be raising so much as a hamster."

Melinda laughed, then lifted one eyebrow as her top lip curled to match. "Maybe a *rat*."

Angel smiled and leaned back again.

"I still don't get why Zack wants to come here," Melinda said. "I mean, I know how tight you guys were, but doesn't he want to be with your old parents?"

"Mom looked into that," Angel said. "Mrs. Mason's aunt is really sick. And when they moved, since all us kids were gone, they dropped out of the foster program. Plus, Mr. Mason's not doing so good either." Angel's throat tightened up. Her mom had told her all that was going on, but this was the first time she'd said any of it out loud. "And Zack wants to be here. He's excited about it. It just works better this way."

Of course, that's what she'd thought the night she ran away. It was all for the better. But Jacob ended up trashing his life, and Zack got taken away. Angel swallowed a lump in her throat and took a deep breath. She would trust that something good would come out of this, and that her parents would make the right decisions, even if it meant not bringing Zack home.

Angel walked into the house after saying goodnight to Ayden. Melinda was curled up on the couch with Shakespeare. His purr oscillated in time with each stroke of her hand.

"He's tasty." Melinda winked and twisted her cheek in a one-sided smirk.

Angel felt heat rise up her neck.

"Sorry." Melinda dropped the smirk. "Didn't mean to embarrass you." Her voice sounded borderline sincere.

"I'm not embarrassed." Angel's voice creaked, and she caught herself reaching for her bangs. It sometimes seemed Gregor's habit had decided to stay behind with her. "We just haven't been together that long."

"Hmm." Melinda curled her legs tighter. "The way he looks at you doesn't say that." She smiled genuinely. "Anyway, where do I crash? I'm wiped out."

"The guest room is down the hall. The door on the right."

Melinda scooped Shakespeare into her arms. "Mind if I borrow him?" She nuzzled his nose with hers. "I forgot my teddy bear."

Shakespeare's eyes closed and his purring ratcheted up in volume as she cradled him against her chest. Angel had never seen Melinda look so sweet.

"He's all yours," Angel said. "Just be warned, when he wakes up, he'll want you up, too, and he'll use any means possible to get what he wants."

"You wouldn't do anything mean to me, would you?" Melinda said, rubbing her cheek against Shakespeare's forehead. She winked at Angel, snagged her backpack from the floor, and headed toward the hall.

Angel climbed the steps to her mother's loft. When she reached the upstairs window, she peered across to Ayden's back yard. The spider web pulsated with the same reds and pinks as the earlier sunset. Angel opened the window, inhaling the scent of the forest. Was Kalek wandering around out there, maybe guarding her house? He seemed so distracted and worried lately. She wouldn't dare tell him Melinda spoke to Doran. He'd flip.

Angel was worried, too, but not about herself. Ayden had looked exhausted when they came back through the Gate. His face had drained of color and his hand actually shook when he held it up to close the Gate. Sarah had said he'd have to choose his Talent eventually. At first, Angel had thought it was because as he grew up one would settle in place and he'd be stuck with it. But now she knew it was because changing Talents was just too hard on him. Maybe it was getting even harder.

Zoe's bark broke Angel out of her thoughts.

"Quiet!" she whispered. Then a little louder as the barking continued, "Zoe, shush!" The hair on Angel's neck rose as she noticed the tone of Zoe's bark, which lowered until it resonated with warning. Horatio buzzed out from where he'd been resting on a shelf, and twittered in her ear.

Angel dashed down the stairs, skidded around the wall, and zipped through the kitchen and out the back door. She ran straight to Zoe, and grabbed her collar. Zoe's fur stood in a prickly ridge down her back, and she curled her lips as the barking turned into a growl. It took all of Angel's strength to hold her back.

"What is it, girl? What do you see?"

Angel's breathing became shallow as she tried to hear and see what Zoe did. She didn't have Kalek's keen Elven ears, but the little bit of Elven blood in her made her hearing slightly better than normal. Still, she noticed nothing unusual. The darkness was only broken by flickering lantern light in some of the neighbors' windows. Angel gazed at each one in turn.

"Zoe, come on. I need to check something out." Angel conjured Zoe's leash from the hook in the hallway, and clipped it to her collar. Horatio chirped and jumped from her shoulder, but she ignored him. The gate creaked slightly as they passed through, and Angel shivered.

She whispered to Zoe, "C'mon, just a little closer." She edged down the street, and stopped at the corner in front of Dark Elm, the road where Doran's house was. Her parents would have a fit if they saw her there. Zoe's stance changed. Had she sensed something?

Angel strained to see down the side road. She could almost make out a difference in one of the houses, but she couldn't be sure unless she got closer.

Her feet fell silently on the dirt road. Zoe's growl was no more than a faint gurgling, but it held more meaning than the fiercest bark. Horatio clung silently to Angel's shoulder. She stepped slowly, and then stopped about halfway down Dark Elm.

The house at the end of the road was set farther back than the others. The trees stood taller and their canopy reached over the roof, blacking out what little starlight there was. Angel's breath caught in her throat, and she gripped the leash in her hand until her fingers cramped.

The illumination flowing out from the windows of the house, Doran's house, didn't have the soft flicker of lantern light. Instead, it shone with the steady glow of an incandescent lamp.

In a neighborhood on an island completely devoid of electricity.

Chapter Twelve

Dreams

Melinda's nose scrunched as she dumped her backpack on the floor. Shakespeare dove from her arms to the floor.

The guest room looked comfortable, but old-fashioned. Mismatched antique furniture lined the flowery papered walls. Frilly curtains looked like puffed sleeves cinched at the either side of the window. Nothing like the rest of the house.

Her gaze fell on the small nightstand that held a heart-shaped hand mirror. It lay face down on a table runner. The blue floral design on the back was faded to almost white in places. The edges were dotted with brown age-spots, and tarnish dulled the ornate silver handle. Melinda shifted Shakespeare under one arm and lifted the mirror. The beveled glass sparkled like fine crystal.

She stared at her reflection. Her eyes looked sunken, and her hair was a stringy black mess. Her pale skin appeared ghostly in the shine of the crystalline glass. She'd strived for that look in the past, but now it made her feel haunted and alone.

She dug a long t-shirt out of her pack and changed into it, tossing her dirty clothes in the corner. Then she settled onto the bed and scooped Shakespeare into her lap. The sheets were warm and soft, and the pillow the perfect firmness. Her mom had spent a small fortune on her bedding at home and it didn't feel half this good. She closed her eyes, but a dog barking right outside her room jolted her just as she began to drift off.

She jumped out of bed and yanked the curtains aside. *That idiot mutt.* What was that thing barking at? She thought she heard someone tell the dog to hush. Angel? Footsteps coming down stairs, and then a door slam. *Good, maybe she'll shut that yappy thing up.*

Melinda climbed back into bed. She pulled the sheets up and snuggled Shakespeare, who had curled up by her pillow. His purring thrummed in her ear, soothing her, as the barking drifted farther away.

Something replaced the barking. Melinda was too tired to sit up, and she didn't want to push the cat away, so she cupped her hand around her ear.

Music?

It was like no music she had ever heard before. Eerie, yet more soothing than Shakespeare's purring. And sad. Like someone remembering a lost love. Goosebumps tingled her arms, and she scooted farther under the comforter. Shakespeare grumbled a protest, and resumed purring when she scratched his cheek.

Melinda couldn't tell if the music stopped, or if she just couldn't hear it over Shakespeare. She strained her ears. Nothing. Her eyelids pulled down despite her resistance. She wanted sleep, but now she wanted to hear the music more.

Still, sleep won. Sleep and dreams.

Melinda stood at the bottom of a hill. People milled around her. They moved as if searching for something, and she felt as though she should be searching with them. For what? There was nothing out of the ordinary in their surroundings. Trees, grass, rocks, sticks, patches of dirt.

An old lady approached her. "Can you help me, miss? I can't seem to find it."

"Find what?" Melinda asked.

The woman's eyes widened. "You don't know?" She stepped back and shook her head. "You don't know? Why are you here?" She moved farther away, her head still turning from side to side. "You should know. How can you not know?" The old lady disappeared into the crowd.

Melinda scanned the area. No one else was even looking in her direction. Their gazes roamed all over the landscape, searching…searching. Melinda cringed as an emptiness ripped at her insides. She could barely catch her breath. What am I supposed to be looking for? Why don't I know?

She couldn't breathe at all, and something dug into her ribs. Heat hit her face and she tried to turn away.

Air finally filled her lungs and she released it again with a shout. "No!" The sharp pain in her ribs increased and her eyes popped open.

Shakespeare stood on her chest, his hind claws poking into her lower ribs. His breath heated her chin. "Mrereow," he said, and dug his claws in deeper.

Melinda gripped his torso and lifted. "You little—ow!" His hind claw snagged her side and she let go of him. He flopped onto her chest, legs tucked under his body, and started purring again. His nose nearly touched Melinda's and he stared directly into her eyes. He blinked.

"That's it?" she said. "You just wanted me awake. You little snot." He licked the tip of her nose, and closed his eyes.

"I warned you."

Melinda turned her head toward Angel, who took a step into the room. That creepy black bug rode on her shoulder like a parrot on a pirate. The thought made Melinda giggle, and Shakespeare bounded from her chest onto the floor.

She pushed herself up until she was sitting. "Man, I had the freakiest dream last night." She rubbed her forehead. "What was with the music?"

Angel took another step. Her brow crinkled just over the bridge of her nose. "Music?"

"Yeah, some kind of weird music was playing right when I was falling asleep. You didn't hear it? You were outside when it started." Melinda leaned forward. "What was that dog yapping about, anyway?"

"I don't know." Angel's eyes looked dark. "There's something strange going on with that guy I told you about. Doran. I need you to tell me the truth. Did you talk to him yesterday?"

"What if I did? What difference does it make?" The feeling Melinda had during her dream returned, as though she suddenly needed to find something she was missing but had no idea what it was.

Angel scowled. "He's up to something."

"How do you know?"

"Kalek told me some stuff about him, and I saw something weird at his house. Just stay away from him, okay?" Angel's gaze moved to the side.

Melinda opened her mouth to protest, but Angel's eyes suddenly bugged out and she darted over to the desk.

“What’s this doing in here?” She lifted the mirror and shot another scowl at Melinda, then turned and dashed out of the room.

Melinda rested her face in her palms. What was that about? It was just a mirror. Whatever. Angel could be all twitchy—it didn’t bother Melinda.

Except that Angel hadn’t heard any music.

How? It had been so irresistible. Like it was calling to Melinda.

Was that why she had such a weird dream? In the dream she’d felt like she should be searching with the others—could it have been the music?

She leaned back against the pillow. That must have been it. But why did she still have that feeling she was missing something big?

Chapter Thirteen

Complaining

"Why does *he* have to come?" Melinda's eyes narrowed to slits as she peered at Kalek through the kitchen door and crossed her arms. His long legs dangling over the banister at the base of the stairs were the only part of him visible from where the girls stood.

Angel grimaced. After three days, Melinda had yet to say a civil word to Kalek. She'd taken right to Sir Benjamin, and even gotten over her initial shock at Spike and Niles, but she treated Kalek with animosity every moment.

"It's his farm, too," Angel said. "He needs to help me with something."

"Ayden can help you, can't he?" Melinda's head snapped over to meet Angel's gaze. "He's got a complex. I'm staying here." She stepped back and plopped onto the kitchen stool.

"Out of the question." Kalek's voice carried through the door. "I don't trust you."

"Yeah," Melinda said, cocking her head to the side, "I don't trust you either! And keep those freaky ears of yours tuned to something other than my private conversation."

Angel clenched her fists in an attempt to hold back her desire to strangle Melinda. She inhaled deeply. "Ayden can't help us. He's spending the day at the University with his mom." That wasn't entirely true. Ayden was at the University, but it was by Angel's request. Partly because she wanted him to take the day easy. Partly so Sarah would notice how pale and drawn he was looking from changing Talents.

She also wanted some time to talk to Melinda alone—or at least what Melinda thought was alone. She needed Kalek nearby, listening in, without Ayden buzzing around. She had wanted Kalek to meet her at the farm, but he'd shown up bright and early that morning and claimed he'd seen something strange—he refused to say what—and insisted on walking the girls to the farm.

"I don't care a bit about your private conversation," Kalek called from the staircase, "but I do care about Angel's safety. I'm going."

The trio trudged along the edge of the road, Horatio zooming in circles around them and Zoe pulling on the leash in Angel's hand.

Kalek kept his distance behind the girls, but Angel knew it wasn't because he wanted to make Melinda happy. He didn't speak at all and kept scanning the forest to their left, his hand jerking toward his dagger every now and then.

Angel glanced back at him for the fiftieth time. He stared straight ahead, ignoring her.

Horatio zipped by and Melinda ducked.

"Does he have to fly so close?" she said.

Before Angel could answer, Melinda cut in, "Yeah, I know. He's here to guard us." She rolled her eyes. "I think I could deal with it if he'd stir up a breeze with those monster wings of his."

"You wouldn't be so hot if you'd wear short sleeves," Angel said.

"Not my style."

Kalek's voice carried over their shoulders. "Then don't complain."

Melinda snorted.

Kalek mumbled something, but stopped before Angel could tune into his words. An eerie silence settled in for a moment, and then Zoe bared her teeth and released a gurgling growl.

Angel's heart thrummed in her ears and she glanced at Melinda, who was scowling at Kalek. He'd poised himself with his eyes closed.

His eyes popped open, and sunlight glinted off their onyx surface as his gaze locked on her. He nodded.

Angel tugged on Melinda's arm with one hand and Zoe's leash with the other. As they stepped forward, Kalek turned back and lolled along the edge of the forest. Angel watched him over her shoulder. Just before he reached beyond her line of sight he slipped into the forest.

"What was that about?" Melinda asked, fortunately with sense enough to keep her voice down.

Angel just shook her head.

"We'll be there soon," she said, lightening her voice with each word, even though her heart felt like a brick inside her chest. "You're going to love Gregor's farm."

Melinda screwed her face up in disgust. "I doubt that. Goats. Ick."

Chapter Fourteen

Surprises

Melinda followed Angel down the long pathway from the road to the farmhouse. Okay, she'd give Angel that the place was cute. She'd never seen grass so green in her life either. Even in her subdivision where the homeowners spent hundreds every month to illegally water their chemical-laden lawns.

But the stench of goats reached her before they'd even circled the side of the house. She pinched her nose.

"Doesn't that bother you?"

Angel just laughed, and led Melinda farther around the house. They stopped at the corner of the back steps.

Kalek popped up from a hedge behind Angel and grabbed her sides. Angel screamed and jumped. Melinda smirked. *Heh. Maybe I could learn to tolerate him.*

Angel turned around with her hands on her hips. She reached out and smacked Kalek's arm.

"Don't *do* that! I hate when you go into stalker mode and I can't hear you!"

Kalek's stony eyes fixed on Melinda. There was a smile behind them. It sent her brain reeling.

Melinda followed them into the barn and found exactly what she'd expected. Hay, wood, animal stink. Ugh.

"I don't do farm work, you know."

Kalek glared at her so intently she could have sworn she felt his gaze pressing into her skin. No smile in those eyes now.

After gathering their tools, Kalek and Angel carried everything outside and started removing the damaged boards that needed replacing before the summer storms hit. Zoe curled up in the shade next to the wall of the barn and closed her eyes. Melinda plopped down on an overturned bucket and started picking her nail polish. Angel frowned at her but didn't say anything.

The nails seemed to slide out of the planks a little too easily, and Melinda wondered if they were using magic to help things along. Angel glanced at Melinda every now and then when Kalek's back was turned, offering a pleading look.

After prying another board loose, Kalek spun around and caught Angel in the act.

He glared momentarily at her, and then spoke to Angel as if Melinda wasn't there. "If she's not going to help, the least she can do is get us something to drink." He lifted his hand, and a small towel flew from the pile of tools and landed in his hand. He wiped his forehead, and then tossed the towel on the ground and started prying off the next board.

Melinda considered ignoring Kalek's request, or snapping back, but watching everything go so smoothly with the help of magic unsettled her. So far, Angel hadn't said anything about teaching Melinda magic, or even seeing if Melinda *had* any.

Still, as she stared at Kalek's discarded towel, she found herself concentrating, willing it to lift off the ground.

Nothing happened.

Maybe going in to get everyone drinks would be less torture than sitting in a smelly old barn. She rose and stomped toward the house.

Melinda stood in front of the kitchen sink, holding a glass in the flow of water. There was no freezer space in the refrigerator—not that it looked much like a fridge, more like one of those antique iceboxes—so they'd have to do with warm water. She figured Angel and Kalek could probably cool it with magic anyway.

Angel had told her enough about magic that Melinda knew it followed laws of physics; and cooling things just meant removing the heat, which would have been a simple process. Her dad was a scientist, after all—*had* been one before he'd gone and disappeared—and despite lousy grades in school she understood a lot more about science than any of her classmates.

A noise caught Melinda's attention, and she leaned over and peered out the kitchen window. A shadow appeared in the shade of the goat shelter. She squinted. *Someone's out there.*

Horatio had been buzzing around the perimeter of the yard, and she'd seem him zip past a couple of times while she filled the glasses. But he seemed oddly absent all of a sudden. Melinda watched the shadow—there was something familiar about the way it moved.

Doran.

Something chilled her hand. She jumped back, dropping the glass in the sink. It didn't break but fell over and spilled its contents down the drain. Melinda stuck her finger in the trickling water. It was cold. Ice cold.

Her heart pounded and her fingers trembled. The water got even colder, *burning cold.* Frost began to gather on the faucet. She yanked her hand away and the water stopped flowing.

What?

She shook the water from her hand and dashed out the back door. She looked over her shoulder at the barn as she headed toward the goat shelter. Angel and Kalek were inside the barn, but could be coming out at any moment. Fortunately, if they did, they'd be working on the other side, where the goat shelter would be out of view. Still Melinda ran as fast as she could.

When she reached the shelter, she slid and nearly fell as she stopped. Doran leaned against a support pole, a playful smile on his face.

"I thought you were coming to see me today."

Melinda smiled. "I couldn't get away from the warden."

Doran flinched.

"Oh, sorry." Her smile dropped, and she bit her lip.

"It's okay." He shifted so he wasn't leaning anymore and stepped toward her. "I'm glad you didn't just ditch me. I was hoping to spend some time with you."

Melinda's heart fluttered. Doran wasn't all gorgeous and exotic like Kalek, but he seemed genuinely interested in her. And he did have pretty eyes. They swirled with color like oil on the surface of a puddle. His voice was soothing, too.

She wanted to answer him, but she couldn't stop staring into his eyes.

Until they widened suddenly. Melinda snapped her head to the side and followed Doran's gaze. Angel and Kalek were running toward them with Zoe at their heels. She'd never seen anyone move as fast and smoothly as Kalek did. In an instant he was at their side. Angel joined him, with Horatio chittering around her head.

Melinda narrowed her eyes at the beetle. *No wonder he was gone. He was off tattling.*

Chapter Fifteen

Shamed

Angel's heart froze at the sight of Doran Ashe. She fought to keep her hands from trembling.

She could almost sense Kalek's increased heart rate, too. She glanced at him. His eyes were slits between curtains of tangles. A lock of hair was pushed behind his ear, exposing the side of his neck where an artery pulsed against his skin.

"What are you doing here?" he demanded.

Doran plunged his hands into his pockets and took a step back. "I came to see Melinda."

The ground rotated under Angel's feet momentarily. *I was right. She did meet him in town.* She looked over at Melinda, whose eyes were wide with confusion and anger.

"You need to leave," Kalek said through clenched teeth. "Now."

Doran backed up a few steps again. He looked brazenly at Melinda. His eyes sent a distinct message: *Are you going to put up with this?* He stepped back again. His movements seemed innocent enough, but his expression was meant to coax Melinda into going with him.

Melinda shot a sideways glare at Angel and stepped from the shade of the shelter into the sunlight.

A loud creaking from above grabbed Angel's attention. She looked up and threw her arms over her face at the sight of a beam breaking free from the roof of the shelter. Something slammed into her, and she staggered back, tripping, and landed hard on her back.

"What the—" Kalek cried out.

There hadn't been a crash. She pushed herself up and gaped at the sight in front of her.

Doran stood with his feet spread and his arms straining under the weight of the beam. Kalek raised his hand, and the beam lifted a couple of inches out of Doran's hands. Doran stepped back, and Kalek let the beam drop to the ground.

Melinda stood off to Doran's side, her hand over her mouth and her eyes huge. She blinked several times and let her hand drop. "Angel, are you okay?"

Angel nodded. "Who pushed me out of the way?" She looked at Kalek.

He barely shook his head as he stared at Doran. "Why did you do that?" The anger in his eyes intensified as he spoke. "I could have caught that with magic!"

Doran opened his mouth, and closed it again. He took another step back. His eyes darted side to side, and then he looked down at the ground.

"What?" Angel asked. "Kalek, why are you yelling at him?"

Kalek spoke to her without taking his eyes off Doran. "I had everything under control! He should have left well enough alone!"

"Kalek, give him a break. He was trying to help." Even knowing what had just happened, she couldn't believe she was defending Doran. There was more to this, but she didn't want to bring it up yet. She'd talk to Kalek later.

She stood up and brushed herself off as she inspected the goat shelter. The beam wasn't a main support and the goats didn't care what it looked like, so no harm waiting to fix it.

"Let's go. The barn's fixed, and we can take care of the shelter later." She glanced over at Melinda, who was staring at Doran like he was a fireman who'd just saved her child from a burning building. All the more reason to get home.

"Not yet," Kalek said. "Not until he answers one question."

Doran's head lifted. He looked at Kalek for only a moment, then let his gaze drift off to the side. He didn't speak.

Kalek glared even harder. "Why didn't you use magic to grab the beam?"

Doran drew his gaze back until it locked with Kalek's.

"Because I don't *have* magic anymore."

Chapter Sixteen

The Mirror

Melinda curled herself into a ball on the bed with Shakespeare cradled in the nook between her stomach and legs. His purring wasn't at all loud enough to drown out Angel and Kalek's raised voices. Even with the door closed Melinda could hear them in the kitchen.

"Kalek, he's been in prison for years! You can't expect him to adjust that quickly. Maybe being in that cell, surrounded by all that electricity, sucked his powers out of him."

"I'm not talking about him *adjusting*—I'm talking about him *lying*."

"You think he's lying about his magic being gone?"

"No, I think he's lying about wanting to see that *friend* of yours. I think he's trying to get to you…or something on the farm. I don't know what." His voice paused. "He's up to *something*, though. I know that for sure."

Melinda scrunched her eyes shut. *He's such a jerk*. She squeezed herself into a tighter ball and Shakespeare squawked in protest. She stroked his neck and he resumed purring.

She sighed and let her eyes open. Angel and Kalek's voices still carried into the room, but their words were muffled. At least Ayden had gone home and couldn't join in. He'd stopped by when they got to the house, and the look he'd given Melinda when Angel told him what happened showed her exactly whose side he'd take.

Angel had asked Melinda to go to her room so she and Kalek could "discuss things." That girl acted like a parent way too often. Even when Angel and Melinda were kids, Angel was always trying to mother her. Melinda had never been able to stop her back then, and she didn't bother trying now. She just went to her room. Let Angel discuss all she wanted. Kalek was a stubborn, pointy-eared freak and he wasn't going to listen to anything *anyone* had to say.

He was jealous, too. Or something. Doran had saved Angel, and without magic. Kalek was too dependent on it. He probably couldn't have stopped that beam any other way. Melinda smiled, imagining the beam landing on Kalek. It made her stomach twist and her eyes sting. She pulled her hand away from Shakespeare, and he stopped purring.

Shakespeare looked up, and when she didn't start petting him anymore, he stretched and jumped off the bed. He padded over to the chair that was sitting slightly pulled out in front of the old, roll-top desk in the corner of the room. He leaped onto the seat of the chair and curled into a ball again.

Melinda watched him, amazed at how content cats always seemed to be, as the voices drifting through the closed door blurred into a background buzz. She settled back against the headboard, and then sat up again when something shiny—peeking through the partially open desktop—caught her eye. She climbed out of bed, walked over to the desk and gripped the knobs. The roll-top was stiff at first, but then suddenly let go and slammed open. Melinda looked over her shoulder. Angel was still yammering at Kalek.

She turned back to the desk and her forehead crinkled. It was the mirror Angel had taken out of the room before. How had it gotten back in here?

Melinda picked it up and studied the intricate floral pattern on the back, and then spun it around by the handle. The bright, shiny crystalline surface of the glass was such a contrast to the tarnished, faded body of the mirror. She tilted it side to side.

Her hand froze. Lines, like static on a TV set, appeared across the surface momentarily, and then disappeared. Melinda stared at the mirror. *What do you do? Are you magic?*

As if in answer to her question, the surface of the mirror fogged and then a scene appeared. A little girl who looked like a younger version of Angel was sitting on a bed, drawing in a sketchpad. She wasn't Angel though—her face was much rounder, and her proportions more like someone petite.

The girl glowered at the sketchbook and then threw it on the ground and started crying. Melinda stared, transfixed by the image. She felt the girl's despair as strongly as if it were her own. *She's upset because everyone else has something special they can do, something more magical than drawing.* Melinda fought against the tears that stung her eyes. She felt sorry for this girl, but something else crept in.

The girl was Angel's mom when she was young. Despite her tears she had everything Melinda had always wanted. Parents who loved her and a friend who watched out for her like an older brother.

She stared, confused.

How do I know that?

It made no sense, but she did *know*. She couldn't read the girl's thoughts but she somehow *felt* the girl's links to those around her.

From deep inside Melinda, anger surged, pressing against the connection.

So what if the girl didn't have a Talent? Melinda had never had magic of any kind.

Her hand squeezed the mirror handle and began to tremble. She opened her eyes and narrowed them at the girl in the mirror. *Pathetic. Be happy with what you* do *have. You could have a mother who doesn't care, and a father who leaves you…*

Every muscle in her body tightened and the mirror shook harder in her hand. Her pulse slammed against the inside of her skull and her breaths came shallow.

She pulled back her arm and flung it forward. The mirror slipped out of her grasp and seemed to hurtle through the air in slow motion. End over end it headed straight to the corner where the bed stood. Melinda sucked in a breath and felt panic crush her lungs.

No…what have I done?

She snapped her hand in front of her, and screamed, "Stop!"

The mirror hung in mid air over the bed.

Melinda's heart pounded. She didn't dare move. She didn't dare think. The mirror hovered, and Melinda couldn't take her eyes off it.

"What—" Angel's voice came from Melinda's left, too loud and clear for her to be anywhere but in the doorway.

Melinda flinched, and the mirror dropped onto the bed.

Chapter Seventeen

Connections

"Melinda! You just…what did…how…" Angel stumbled for words while the image of her mother's mirror fixed itself in her mind. It had been *floating*. Until she'd opened her mouth and broken Melinda's concentration.

Melinda stared at the mirror on the bed.

"I-I don't know. It just sort of stopped when I said 'stop' and then it hung there."

Wait. That didn't make sense. Anger stirred in Angel's chest.

"Stop? Stop what?" She stepped all the way into the room and grabbed Melinda's shoulder, turning the girl to face her. "What were you stopping?"

Melinda's eyes darkened.

"Tell me the truth, Melinda." Angel squeezed Melinda's shoulder. "How did you even get that mirror? You took it from my parents' room!"

"No, I didn't. It was here, in the desk. I swear, I haven't set foot in their room."

Angel took a deep breath. For whatever reason she believed Melinda. The girl looked guilty about something, but her eyes told Angel she was telling the truth about this.

"Fine, but you were doing something else. So tell me."

Melinda flinched, and Angel realized her nails were still digging into her shoulder. She let go and dropped her hand to her side.

Melinda rubbed her shoulder. "I wasn't doing anything. Not at first. I just picked up the mirror and this picture showed up. Your mom?"

Angel nodded.

"She was upset about something. It made *me* upset, and I threw the mirror. I wasn't thinking, I just got mad. But then I realized what I'd done, and I just screamed 'stop' and it did." Melinda's eyes widened. "It stopped."

Angel took a deep breath. How did the mirror even get in here? And why was it showing Melinda stuff when it had never worked for *her*? Not. Even. *Once*. It was *her* mother's diary, and she'd always assumed her mom had it locked so no one else could see the images it held. Now she knew it was locked for *her*, but not necessarily anyone else....

She shoved the thoughts aside as another vied for attention.

Melinda could do magic.

Angel had thought half the time Melinda would eventually realize she didn't belong here and ask to go home. But Melinda could do magic. That meant she could stay. The implications jumbled in Angel's head...Melinda leaving her home for good, Melinda's mother's reaction, where Melinda would live....

Angel walked over and sat on the edge of the bed. She picked up the mirror and stroked the handle, gazing into the smooth glass that only reflected her own confused face.

Angel looked up again. Kalek stood silently in the doorway with Horatio perched on his shoulder. Zoe's barking carried faintly through the closed window.

She turned to face Melinda. "You said this was in the desk?"

Melinda nodded.

"I wonder how it got there." Something scratched at the back of Angel's thoughts. "Unless..." She glanced over at Kalek. "Lucky said we might have one, but I never saw any signs. Maybe he was right."

Kalek laughed. "You think so? I still think he's making up some of that."

"Sir Benjamin and I looked them up, though. They're real. Lucky would be able to see them. He saw Dr. Randall."

Kalek laughed again, a strange stifled laugh, and Angel followed his gaze. Melinda stood staring at them both like they'd suddenly started speaking a different language.

"Lucky is someone from town. He can see things that are invisible.

Remember the story I told you about Dawric and Gregor, and how we'd found the unicorn—"

Angel's words were cut off by Kalek's hand over her mouth. She hadn't even realized he'd stepped up behind her. His voice came from over her head as she sat trapped on the bed, shoulders pressed against his stomach.

"Do you want the long version or the short version?"

Melinda smiled. "Short."

"Then let me tell you."

Angel struggled under his grasp, but he wouldn't let go. She opened her mouth as if to bite him.

He leaned over her shoulder until his curls hung in front of her face. "You hurt my hand so I can't play and I'll conjure you someplace where no one but *you* can find you."

He let go and laughed.

"Hmph! You can't conjure *people*," Angel said, wiping her mouth.

"Maybe *you* can't..." Kalek raised his eyebrows.

Was he showing off? For Melinda? Had her using magic suddenly changed his mind about her? It was obvious what Melinda thought about *him*. The way she'd gaped at him the first time they met had said it all. Kalek couldn't have missed that, but until now he'd seemed completely repulsed by her.

"Don't be such a jerk, Kalek."

"I'm just trying to spare us another long-winded story." He turned to Melinda. "Lucky can see things that are invisible. Everyone thought he was making stuff up all the time. It drove him to drink like a fish and become the town laughingstock. He saw Dr. Randall, though, when Dawric was on the island and everyone realized he wasn't a nutcase. Now he owns a barber shop."

Angel looked at Melinda's still-confused face and rolled her eyes. "Well, that helped a lot, didn't it? Much better than my version. Melinda, Lucky used to see these little creatures he thought were leprechauns. They're small and green, and he never got a good look at one because they move really fast. No one else can see them because they're invisible to humans. But when Sir Benjamin and I talked one day about how Lucky had seen someone with the unicorn, we realized he'd actually seen Dr. Randall while he was invisible. That was his Talent, only we'd never known.

"Anyway, we spent days looking through books about magical animals and discovered that what Lucky thought were leprechauns were actually clurins." She turned and glared at Kalek. "They're real. They're kind of like lemurs, and they move stuff around." She faced Melinda again. "You know how it seems like you're always losing little things when you know exactly where you put them? Well, clurins can be responsible for that. It's some kind of defensive behavior that throws off predators. Sir B doesn't quite understand it all."

The confusion didn't disappear, but a strange expression crept onto Melinda's face. She kept her gaze just off to the side and tilted her head.

"So, people can go a long time without knowing their own Talent?"

"Sometimes," Angel said. "My mom didn't know hers until she was thirteen, and she only found it by accident."

Kalek cleared his throat, and when the girls turned to face him, he smirked. "Your parents are home," he said.

Chapter Eighteen

Brothers

"Zack!"

Angel's heartbeat thudded in her ears as she ran past her parents and wrapped her arms around her little brother. Zack's arms squeezed her waist and she breathed in the sweet scent of his hair. Zack beamed when she finally released him, and she turned to hug her parents.

Kalek stepped in and wrapped her mom in a bear hug, and shook her father's hand.

Melinda stood to the side, staring at the floor, one hand in her pocket and the other fiddling with the end of the belt slung around her hips.

"Mom, Dad, this is Melinda," Angel said.

Her mom smiled. "Hi, Melinda. We kinda figured that's who you must be." She winked at Angel. "We're so glad you're going to stay with us for a while."

Melinda raised her head and spoke softly. "Thank you, Mrs. Mas—, I mean…"

"Kleidon. But, please. Call me Caryn."

"And call me William." Angel's dad reached forward. Melinda took his hand, looking very unsure, and shook it.

Angel asked, "How did you get back so quickly?'

Her mom stepped over to the couch and sank into the cushions. She released a contented sigh. "The paperwork was processed before we even got there."

Zack grabbed Angel's hand. "I told Uncle Clarence and Aunt Ivy if they didn't let me go, I'd start flunking school on purpose and I'd embarrass them all the time. And that I'd never do another contest, ever."

"And that's all it took?" Angel thought back to the stodgy couple she'd met that day, and the way they'd talked about Zack. He was just a toy to them, but was he one they'd so easily throw away?

Zack's eyebrows rose as he gave a mischievous smile. "Well, I kinda had to prove it to them, too..." His eyebrows lowered. "Aunt Ivy locked me in my room after I threw a tantrum at their stupid country club, so I threw all my trophies through the window."

"*Through* the window?"

Zack smiled, mischief gleaming in his eyes. "Yeah, the glass went *everywhere*!"

"Zack, I can't believe you—"

"Uncle Clarence threatened to beat me for it, but I told him I'd take pictures of the marks and post them online."

"Zack—"

"He knows I can do it, too 'specially after I told him his password."

"Zack!"

He snatched his hand from hers and crossed his arms. "I *never* want to live with them again. They don't want me now, either. Uncle Clarence sent money to some friend of his and said that took care of it."

Angel's mom leaned forward, eyes wide. "Zack, what do you mean he gave money to a friend?"

"Told ya," Melinda said as she looked pointedly at Angel. "He paid to *get* Zack, he paid to get *rid* of him."

Angel's mom opened her mouth, but before she could speak her father said, "It doesn't matter. We did nothing wrong. I'm just grateful it's all taken care of. The important thing is Zack's here and away from those horrible people."

Zack nodded. "Yeah. That's what Mom and Dad said. They're glad I'm going to be someplace I can be happy." He squeezed her hand and then a grin spread across his face again. "But they understand. I told them about you being magic—"

"You told them?" Angel's heart began to pound and she looked at her parents.

"It's okay, Anna," her father said.

She turned to him. "You *knew*?"

Her mother moved toward her. "Anna, calm down...."

"But—"

"Anna, *listen*," her mother said. "*They* already knew. Well, sort of. Their son saw you leave that night. One of the older boys, Jacob, I think. No one believed him at the time, but he saw you step through the Gate."

Melinda grabbed Angel's arm and whispered, "Toby told me something about that. Jacob said you'd just disappeared that night, and that he meant it *literally*. We thought he was pulling another prank."

Heat rose into Angel's neck and her pulse throbbed. Jacob had seen her. Maybe that's why he'd gotten so messed up. He'd finally tried to tell everyone something serious and they took it as a prank. But it had paid off for her. The Masons believed her, were happy for her, and for Zack.

Angel took a deep breath and looked down at her little brother. He gazed up at her with sparkling eyes.

"We went through a portal, Angel. It was *so* cool."

"That's awesome, little man. I've never even done that. I've only been through little Gateways."

"Yeah, but those can take you anywhere, right?"

Angel nodded, and pulled Zack into her arms again. "I missed you so much," she whispered into his strawberry curls. His arms wrapped around her waist, and tears finally pushed past her lids. Tears of joy, fear, relief…a million emotions swirling through her.

When she pulled away, Angel looked around the room. Her parents sat on the couch, her father's arm around her mom. Kalek had stepped out of the room, and Melinda had moved to the corner, shoulders hunched and eyes downcast.

Angel's mom pointed to the chair adjacent to the couch. "Sit down, Melinda. Tell us a little about yourself. Anna's talked about you so much. She said you write."

"Um, I used to. Not for a long time, though." Melinda peeked out the corner of her eye at Angel and moved toward the chair.

"Hey, I need to go check on Kalek," Angel said. She turned to Zack. "Come with me, little man. Kalek's going to love you."

They walked into the kitchen to find Kalek gazing out the window toward the forest. He must've heard them enter, but he didn't move.

Angel motioned for Zack to go sit at the table, then stepped over and put her hand on Kalek's shoulder.

"Are you okay?"

He breathed in deeply and exhaled. "I'm fine. I just miss her. I won't get my reunion until I've moved Beyond." He turned to face Angel, onyx eyes wet and shadowed. "I miss her so much. And Gregor. They should be here. It isn't fair. And it's all *his* fault."

She knew he meant his father. She also knew he was wrong, but nothing she'd said made him see that. She squeezed his shoulder. "Come meet Zack."

By the time Angel's parents and Melinda walked in, Zack and Kalek were laughing hysterically as Kalek levitated apples into a circle and made them spin like a Ferris wheel.

"It's late, boys," Angel's mother said, grabbing a basket off the counter. She plucked the apples one by one out of the air. "Time for you to go home, Kalek. And the rest of us need to get to bed."

Angel's dad nodded, and covered a huge yawn with his hand. "I'm beat. 'Night all," he said, and left the room.

Her mom, Melinda and Zack stayed in the kitchen while Angel walked Kalek to the front door. He stopped with his hand on the knob and turned to her.

"Do you ever miss Gregor so much you think you could see him if you really tried?"

The question stunned Angel; she shook her head and ran her fingers through her hair.

Kalek raised an eyebrow at her.

Had he seen something? The guy in the forest with hair like Gregor's? She still hadn't told Kalek about that. It hadn't happened again, but maybe…

"I miss him a lot." She paused, chewing on the corner of her mouth. "I did think I saw him one night. But it was someone else. Must have been my mind playing tricks."

"Yeah, well, there are a lot of guys who could be mistaken for Gregor. But there's no one like Siophra."

Before Angel could say anything, he turned the knob, swept across the porch and disappeared into the night.

Angel stood in the doorway staring after him, until movement caught her eye. A shadow, a person standing below the streetlight. He ran his hand through a tuft of wavy hair and took off running.

Chapter Nineteen

Recurrences

Melinda followed Angel and Caryn up the stairs to the loft. No way was she going to bunk in Angel's room with that zoo of hers, and Zack needed the guest room. Angel shifted the rolled-up pallet under her arm and Caryn moved to the center of the room. Every inch of the place was covered in art stuff.

Caryn turned around slowly, searching for the best place to put Melinda's pallet.

Man, Caryn looked so much like Angel. Same red hair, same dark-dark brown eyes, same fair skin. But Angel practically towered over her mom, who couldn't have been more than five-foot-three. It made sense, as tall as her dad was, but her height seemed to be the only thing Angel got from him.

Caryn finally pointed to the corner of the room that wrapped around the other side of the stair railing. She told the girls goodnight, then headed back downstairs.

Melinda plopped down on the floor and sat cross-legged while Angel cleared away some of her mother's art supplies to make room for the pallet. "Zack's a good kid," she said.

"He's the best," Angel said. "I missed him so much. I still can't believe he's here. I can't wait until Ayden meets him!" Angel moved the final stack of canvases and let out a big sigh. "I've been so freaked out this whole time that it was all going to go wrong, and I'd never see him again." She turned and stared at Melinda. "I don't think I ever thanked you for keeping those bullies away from him."

"Don't worry about it. It was fun." Melinda smiled. "Kids like that need to be put in their place. And…well, that was cool what you did, too. Making your teeth pointy like that. I didn't think you had it in you to be wicked."

"I'm not! But that kid—urgh—I wanted to strangle him for messing with Zack."

Melinda laughed. "There's hope for you yet."

"And you, too." Angel's voice rose with excitement. "You can do magic! I can't believe it. And so fast. We'll have to try some stuff tomorrow. Too bad Gregor's not here. He was the best teacher."

Melinda thought about how she'd stopped the mirror in mid-air. What else would she be able to do? Would she have a Talent like everyone else? Maybe she'd be able to pick hers, like Ayden. Of course, Angel made that sound like it was really rare. And Ayden looked beat from changing his Talent. Maybe it wasn't such a great thing.

"Are you worried about Ayden?" Melinda asked.

Angel dropped to the floor and crossed her legs, facing Melinda. When she spoke her voice cracked like she was holding back tears. "Yeah. I'm thinking he must have changed his Talent again, so he's not a Gate-maker anymore. And that change really wore him out."

"You don't know if he's changed?"

Angel started crying. "No…I've been so focused on Zack. I can't believe what Ayden's putting himself through to help me."

"Maybe you should spend the day with him tomorrow. Just the two of you."

Angel sniffed. "But Zack…and you…"

"Don't worry about me. I can hang out here. You could take Zack into town. He'd probably spend so much time exploring and playing with Niles, you'd have some time to talk to Ayden."

Angel sniffed again. "How did you get so smart?"

Melinda didn't speak. How could she not be smart with her dad the scientific genius that he was?

"Melinda, you okay?"

She looked up at Angel and inhaled. "Just because I hated school doesn't mean I'm stupid."

"I never said you were."

"But you thought it. Everyone thought it."

Angel shook her head. "No, I didn't. And if anyone else did, it was because you made them think that way. Why do you think I was always nagging you about school and stuff? I knew you had it in you."

Melinda lowered her gaze. *Had it in me. Yep, Dad would agree with that.* He'd hounded her all the time about how everything about her was predestined because of her genes. Every facet of her personality and appearance was supposedly controlled by little strands of nucleotides. She hated that thought, and she swore she'd be who she *wanted* to be. Even if it made her dad angry, and her mom turn away from her. Even if it made everyone think she was stupid.

She looked back up. Angel was staring at her.

"Don't look at me like that. Having people think I was stupid had its advantages, you know. Remember how I used to tell fortunes and all the kids thought I was a witch? It's because I studied up on body language and stuff, and knew all the right questions to ask. No one thought I was smart enough to do that, and they figured I must have actually been psychic or something."

Angel narrowed her eyes. "Yeah, I remember. It bugged me that you were always scamming everyone." Then her expression softened as one side of her mouth curled. "Well, except for Cassie. She totally deserved it!"

Melinda laughed, but she felt the tiniest tug of guilt. Even now, she was working out a way to scam the very people who were trying their best to help her.

She *had* to see Doran.

Those eyes…they'd looked like the swirling rainbow of oil on water at the farm, but when she'd first met him they were the green of a Silver Spruce. He'd said he didn't have magic anymore, but how did his eyes change color like that?

The guilt popped like a bubble.

"Really, Angel, I'll be fine. Go spend time with your boys tomorrow." She nodded toward the pallet. "Time for bed, I guess."

Angel stood. That sappy look on her face made something in Melinda's stomach twist.

"Thanks, Mel. Oh, and the day after tomorrow we're going to work on your magic." She smiled and headed downstairs.

Melinda curled up on the pallet. The shadows in the room hung in strange shapes and the wind blowing through the open window carried a melodic lilt. Could that be the music she'd heard before? It sounded mournful, empty. Melinda fell asleep aching from the desire to learn more about Doran and her own magic, hollow inside from the need to discover something. She just didn't know what….

She stood at the bottom of the hill again, surrounded by people. As before, everyone was searching, searching. No one seemed to notice her. She scanned the crowd for the old lady who had spoken to her before, but she didn't see her anywhere.

She looked up the side of the hill. People were climbing, stumbling, and falling back down. They grabbed at each other and at the ground, crying out as they slid back to the bottom of the hill. One man bore down hard on a walking stick, but it seemed the harder he pushed it the more he slid.

Melinda swung her head from side to side, frantic. Something was on that hill, and she had to get to it. But there was no way up.

She'd never make it.

She woke with a start, gasping, and spun herself into a sitting position. Her heart hammered away as it had in the dream, a frantic beat that droned her need to find what she was searching for.

But what was it?

"Are you sure you want to hang out here with my parents?" Angel asked as she stood by the front stairs.

Melinda sat on the couch with a notebook in her lap, working on a poem. Caryn's question about her writing had hit something inside her, and phrases swam around her head all morning. The only way she could get them out was to write them down.

"Yeah, I've got this to work on. And your parents have a lot to do. Maybe I can help."

Angel lowered her eyebrows and bit her lip.

Melinda had banked on Angel's desire to spend time with Ayden and

Zack being stronger than the desire to keep tabs on her. Besides, Caryn and William really would be around, so Angel couldn't protest without making them think she didn't trust *them.*

"Okay, then," Angel said. "If you change your mind, tell my dad. I'm sure he'd be glad to call Romeo and Juliet over and ride into town with you."

"Yeah, right. Horses. Don't think so." Melinda scrunched her nose for effect. She didn't want Angel keeping a lookout for her in town. "Now get out of here."

Angel slipped into the hallway, looking irritated.

Melinda looked down at the poem in her notebook.

She's a t-shirt—mobius light
Plays her flesh like an instrument
Dies in a turn—
In a James Joyce conjunctive slide

She becomes the speaker ride
Bathes in a circular science of rhythm
Time slips in snared moment
And joins the hologram in a laser touch

The stillness in movement
Occupies her center
Defies gravity with mass's redefinition

She didn't know what it meant, but it was the first poem she'd written in over a year. Actually, now that she was thinking about it, she hadn't composed a single poem since her dad disappeared. It felt good to write again, even if it was probably total garbage. She closed the notebook and set it on the couch as she stood.

Caryn and William were in the kitchen when Melinda walked in. A huge stack of pancakes sat in the middle of the table. The aroma wafted across the room and made Melinda's stomach growl.

"Mornin', Melinda," William said. Caryn nodded, chewing a mouthful of pancake. She pointed at the stack, eyeing Melinda as if to say *help yourself.*

Melinda grabbed a plate and several pancakes and took a seat at the table. She felt oddly comfortable around Caryn and William. They seemed so normal, but not stuffy-normal like most of the grown-ups she knew. They bordered on hippy, with Caryn's long red hair pulled back in a braid, and her fingers always spattered with paint. William's blonde hair was short, but the way it stuck out gave the impression of length, and he dressed in jeans and a t-shirt with a pair of glasses sitting crooked on his nose.

Caryn swallowed a bite of pancake. "Angel told us you didn't want to go with them today."

"Nah, I've had her all to myself for days now. She needs some time with Zack and Ayden."

"Very perceptive of you," said William. "And considerate. I'm sure Angel will appreciate it." He pulled his glasses off and wiped them with the edge of his t-shirt, then plopped them back on his nose as crooked as before. "So, then...what are you planning to do today?"

"Well, actually, I figured I'd write to my mom. And since my cell phone doesn't work out here..."

"You're welcome to use our phone," Caryn interjected. "It does connect with outside lines."

"Thanks," Melinda said, "but my mom would never answer unless it's my number. Even then, she might not. She's always so busy. I'll write her. Then she can read it when she has time."

Caryn and William gave her looks that didn't quite mask their sympathy. Melinda felt a lump form in her stomach, which she tried to blame on the lameness of her excuses.

"Well, when you're done writing, maybe you can come up to the loft—have you ever modeled for a portrait?" Caryn asked.

The lump tightened when Melinda realized she's just painted herself into a corner. She'd gotten rid of the prying eyes of Angel and Horatio, and who knew where Kalek would be spending the day...but what about Caryn and William? Melinda was used to adults who didn't notice her. Angel's parents were looking right into her, though, and expecting to actually spend time together.

Melinda swallowed. "Um, no, I haven't..."

"Well, it would really help me if you'd pose for me. I've been wanting to finish a painting I started a while back, and you have just the right coloring."

This was a disaster. She now had the complete attention of two people who worked from home. She picked at her nail polish. *I'm never gonna get out of here to see Doran.*

At the end of breakfast, and after scribbling a quick note to her mom, Melinda still hadn't figured out a way to sneak off. She followed Caryn up to the loft, tossing her notebook on top of her pallet. Caryn bustled around, grabbing paints and brushes, and then set a half-painted canvas on the easel in the middle of the room. Melinda tried to take a peek at the unfinished painting, but Caryn shooed her away.

"Oh, no! The subject never gets to see the work until it's complete." She smiled and winked as she pulled on her smock. Then she pointed to a stool in front of the open window. "What I need you to do is sit over there, facing the window just slightly. I want a view of your face, but more of a profile."

Melinda sat on the stool and tried to position herself as Caryn had asked. Caryn moved Melinda's shoulders and head as if she were sculpting her, *tsk*ing now and then as she stepped back to check Melinda's positioning. After several minutes Caryn finally seemed satisfied and stepped behind the canvas.

"Let me get the angles of your face right, and some of the major shapes drawn, and then you'll be able to move a little and talk. I'll be quick."

Caryn wasn't kidding. It took her less time to sketch Melinda than it did to position her. Melinda was almost disappointed when she broke the silence.

"Alright, you can relax a little."

Caryn talked the entire time she worked. Half the time her words were muffled from what Melinda presumed was a paintbrush stuck in her mouth. She couldn't see Caryn from the angle she faced, but sensed the woman's concentration as if it were a presence in the room.

Caryn asked Melinda about Angel when they were friends as children. At times Caryn's voice nearly broke. Caryn and William had gone seven years without their daughter. That had never really dawned on Melinda before. Her own parents seemed to always be glad to be rid of her when she wasn't around.

Heat rose inside her, and she found herself fighting the urge to jump off the stool and run out of the room. Angel had more people who loved her than Melinda could ever hope for—two families in two different parts of the world. Melinda blinked back tears. *She would not cry.* She was strong.

Once she got a handle on how to do magic at will, she'd leave Angel's house and show everyone she could take care of herself.

Every twenty minutes, Caryn announced that Melinda could get up and move around. Then she had Melinda take her seat again while she worked. Finally, after a couple of hours, Caryn suggested they go down for lunch.

Melinda stood and stretched.

Shakespeare popped his head out from behind a stack of canvases and mimicked her. Then he pranced over and wound himself around her ankles.

She picked him up and carried him down to the kitchen, where she shared part of her tuna sandwich with him while Caryn and William talked at the kitchen table. Their voices faded into the background as Melinda's mind wandered to how to meet Doran.

William's voice jolted Melinda out of her daydreams.

"Maybe Melinda can help me. You two can always finish the painting later."

"Help what?" Melinda asked.

William leaned back in his chair. "I need to find some materials for tools I'm making. Would you like to join me?"

Melinda stared. "Um…does that mean we have to ride the horses, because I—"

"Oh, no! We just need to walk out the back door into the forest."

Melinda's mind spun. She really couldn't care less about the forest, but if she went out there with William maybe she could steal off for while. It looked like a place where she could easily claim to get lost. She'd just have to pay attention to what direction they were heading, so she could find her way back to the neighborhood and down the street to the house Angel said belonged to Doran.

"Yeah, that sounds cool." Melinda forced a smile. "Can we go now?"

Chapter Twenty

Finding Trouble

"He's really got a pet dragon?" Zack's eyes bulged. He bounced rhythmically on Romeo's back; Ayden's arms stretched forward on either side of him and gripped the reins.

Angel rode next to them on Juliet. "You bet. Actually, he's got two, but one is half cat."

Zack's eyes widened even more. "Whoa…that's cool. I can't wait to get there!"

He'd said that about everything. He couldn't wait to walk in the forest and check out all the magic insects; he couldn't wait to see Angel's mom's paintings and her father's tools; he couldn't wait to try magic; he couldn't wait to be homeschooled again…

Angel smiled. It was so good to have Zack in her life again. It felt as if no time had passed. He'd only changed in that he was a little taller, and his face had thinned down making him appear not so much a little boy. Angel almost felt as if things couldn't get better. Almost.

She slid her gaze over to Ayden. He looked pale and tired. He smiled at her, but there was something not right about it.

Angel swallowed and tightened her grip on the reins.

"Ayden, um…I was meaning to ask. You changed Talents again, didn't you?"

He nodded. "I knew it kind of bothered you that I had Gregor's Talent."

What?

"No, it didn't!" she blurted out.

Did it?

"It's okay, Angel. I'm not jealous or anything. I know he was like a brother to you."

"But you're exhausted. You need to pick something and keep it. I'm getting worried."

"Yeah…so's my mom. She gave me a massively hard time about it. I mean, she's glad I helped you and all, but she's watching me like a hawk. The way she did when I was little and she first discovered what I could do. I'm surprised she let me out of the house today."

After dropping the horses off at Old Man Brady's, Angel, Ayden and Zack walked into the town square. Zack did exactly as Melinda had predicted. He oohed and aahed over everything, asked question after question, and took off running toward *The Professor's Roost* the second he saw the sign in front of the little stucco building with the toadstool-lined walkway.

Angel and Ayden ran to catch up. Horatio whipped in front of them and chided Zack.

"Oh, leave him alone," Angel said to the beetle. "He's a little boy! You're taking this whole guardian thing way too seriously."

Horatio chirped indignantly, and zipped through the door into the bookstore.

Sir Benjamin looked up from his jigsaw puzzle as they entered. "Angel! What are you doing here?"

"Why do you always ask me that? You never did that to Gregor, and he came here all the time."

"I know, but he didn't work here. Seems like you'd get tired of this old place." He turned toward Zack. "Who do we have here?"

"I'm Zack! You must be Sir Benjamin! Angel told me all about you. Do you really have two pet dragons? Is one of them really part cat?"

Sir Benjamin chuckled and rose from his seat. "Well, why don't you go behind the desk and see for yourself, young man?"

Zack wasted no time and disappeared around the desk. Moments later his voice rang out across the room. "Holy cow!"

"Well, if they were sleeping before, they're not now," Angel said. She and Ayden walked over and sat at the puzzle table.

Angel grabbed the puzzle box. "I didn't know you'd started a new one…Hey, this is *Mori Zede*!"

Ayden's eyebrow rose. "Huh?"

"The Elven Temple," Angel said.

Ayden nodded and started looking for pieces.

After a while, Angel found herself watching Sir Benjamin. He stared at the same puzzle piece without attempting to place it. She reached out and touched his arm. He jumped as if startled.

"Are you okay?"

Sir Benjamin put his hand to his heart. "Oh, dear. Yes, I'm fine. Just...lost in thought." His eyes looked shadowed again.

Angel didn't like it.

"Is it the notebooks?"

Sir Benjamin hadn't mentioned them in a while. She'd been so caught up in her own life she'd forgotten all about them until this moment.

He looked at her as if processing her words, then finally said, "You know, I meant to tell you, I can't find them. I've been keeping them in the back room, and only bring them to my desk when I read them. Last time I went to get them, they weren't there. I thought maybe I'd left them in the desk, but I can't find them there either. I've searched half the bookstore. Do you think you can help?"

"Sure," she said. Easy. The notebooks had to be in the bookstore; and even if Sir Benjamin had accidentally taken them home, his house was close by, so Finding them would be quick. She concentrated, relaxing, letting the power of her Talent surge through her.

Nothing.

She concentrated harder, imagining the leather covers, the scratchy writing.

Still nothing.

It didn't make sense. Maybe if she tried focusing on just one of them…

No, still nothing.

Angel's eyes popped open. "I can't Find them!"

She tried Finding Niles's hedgehog. The image of the toy popped instantly into her head—it was in Zack's hand, behind the desk, about to be tossed for Niles to fetch. She tried Finding Zoe. Immediately an image formed of the Boxer in her back yard, barking furiously at a squirrel running along the top edge of the fence.

"It's working on other stuff, but not the notebooks."

Ayden grabbed her hand. "Let me help."

Angel cocked her head to the side. "What?"

He squeezed her fingers with one had and stroked her forearm with the other. Angel stared into his stormy blue eyes as he spoke.

"Remember, I changed my Talent before. I chose Enhancer. I can make your Talent stronger."

The sound of glass shattering snatched their attention.

Sir Benjamin stared at the shards of his teacup scattered on the floor. "I'm sorry. It just slipped. I'm fine." He waved his hand and the shattered pieces slid across the floor and formed a pile. "I'll get that in a minute." His hands were shaking.

Angel didn't like the expression on his face. The notebooks hadn't seemed to bother him before—why did he look so distressed all of a sudden? She turned back to Ayden. "It's not going to tire you out, is it?"

"Nah, only the change does that. Using the Talent is fine."

Angel chewed the inside of her cheek while she considered what he'd said. Making the Gates seemed to affect him, but he was already worn out. This might be different—Enhancing meant adding his power to hers, so maybe it wouldn't be so hard on him. She listened to Zack's giggles as he played with Niles and Spike. Finally, she agreed.

"Okay," he said. "Here goes."

This time she got an image, but it was like TV static. She saw the notebook only vaguely, and could not pinpoint its location or see anything around it.

"It's like there's interference," she said. "I've never had that happen before. Do you think it's got some kind of enchantment to protect it? Something Dr. Randall put on it?"

Sir Benjamin had returned to his seat, looking somewhat calmer. He shook his head, but his eyebrows furrowed. "There could be something…"

"What?" Angel and Ayden asked simultaneously.

Zack appeared from behind the desk. "Hey, Angel, these dragons are awesome!"

Angel turned to face him. "Glad you're having fun, little man. Did Spike go back to sleep?"

"Hah! He only woke up for a second when I first went over there. Wow, I could look at him all day. The texture of his scales is amazing."

Texture? They looked like smooth metal.

Niles sprang from behind the desk, carried his hedgehog over to Zack's feet and dropped it. Zack tossed it to the back of the room, and then followed the Cagon back behind the desk.

Angel turned back to Sir Benjamin. "Sorry, Sir B. What were you saying?"

"Well, I got to thinking after that Doran fellow came here the other day. I know what I said about him, but I just found out something new. Roger told me Doran worked at the hardware store a short while. A very short while—only a few days, actually. Roger caught him swiping some seed packets. Roger took them from him, and told him to take the afternoon off without pay.

"The thing is, Roger said when Doran left, he realized the boy had been pulling one over on him. When he looked in his hand, the seed packets were really a small set of tools. It was as if Doran made Roger see them as something else."

"What did Roger do?" Angel asked.

"Fired him. He could have done more, but he said Doran had plenty of chance to steal money and hadn't so Roger let him off easy. He never told anyone about what happened to give the boy a chance to straighten out on his own."

Ayden moved closer to Angel. "What does that have to do with the notebooks?"

"Well," said Sir Benjamin, "if he can make people see what's not there…" He shook his head and rubbed his beard. "I can't believe I'm saying this, but maybe he took the notebooks and has them disguised."

Angel swirled a puzzle piece around on the tabletop. "I can see why that might mess up my view of them, but it doesn't explain why I can't pick up the location."

"Or why he'd take them," Ayden added.

"Right you are," said Sir Benjamin, "but that's the only explanation I've got."

Angel looked closely at Sir Benjamin again. The creases in his forehead were deeper than she'd ever seen. He was almost as pale as Ayden, too.

What had she been missing while her thoughts focused so strongly on Zack and Melinda?

Angel pried Zack away from Spike and Niles so they could explore the rest of the town square. Zack begged to return the next day. Sir Benjamin, of course, told him to come back as often as he'd like. Zack beamed.

"I want a pet dragon!" he said as they walked out the door.

Angel looked over her shoulder through the front window of the bookstore. Sir Benjamin sat at the puzzle table again, staring at the pieces with a strange, mournful expression.

After shopping for an hour among the stands of arts and crafts, they passed back by Sir Benjamin's. She stopped walking and took in the sight of him still staring solemnly at the puzzle in front of him. Ayden's hand slid into hers, and he leaned over her shoulder.

"He looks as if he's seen a ghost," he whispered.

Chapter Twenty-One

Forest Hunting

Melinda tromped through the forest behind William. He'd been rambling on ever since they left the house, pointing out plants and bugs, explaining all their magical properties. Who cared? Plants were just plants, and bugs…Ick.

Every once in a while William would pick up a branch, rock, leaf, or even a bird feather. He'd pull up his glasses and hold the object close to his face. With an *m-hm,* he'd toss it back on the ground, stuff it into his own bag, or hand it to Melinda to put into the bag she was carrying.

As she stood waiting for him to examine another rock, impatience stewed inside her. She hadn't found the slightest opportunity to slip away, and her boots were rubbing blisters.

"William, think I could sit down a minute? This bag is getting heavy."

He squinted at the rock in his hand while he held his glasses up out of the way. "Oh, Melinda, I'm sorry." He tossed the rock to his side and let his glasses flop back down to his nose. "You're probably not used to trucking around like this, are you?"

"I walked around town a lot at home, but it's different, yeah."

William looked around the area and then pointed. "Over there. A fallen tree. Perfect sitting place. You can leave the bag here. I noticed a Bronze

Oak just a few yards off"—this time he pointed in the opposite direction through denser brush—"that I'd like to check out, see if there are any fallen branches. You go ahead and rest a minute.

"Oh, and here…" He held out his hand, and a glass jar filled with water appeared in his palm. He handed her the jar, and then conjured a second for himself, holding it up as if making a toast. "I'll be back in a sec."

He turned and headed through the brush.

Melinda stood, stunned for a moment. Now was her chance. She moved toward the log, and then turned to head back in the direction they had come from. She stopped cold, feeling as if she was being watched.

She looked over her shoulder. Her eyes widened and her heartbeat quickened. Doran was sitting on the log.

He stood and beckoned, then jumped over the log and headed into the trees behind him.

Melinda followed, and caught up to him just as he reached a patch of the forest where the canopy hung low and dense, blocking out much of the sunlight. Branches swayed above them, scraping against each other in a whisper.

"What are you doing here?" Melinda asked.

Doran shrugged. "I saw you two coming out here, so I followed."

"But, I didn't even hear you."

He tilted his head down and she couldn't see his expression. His voice was strained when he spoke. "I got pretty good at sneaking around…you know…before…"

Melinda rolled the water jar between her palms. "That's…cool."

Doran slunk deeper into the shadows.

"I have something I want to show you. A place…someplace special I've never shown anyone."

Melinda shivered at the sound of his whispered voice in the silence of the forest.

"Why me?"

"You're special."

"How can you say that? You just met me."

"I feel like I've known you for a long time. You seem really familiar to me…"

Melinda bit the corner of her mouth and started picking at what little was left of her black nail polish. *I can't believe it. Guys use cheesy pick-up lines even in magic-land.*

"Okay, show me."

Doran nodded and started walking. Melinda followed, William's voice barely audible through the trees, calling her name.

The forest felt completely different with Doran. When Melinda had arrived on the island, it was foreign and strange. She hadn't gone back into it until coming with William, and it was more like a school field trip. With Doran it held mystery. Maybe because the path he chose was filled with shadows. Maybe because the sounds around them were eerily muffled, and Melinda began to imagine the creatures that might be making them.

They continued weaving through trees, cutting across clearings, and ducking under branches until the trees opened up to gravelly terrain.

In the distance, thunder cracked, and almost instantly a light mist of rain began to fall.

"This way." Doran turned to his right, where the ground inclined. He turned again, left, and a rocky hill with a large, black opening appeared before them.

Melinda quieted her breathing, afraid any noise she made would echo through the silence and into the cave.

Doran smiled and ducked his head to the side. When he glanced at her again, his eyes flashed golden brown. "It's a dragon cave. Abandoned now. Nearly every living thing has been cleaned out of this area."

Melinda stared straight ahead, waiting for Doran to explain more. An empty cave was nothing special, even if it had belonged to a dragon once. Not all dragons were like Spike, domesticated and dog-sized; but visiting where a big, possibly vicious dragon *didn't* live anymore seemed hardly adventurous or "special."

Without another word, Doran stepped into the cave. Melinda hesitated, but the mist turned to droplets, and then seconds later to heavy drops. She ducked into the cave.

Despite the blackness of the entrance, the inner walls sparkled with miniscule flecks of golden light. Melinda moved closer to the walls, expecting the glowing specks to be tiny pieces of metal…

She gasped, the sound lost amid the thrum of pouring rain.

Thousands of tiny butterflies covered the walls. Most of them were less than a half-inch across, and their wings flapped with a hypnotic rhythm. Those tiny, tiny wings, glowing, sparkling like miniature angels, dancing to an otherworldly music—

She jumped when Doran's voice came from directly over her shoulder. "They glow exactly like the flesh of a Fire Nymph."

Melinda remembered Angel telling her about a Fire Nymph luring her into a dangerous part of the forest. Angel had described it as a glowing, dancing plant shaped like a human—both beautiful and frightening—but she'd also said some of them were good.

Doran shuffled behind her, and she turned around. He gazed at the walls as if at something sacred that he desperately wanted to touch but didn't dare. He swallowed, and licked his lips. "Like a Fire Nymph…because they *are* part Fire Nymph."

"O…kay…" Melinda tightened her grip on the water jar, and released a nervous laugh.

Doran spun to face her. His eyes were narrowed at first, but his face relaxed almost immediately.

"Sorry," Melinda said, her laughing stopped short.

Doran's eyes gleamed copper.

She cleared her throat. "I just…it's…well, how can they be part Fire Nymph?"

Doran's eyes flared. He rubbed the back of his neck, and exhaled loudly. "When I was…in jail…the man next to me, in the cell on the other side of the wall, told me things. He's a scientist, and he'd been doing experiments." The copper blazed brighter. "Brilliant experiments. He was hybridizing animals, trying to combine their powers—"

"You mean that freak Angel helped catch a couple years ago?"

Doran's face contorted and he raised his fist in front of his face. "He's not a freak! And your little friend Angel had no clue what she was doing!"

Melinda jumped back. She glanced at the cave entrance just as Doran moved to block her path. The water jar slipped from her hand and crashed to the ground.

"Why are you so hung up on that guy?" she said. "You met him in jail, and he…he killed someone…that Elven girl." She focused on the diminishing rain as she moved slowly toward the open forest.

"He was the only one I had to talk to for the last two years," Doran said, head hung and his voice pained. "He didn't mean to kill her. She only got in the way. No one understood him, or his research. But he told me all about it, and about this cave. He told me that if I came here I'd see that he finally succeeded, and that I should show someone I trust."

"Why me? You just met me—you can't possibly trust me already."

Doran tilted his head enough for Melinda to see his eyes, which were now a silver gray. "Because I thought you'd want what he can give you."

"And what is that?"

"Magic."

"I don't need him for that."

Doran's brow creased. "You can do magic?"

"Yeah."

"But you're—"

"But I'm *what?*"

"Unempowered."

"That's that stupid word Angel used. But she said you can *become* Empowered. I guess I did." Melinda stopped inching her way out. She had magic—and he didn't. Even if she couldn't control hers yet, he didn't know that.

Doran stepped away from the cave entrance. "You have magic, and you didn't have to take it. That just doesn't make sense."

Melinda glanced at the trees outside the cave entrance. "I gotta go," she said. "William's probably looking for me."

"Will you come again?"

His eyes had turned green again. They were beautiful when they were green, like a field in spring.

No harm done. He's scared, and alone. No one to talk to for two years except that crazy Dr. Frankenstein.

"Yeah."

She reached to touch his arm.

He pulled back, out of her reach, and raised his hand up to the cave ceiling. A cluster of butterflies settled onto his fingertips.

"They'll lead you back," he said as the butterflies lifted from his fingers and flickered toward the cave opening. "Go. Now. Or your…friends…will get worried."

Melinda nodded, and dashed out of the cave, chasing after butterflies too small to be able to move so fast.

She ran through the forest, dodging dripping branches, sliding on the wet earth, and trying to block out the eerie animal calls. Nearly breathless, she reached the clearing where she had last seen William and called his name.

"Melinda!" Caryn called from close by.

"Over here!" Melinda cried.

Caryn and William appeared at the edge of the clearing. Caryn dashed over to Melinda and wrapped her arms around her. She and William seemed so dry—had they used magic to keep from getting soaked in the rain?

"Where have you been?"

William's stare pushed Melinda's gaze to the ground in front of her feet.

"I saw something…some kind of animal. I followed it, and I guess I got lost. And then it started to rain, so I hid inside…I mean, under…"

"Melinda." Caryn gripped Melinda's shoulders. "You can't do that in this forest. You don't know what's out there. You don't know how to use your powers yet."

Melinda's head snapped up.

"Yes," Caryn said, "Anna told us. We would have offered to help you with your magic, but Anna wants to be the one. For now, anyway."

William stepped up next to his wife. Nothing of the playful William showed through. "Let's go. She's probably home by now."

Melinda followed them back to the house, with one question niggling at her the whole way. Why had Doran been so sure she was unempowered?

Chapter Twenty-Two

Warnings

"I wonder what's taking them so long?" Angel asked as she paced the living room.

Zack and Ayden were playing checkers on the floor. Horatio zipped from window to window, chirping angrily.

Ayden looked up and scowled. "Stop chewing your fingernail."

Angel snapped her hand away and crossed her arms. Seconds later her finger was hooked in her mouth again.

The door burst open, and a damp and ruffled Melinda tromped through, followed by Angel's somber-looking parents.

"Anna, can we talk to you?" her father said, as her mom instructed Melinda to go dry off and change clothes.

Melinda's face clearly showed she was not used to being parented, but she headed upstairs to the loft.

Angel followed her parents into the kitchen, where her mom began pulling food out of the icebox. Her father sat on one of the barstools and patted the other. Angel sat next to him.

"Where were you guys?" She gripped the edge of the barstool to keep from gnawing on her fingernail.

"Melinda took off while we were out searching for materials in the forest. She said she got lost, but I think she's not telling the truth."

Angel's mom nodded in agreement. "Anna, we know she's been through a lot, and we want to give her the benefit of the doubt and help her get through these adjustments. But we can't tolerate her lying."

Angel bit the inside of her cheek and squeezed her eyes shut. "I, um, think I know where she ran off to. She's been meeting up with Doran Ashe."

A crashing noise made Angel jump, and her eyes popped open. The plate her mother had been holding was on the floor, scattered in dozens of jagged pieces.

"And you didn't tell us right away?" Her mother's voice crept higher with each word. "Anna, what were you thinking?"

Her father stared at her, then pulled off his glasses and wiped them on his shirt. "Baby girl, I'm disappointed." Despite his casual actions, his voice was more stern than she'd ever heard.

Angel's heart twisted with remorse. "I thought I could stop her from seeing him. I've been talking to her, warning her. She hasn't gone looking for him before, but he showed up at the farm the other day. Mom, he lost his magic. He seems really upset about how his life has turned out. I don't think he's—"

Her father's fist slammed on the counter. "He's a professional thief and liar, Anna! Not to mention Melinda is not even sixteen and Doran's—"

"Actually, Dad…she's almost eighteen."

"What?"

Angel sighed. "She missed the birthday cut-off by like two days when she started school, so she kinda got stuck in the year behind. And then she got held back for missing too much school one year when she was really sick. She's never really been into the school thing anyway, so she didn't push to get moved ahead."

Her parents stared at her.

Angel slid off her stool and crossed her arms. "Anyway, I didn't say we were going to spend time with him. And I *did* warn Melinda about him. I just don't think we're in real danger from him, that's all. Plus, in a few months, she'll be an adult and there will be nothing we can do. But I'll talk to Melinda again."

She took a deep breath and tightened her grip on her elbows. "Besides. Kalek told him off. Doran's got to know he doesn't have a chance against someone as powerful as Kalek. I'm sorry. Really. I just didn't want you guys worrying."

Her mom rubbed her temple and sighed. "We're *going* to worry. Just because he did his time and seems sorry doesn't mean he is. He still has to prove it."

"How can he prove it, though, if no one gives him a chance?"

Angel's father leaned against the counter and looked over his glasses "We can't pretend he never did anything wrong. And we have an obligation to keep you and Melinda safe."

Angel nodded. "We'll be careful."

"It's more than you just being careful," her mom said. "Melinda's living in our house. We're going to have to talk to her about this."

"Mom, no." Angel shook her head. "No, please. Let me. You don't know Melinda. You don't..." She huffed. "She's never had to listen to adults, and if you start coming down on her right now, she's going to just push back harder. But I *know* her. I'll find a way to keep her away from him."

Her father frowned. "This isn't a game."

"I know it's not. And I'll tell you if I think she's planning on sneaking off again or anything, I promise. But please...just give me a little while before you step in. Please."

They looked at each other, and her mother's head tilted slightly to the side. The look said, *I'll let you make the call on this one.*

Her father turned back to Angel. "We'll back off for now, but you will come to us if you suspect anything. Anything—you hear?"

"Yes, sir."

"So, you're saying your parents think I'm a sneak and a liar, and now they want you to babysit me even more?"

Angel stared at Melinda's back as Melinda stared out the window in the loft. The amber glow of the setting sun framed her silhouette.

"That's not what I said at all. I told them about Doran, but I said they don't need to worry, that I'll be with you—"

Melinda swung around, her eyes blazing with anger. "*Wrong.* That is *exactly* what you said!"

"You did sneak off with him, didn't you?"

"I got lost. That's all. It's not my fault it rained and your dad was off playing pick-up sticks."

"Don't you even try to blame this on my dad!"

"Why not? My dad's a loser...*was* a loser...Maybe yours is, too, and you just haven't found out yet."

Angel jumped to her feet, and balled her hands into fists. "You're horrible! I was sticking up for you! I let you come live with me. My *parents* let you come live with us, and this is how your repay us? You're welcome to go home any time!"

She spun on her heel and stomped down the steps. *She deserves to have a rotten murderer for a father!*

Ayden's eyes widened as she cut through the living room. "Angel, what's wrong?"

She ignored both him and Zack, who knocked over the checker set as he stood up and stepped toward her.

She ran through the empty kitchen and out to the back yard, letting the door slam behind her. Zack and Ayden's voices followed her as she jumped the fence and headed into the forest. Horatio appeared and buzzed circles around her head, his chirping like a whine in her ears.

"Leave me alone!" She swatted at him, and dove between two trees onto the familiar path that led to *Mori Zede*.

The stone steps of the ancient Temple cooled Angel's skin as she leaned against the base of a half-crumbled pillar. What was left of the broken walls still stood amazingly high and cast the portico in darkness as it blocked out the faint light from the setting sun. All around, chirps and caws clicked through the clearing, echoes of the animals in the surrounding forest. A hint of a breeze fluttered the hair around her face.

Who would come after her first? Her parents were probably furious, but they'd most likely send Ayden. Her ears were keened for crunching of footsteps, but she felt Kalek's approach without ever hearing him.

"Don't ask," she said.

"Ask what?"

"Why I'm here. And if you value your life, you will *not* lecture me about being in the forest at night."

Kalek slid next to her on the steps and put his arm around her shoulders. "I won't lecture, but there's no way I'm letting you walk home alone."

Angel huffed. "Don't worry. Ayden will be along any minute, I'm sure."

"You're not here because of him, are you?"

"Of course not!"

He squeezed her shoulders. "Good. I'd hate to have to kick his—ow! Don't hit me, I'm on your side."

Angel laughed and patted his thigh where she'd smacked him. "I know you are. Even if you have been a pain lately."

"Me?"

"Yeah." She laughed. "But your kind of moody I can deal with most of the time. Melinda, though…."

"Oh. Her." His voice scraped like a dagger being unsheathed.

"I thought you were actually beginning to like her?"

Kalek didn't reply, and when Angel opened her mouth to speak again, he touched her lips with his finger.

"Someone's just outside the clearing," he whispered.

Ayden burst out from between two trees and ran toward them. His damp bangs clung to his forehead and he searched her face with worried eyes as he sat down next to her.

"Angel! Why did you take off like that?" he asked.

Kalek moved to perch on a nearby pillar.

"Why don't you ask Melinda?" Angel said.

"I did. She didn't answer. She just started crying and told me to find you."

Chapter Twenty-Three

Crystal Clear

Melinda sat on her pallet with her knees pulled up to her chin. She raised her head, grateful for the darkness in the loft. The only light was a faint moonlit haze from the window on the other side of the room. She wiped her tears and took a deep breath as she shifted position on her pallet.

Angel stood by the railing at the top of the stairs, arms crossed.

"I'm sorry," Melinda said between sobs. She'd been crying ever since Angel ran out. She hated it. Why did she keep losing it on this ridiculous island?

"I never should have called your dad a loser. I didn't mean it. He's nothing like my dad. My dad would never have spent years searching for me. He never even spent enough time with me to notice when I was home."

Melinda could barely see Angel's face, but she didn't need to. She knew the girl had that pitying expression she always got when Melinda talked about her dad. Something in Angel's eyes always said she knew more than she was letting on. Melinda's dad may have been a complete slouch of a father, but Angel looked at her as if she'd been raised by wolves.

"I'm sorry, too." Angel moved toward Melinda, then stopped and ran her fingers through her hair. Sighing, she stepped back and leaned against the railing. "Hey, why don't we have some official magic lessons tomorrow?"

Melinda's shoulders relaxed and she wiped the tears that ran down the sides of her nose. "Only if you promise Kalek won't be there."

Angel shook her head. "I'll make sure he stays away."

The tone of her voice told Melinda she was irritated, but Melinda didn't care. The last thing she needed was Kalek watching while she made a fool of herself. And she was sure that's exactly what she'd do.

"What about Ayden?"

"He's helping his mom tomorrow."

"And Zack?"

"I don't know. My mom and dad may want to work with him. Mom said something about magic being really unpredictable in kids his age, and since he's never tried it before…"

Melinda shifted to the side and leaned on her arm. "Your mom told me you wanted to be the one to teach me, but I haven't done real magic either. Not on purpose."

"Yeah, but it's different."

"Why?"

"It just is. Don't you want me to teach you? Don't you think it will be fun? Like when we were kids."

"You mean you bossing me around?"

Melinda braced herself for Angel to get mad, but she actually laughed.

"I thought you weren't going to boss me around," Zack said.

Melinda smirked. "She said the same thing to me."

"I did not." Angel set the rock on the tree stump for the twentieth time. "I never said anything. *You* said I'd boss you around. Besides, I thought I'd just be teaching Melinda today, not both of you."

"It's not my fault your dad has to work, and your mom's sick. So don't take it out on me." Zack pouted like a scolded puppy, lip sticking out, but his eyes glistened with mischief.

His words hit Melinda like ice. Caryn was sick, no doubt because she'd been out in the rain searching for Melinda, and William was behind schedule for the same reason. She picked at the remnants of her nail polish and kicked a pebble across the dirt. The clearing they worked in was just outside Angel's back yard and Melinda was grateful for the privacy, but she felt open and exposed nonetheless.

"Don't complain." Angel waved her hand, sending the rock in a circle around the clearing. "I could have you cleaning dishes like I had to do for *my* first lesson. I was trying to start ya'll off with something fun."

"Floating rocks around? That's what you call fun?" Zack poked Angel in the ribs. "I want to learn how to conjure insects into my hands so I don't have to chase them down anymore. I want to fly up into the canopy and check out those cool spider webs. I want to do that trick Ayden did with the sand when he turned it into a magnifying glass."

Melinda sighed. Zack had nothing to complain about. He'd managed to get every shape and size rock to lift off the tree stump, and land wherever he chose. Melinda, however, hadn't made even the small one in her hand do more than wobble.

"You said the magnifying glass wasn't strong enough." Angel waved the rock over until it hung just out of her reach.

"Well, duh. If you can see stuff up close anyway, why would you need something that weak? I'm just talking about the way he can transform—"

"What do you mean?" Angel asked, her rock now hovering right in front of Melinda.

Melinda snatched it out of the air and looked at Zack.

"Well, like that piece of grass right there. Can't you kind of zoom in and see the orange stripe down the middle?"

Melinda watched Angel's face twist in confusion.

"It's just grass."

"Yeah, I know, but I can see it like I'm looking through a microscope. Try it!"

"I can't, Zack. I've never been able to do that…" Angel gasped and grabbed Zack's arm. "Zack! It's your Talent. You have some kind of super-zoom vision or something!" She smacked her palm against her forehead. "Now I get it. That's why you were so good at finding bugs."

"I thought I just had really good eyesight," he said, his eyes still glued to the ground.

Melinda concentrated, but saw nothing different. This wasn't fair at all. She hadn't even mastered floating a stupid pebble, and Zack had already found his Talent.

Angel squealed, and dragged Zack to the edge of the clearing. "Try it on something else. What does the tree bark look like?"

"It's got tiny spines all over it."

"How about over there?"

Melinda followed Angel's gaze to a patch of grass several yards away.

"Do you mean the toadstool or the ladybug that's sitting on it?"

Angel squealed again, and Melinda had to fight to keep her feet planted.

"That is so cool!" Angel grabbed Zack's hand and hurried toward the house without even looking in Melinda's direction. "Let's go tell Mom and Dad."

As they disappeared between the trees, Melinda squeezed the rock in her hand. This just wasn't fair at all. She squeezed harder, until her hand burned from the effort. She relaxed her hand, but the burning sensation didn't stop. Looking down at her palm, she gasped.

The rock was crystal clear.

Melinda entered the kitchen through the back door. Angel and Zack sat on the bar stools and barely looked over when she stepped inside. Zack was chattering away, but stopped when Caryn shuffled in from the hallway. Her cheeks were flushed and she hugged a bulky bathrobe around herself.

"Mom, you didn't need to get up," Angel said. "I was just so excited about Zack finding his Talent I forgot you weren't feeling well."

Caryn sniffed and wiped her nose with a tissue. "I'm actually feeling better, and I'm tired of staring at the ceiling in my room. I think when I get over this cold, I'm going to paint a mural up there." She smiled, a twinkle in her puffy eyes. "Now tell me all about it."

Angel recounted all the things Zack had homed in on while Melinda sat at the kitchen table examining the crystal she had made from the rock. It was perfectly smooth and symmetrical. She turned it in every direction while Angel droned on about Zack's brilliance. Little did they know she'd just done exactly what he'd wished he could do.

But how? And why did her magic only seem to come out when she was mad?

"We'll have to figure out what to call your Talent," Caryn said

Zack's eyes widened. "You mean I can pick? Cool…" He scratched his chin like a little professor deep in thought.

Melinda swallowed a lump of jealousy.

"I can be a Zoomer! Or an Optimator…or a…a…Visionary!"

Angel laughed and ruffled Zack's hair. "Visionary? Please. I think not. And those other names make you sound like a superhero."

"How about Magnifier?" Melinda said.

Zack turned to her and scrunched his mouth to the side. "Hm…Magnifier. That's good. Yeah, I like that. Sounds scientific, too."

"What's that you've got?" Caryn asked.

Angel snapped her head around and gawped. "Where did you get that? It's gorgeous!"

"I, um, found it out in the forest." Melinda's stomach squeezed tight. What was she doing? She should be happy about this. Proud. She should be showing off what she could do, not lying. But…she still couldn't control it.

"You did not." Angel crossed over to the table and sat by Melinda. "Crystals like that don't just lie around on the forest floor. I would have noticed it when I was looking for rocks for us to practice with."

Melinda sighed, and plunked the crystal in front of Angel. "Then you tell me where it came from."

Angel picked it up and examined it. "Wait…this *isn't* a crystal. It's one of the rocks I picked. I chose each rock for a different reason. The shape of an object affects the way it lifts. I remember thinking how perfectly shaped it was, and how its symmetry might make it easier for you. The only flaw was a ridge exactly like the one this has." She looked up and gazed directly into Melinda's eyes. "You turned it transparent."

Angel's face lit up with a smile.

Melinda couldn't help but mirror it. Then the smile fell. "But I can't do it again. It only happens when I'm mad."

"You mean like with the mirror?" Angel's eyes narrowed.

"Yeah." Melinda glanced at Caryn and then looked back at Angel. "And when you and Kalek sent me in to get drinks that day at the farm. I think I made the water cold."

Angel's eyes widened again. "You didn't tell me that."

"I forgot about it, 'til just now."

Caryn shuffled over to the table and took a seat. "Melinda, it's perfectly normal for magic to come and go like that, and coincide with strong emotions. You're certainly not the first to struggle."

Melinda lowered her eyes and shifted in her chair. She remembered what Caryn's mirror had shown her. Caryn had struggled with finding her Talent, and she'd grown up in this world.

Melinda and Angel stood at the loft window watching the spider web in Ayden's back yard spin in flashes of metallic gold and silver. The sun had been down for a few hours. The moon and stars were completely blacked out by thick cloud cover, making the spider web's light all the brighter.

The floor creaked as Angel shifted her weight. "Why did you look so freaked out when my mom told you other people struggle with magic? Didn't it make you feel better?"

"It did. I just…it's just weird thinking of your mom as a little girl, that's all."

"My mom? What are you talking about?" Ice filled Angel's voice, and Melinda turned to see her glaring out the window.

"The mirror."

Angel turned toward Melinda. Her voice was melancholy, but her eyes were sharp with anger. "Why did it show you things, but it's never shown me anything?"

"How would I know? I was just looking at it, and it kind of clicked on, like a TV or something." Melinda's heart started to pound. "It freaked me out. I *felt* how upset she was, and it pissed me off and I threw it. Is that what you want for yourself?"

Angel blinked and her fingers shot to her bangs. She jerked them away and stared at her hand as if it didn't belong to her. Then she laughed, a sad, somber laugh, and the anger in her eyes dissipated. She took in a deep breath and sighed. "I've held that mirror a hundred times. My mom told me a long time ago that it was like a diary, and that it would be mine someday. She said it only opens for the person it's meant for, at the time it should be handed over. I just figured it wasn't time yet. I never thought for a minute I was the wrong person."

Melinda's brain rocked with the thought—Angel was jealous of *her*.

Angel who had everything.

Angel's head suddenly popped up, and she smiled. "Hey, Kalek must be at the Temple tonight. I can hear him playing."

Melinda strained her ears, but heard nothing. She leaned out the window, and Angel grabbed her arm.

"Don't hurt yourself. You probably can't hear him. I can barely pick it up. There's something about me having a drop of Elven blood that makes my hearing a tiny bit better than normal and I can pick up his music if the wind is just right."

But Melinda had heard music coming through that window before, and even heard it one night when Angel said she hadn't. That didn't make sense.

"What does his music sound like?" she asked.

"Hold on a sec, and I'll show you." Angel dashed down the stairs and returned a minute later with a huge red rose. It looked real in every way, but too perfect to be real at the same time.

"What is that?"

Angel laughed. "I guess you could call it an Elven CD. It's how Kalek's band records their music."

"It looks like it's alive."

"It is. It's infused with magic I couldn't even begin to explain to you. *I* don't even understand it. Ancient Elven secret, I suppose. Anyway, you won't get the full effect, but it's still beautiful. Just stroke the petals."

Melinda ran her finger along one of the petals. It was softer than anything she had ever felt before. Immediately a melody played as if it came from the walls around her. Haunting and beautiful…

"That's the music I've been hearing at night. It always seems to make me have strange dreams."

Angel looked confused, but shook her head and smiled. "Well, maybe you're meant for this place after all."

When the music stopped, Melinda held the rose out for Angel to take.

Angel shook her head. "No, you hang on to it."

As she lay in bed that night, Melinda held the rose in one hand and the transparent rock in the other. As sleep crept up on her she set the rose on the table she'd been using as a nightstand. The music stopped playing, but moments later, the same melody drifted through the window as it had before. Melinda clutched the rock to her chest. *I just want to know how to control all this.*

Soon her eyelids became too heavy to hold open.

The hill loomed as majestic as before. People milled around everywhere, bumping into each other, clawing past one another. Melinda felt the same desperation to reach the hilltop, and the same uncertainty as to why. She stared at the top of the hill, so distant and hazy.

If only she could see what was up there. If she had Zack's Talent she could home in on it. But she didn't have any Talent at all. She barely had magic. She didn't belong among these people.

Yet the hilltop called to her. She squinted and concentrated. A flash of light appeared at the top. The purest white light she'd ever seen, but so far away. She could never reach it.

Still, something inside drove her to try.

She kept her eyes locked on the light and took a step. Her foot caught on something, and she stumbled. She should have fallen, but instead drifted toward the ground, impossibly slow, her neck craning to keep her gaze focused on the light. She reached her other leg forward to catch herself, and ended up off-balance. When she pulled her gaze away from the hilltop, she slammed to the ground.

She scrambled to her feet.

The light was gone.

Chapter Twenty-Four

The Lee Side

Angel's mom perched on the top step of a short ladder, stretched just far enough to make Angel nervous. She held her reprimand, knowing it would go unheeded anyway.

An array of colors already filled a good portion of the ceiling, in bursts of varying sizes. Bits of green haze filled some of the background space. Nothing had real detail, but the general idea of *flowers* was obvious.

"That's looking great, Mom. But I gotta say, I thought you'd paint the *sky* on the ceiling, not a garden."

Her mom laughed, and spoke over the paintbrush she clenched between her teeth. "All I could envision when I lay here yesterday was flowers. Besides, who wants to paint what you'd *expect* to see on a ceiling?"

Angel jerked at the sudden sound of footsteps in the room, and swung her head to see who it was. Melinda stood just inside the doorway.

"Ayden's here." She waggled her eyebrows a couple of times and winked at Angel.

Heat started at the base of Angel's neck, and she glanced up at her mom, who was thankfully engrossed in her painting.

She turned back toward the doorway and found it empty. As she took a step back, she said, "Are you sure you don't want me to get the other ladder?"

"No, the other one is too big. Now, go on and see Ayden. I'm fine up here without you supervising, I promise."

Angel found Ayden and Melinda sitting on opposite ends of the couch in the living room, while Zack knelt on the floor tying his shoes. She sat down next to Ayden, and he leaned over to kiss her cheek. Angel caught Melinda winking at her again over Ayden's shoulder. *What's with her?*

She blushed again. *What's with* me*?*

"Are we gonna do more lessons today?" Zack asked as he stood.

"Sure, little man," Angel said as Ayden slid his hand into hers. She squeezed his fingers. "But we're going to do it while we walk to *Mori Zede*."

Zack's eyes widened and he squirmed as if fighting the urge to jump up and down. "Yay! I was reading about the Temple in one of your dad's books. There was only one picture—well, it was actually a drawing—and the walls looked miles high. It's solid stone, and the windows are stained glass made by an Elven artisan who had a Talent that made them completely unbreakable—but of course they did break, so that had to have been one powerful blast that took it down—"

"Zack, *breathe*," Melinda said. "You never talked this much before. I think Angel's rubbing off on you." Her grin and her excited tone of voice betrayed her words, and Angel ignored the dig. Melinda was actually *smiling*.

Ayden leaned forward. "That's the Temple in Sir Benjamin's puzzle, right? The one where Kalek likes to practice?"

The light in Melinda's eyes snapped off instantly.

Angel tried her best not to scowl. "I figured you'd want to go see him play for real after last night."

Melinda remained silent.

"It's better in person. You can't experience his music when you listen to it from the rose."

"Experience it?" Ayden said.

Angel squeezed his hand. "You'll see."

"Come on, Melinda," Angel whispered as they hiked through the forest trail to *Mori Zede*.

Thick trees lined the path. Mossy plants climbed many of their trunks, a deep, rosy purple punctuated with tiny black flowers. Fern-like plants rustled at the base of the trees, and long, spindly branches tickled each other across the bright blue sky above.

Zack skipped ahead, tugging Zoe's leash, while Ayden stayed a few steps behind them all.

"I know you're mad at Kalek for telling off Doran," Angel said, "but he's just looking out for you. For all of us."

"Doran's just a guy." Melinda's words came out like ice.

Angel gritted her teeth and blew out a breath. Melinda ran hot or cold, no in-between. Never any warning before she changed gears. *How am I supposed to help her control her magic if she can't even control her moods?*

"He likes you. I want to give him a chance, but my parents are worried. I promised them we'd be careful."

Melinda turned her head and glared. "You can promise them *you'll* be careful. But you can't promise for me." She looked straight ahead again. "Besides, how's dragging me off into the woods being careful? I thought your parents didn't want us going any farther than the forest right behind your house."

"We've got Ayden with us."

Horatio dug into her shoulder and chirped in her ear.

"Yes, you too, Horatio. And Zoe. And Kalek will be at the Temple. Plus, with Doran having no magic, he can't use his Talent against us." Angel tried not to let her thoughts wander to the light she'd seen coming from his house. Was there something in there he could use against them?

"His Talent?"

"Sir B said he can make things look like other things…He kind of makes your brain see something as different than it really is."

"You mean he *could. If* he had magic. Which he doesn't."

Angel ground her teeth and snapped, "Didn't I just say that?"

She exhaled to calm herself. She'd never help Melinda control her emotions if she didn't get a rein on her own. But the thought she'd been holding back had entered her mind against her will—*Doran is hiding something, and I'm helping him by not telling anyone about that light.*

She wanted to believe Doran sincerely regretted losing his magic, for Melinda's sake. But he'd never have magic again if his house was wired with electricity. He had to know that. Which meant he didn't want it back.

That scared Angel more than anything.

Melinda shot a look over her shoulder, then whispered. "Ayden's looking a little stronger, at least."

"Yeah," Angel whispered back. "He hasn't changed his Talent since right after we got back from getting you. Sarah and I have been harping on him about it. That's one of the reasons she's been asking him to help her so much, I think. To keep an eye on him. She said she wants his next change to be the last."

"Must be nice to be able to pick your Talent." Melinda quickened her pace, aimed straight at Zack and Zoe. As Melinda moved away, Angel thought she heard, "Must be nice to have a Talent at all."

Two Elven musicians stood next to Kalek, both dressed in tunics and leather pants. Angel knew the one with straight hair and boots up to his knees—Drazen—but the other guy she'd never seen before. His hair hung to his waist in thick dreadlocks, and tattoos webbed across his left hand. All three of them were looking over one of the instruments.

"This is awesome!" Kalek's voice carried across the clearing as Angel and Ayden caught up to Melinda and Zack. He turned the instrument—a flute?—in his hands. "Your father did an amazing job on this, dude."

He put the flute to his mouth and played a few notes. Several dragonflies appeared in mid-air, and then disappeared at the end of the last note.

Kalek handed the flute to Drazen as Angel ran up the steps.

"Were those real dragonflies?" she asked. "What happened to them when you stopped playing?"

Drazen smiled. "Oh, yeah, they're real. They just went back to where they were before. The flute summons them when it's played." He lifted his gaze to the spot where Melinda, Ayden, and Zack had gathered at the base of the steps. "I'm Draz," he said, and then turned to join the other musician.

"I brought everyone to hear you play," Angel said to Kalek. She glanced over at the other two musicians. "Who's the new guy?"

"That's Mark."

Angel laughed. *I didn't know Elves ever gave their kids normal names…*

"What?" Kalek asked as he picked up his guitar.

"Nothing."

"Well, then. Let's rock."

Chapter Twenty-Five

Power Surge

Melinda stood slightly behind Ayden and Zack, staring up at the enormous Temple walls rising from the wide steps. Sunlight glinted off the dagger-sharp colored glass that jutted up from the broken windows. The uneven top of the building opened up to the sky like the maw of a great stone dragon.

She stepped back, shivering. Not from cold—prickles of electricity flowed through her, traveling just beneath her skin. She felt *alive,* and yet incredibly small as her neck ached from holding her head back to see the full height of the wall. Dizziness washed over her, and she swayed, shifting her foot to the side to keep her balance.

There's power here.

She lowered her gaze to the front of the building. The steps led up to a wide portico. The wall should have had an entrance, but there was no sign of one. Angel had told her about a night when she and Gregor had created a Gateway where the door used to be, and then the opening filled in with stone. The Gateway led to *Beyond*, as Angel had called it. Had she meant Heaven? Melinda hadn't really paid attention to the story. Now she wished she had.

She let her gaze roam to the group at the top of the steps. The sight didn't quite compute. Three guys with pointy ears and long hair, dressed like heavy-metal-meets-Lord-of-the-Rings. At a *Temple.*

Kalek shrugged the strap of a sleek, black guitar over his shoulder while the guy with straight hair picked up a flute and the one with the massive dreads sat behind a strange-looking drum set.

He looked out over the group gathered in front of the portico and his mouth slid into a half-smile. "Well then. Let's rock."

The music was exactly as Melinda had heard before. Haunting. Amazing. The beat eased her into the song at first, slow, beckoning. As it picked up, it drove her pulse the way good music should. She allowed her shoulders to move and her head to bob in time with the drums. But she didn't see much difference between this and the music from the rose, other than it coming from the open air rather than the walls inside Angel's house.

She peered around, confused by the others' faces. Angel's eyes were closed, a rapt expression lighting her face. Ayden's head dropped just enough for his hair to fall forward and block Melinda's view of his eyes; but she guessed they were closed. He swayed slightly to the beat of the music. Zack looked ready to burst from excitement, eyes closed but eyebrows raised, mouth held tight as if he wanted to sing along but didn't dare.

Kalek and the other two looked like nothing more than ordinary musicians, jamming out. The only thing that struck Melinda as odd about them, other than the strange choice of instruments, was the lack of a power supply and amp for Kalek's electric guitar.

As the music slowed down again, Melinda noticed movement along the edge of the clearing. She squinted against the sunlight, trying to make out the shadow that ducked in and out around the base of a tree.

Doran.

Why was he sneaking around over here? He had to know Kalek wouldn't want him here, and this time Kalek had backup. The dude with the dreads looked like he could break Doran in half just by looking at him.

The music stopped completely, and Angel ran over to Melinda, eyes bright and a grin pouching her cheeks out.

"Wasn't it awesome? Didn't you love the part where you flew over the beach? That was my favorite!"

Melinda's lip curled. "What are you talking about?"

Angel's expression fell, and she tucked her hair behind her ears before crossing her arms. Shaking her head slightly, she said, "You didn't experience it, did you?"

"It was a great song. That part right in the middle totally rocked, but I don't know what you mean about flying over the beach."

Angel's head turned to the side as Ayden stepped up and put his arm around her. He looked completely rested; the shadows under his eyes were gone and he didn't look so pale anymore. It was if the music had zapped away his fatigue.

Melinda shot a glance at Zack, who was chattering away with Kalek and his friends. The three Elven guys laughed at something he said and Kalek rustled Zack's hair.

Melinda felt like more of an outcast than ever. That pitying look popped up on Angel's face again. Melinda started to pick at her nail polish and found none left. She reached down to her pocket where her cell phone was clipped and picked at the flap of its case instead.

Ayden's eyes narrowed. "Why are you still carrying that thing around?"

Melinda shrugged. "Habit, I guess. It hasn't worked since I got here."

"You haven't been wearing that," Angel said. "I haven't seen it on you since the day we went and got you."

"Well, I still just grabbed it today by accident." She flipped the case open and pulled the phone out. "See, the battery is even dead."

Angel took it from her hand and scrunched her nose. "No it's not."

"It was the other day!" Melinda snatched the phone back and looked at the screen. Sure enough, it had a slight charge. "I swear, the other day the screen was black. It was totally dead."

Angel's face screwed up and she glared at the cell phone and clicked her tongue. Melinda snapped it back into the case just in time for Kalek's face to appear without warning over Angel's shoulder. Didn't he ever make noise when he moved?

"What are you three talking about so secretively over here?" His grin flattened into a stern line when no one answered. He looked down at the cell phone case Melinda was picking at again.

"You can't use stuff like that here, you know."

"You have an electric guitar."

"Totally different. Phoebe's all prime wood and high-quality steel." He nodded his head toward her hand. "*That* is a piece of plastic junk."

Melinda stifled a laugh. "You named your guitar *Phoebe*?"

Kalek ignored her and continued his disdainful stare at her cell phone.

"Well, maybe I should name my phone, and that would make it okay to have on this backwards island. Or do I have to make it ring with magic?"

"Melinda, Kalek, come on," Angel said, looking back and forth at them.

"No, she's right." Kalek looked up with challenge in his eyes. "Go ahead. Let's see you do it and I'll drop the whole thing."

Melinda's heart seemed to stop. She forced herself to breathe. *Oh, crap. What have I done?*

Kalek leaned forward like a cheetah about to pounce. "Come on. You got that mirror to fly across the room. You can do this, can't you?"

Melinda swallowed, her eyes burning as she fought back tears.

"Kalek, what are you doing?" Angel stepped between them.

"The mirror was a fluke, Angel. I watched her while I played just now. She didn't get anything from my music. She's completely closed off from it." He turned toward Angel. His voice was ice. "You know what that means."

"It's not what you think," Angel said. "It's not her fault, and it certainly has nothing to do with her cell phone."

"I know that!"

"Then why give her such a hard time?"

This time he turned to Melinda and locked his eyes with hers. "Don't think for a minute Angel never told me about the 'magic' you thought you could do when you were kids. If you think that…" He inhaled through his teeth. "If you think that will be tolerated here, you're sadly mistaken."

"Is that why you've been such a jerk to me this whole time? Because I used to play with Tarot cards and stuff?" Melinda laughed, but held her stare. "It was just for fun, you idiot. A way to scam money off my friends."

Kalek turned back to Angel. "She's clueless, isn't she? It all started when she got here. And it better stop soon." He stalked off to the Temple steps.

"What started?" Melinda asked.

Angel's eyes darkened. "I don't know."

Melinda hung at the edge of the clearing near the path while Angel and Ayden said good-bye to Kalek and the other two. Zack jumped up and hugged Kalek, then shook the others' hands before hooking the leash back on Zoe and running over to join Melinda. Angel and Ayden walked hand in hand toward them.

Kalek waved one more time to Zack, then turned around, reaching toward his guitar. He stopped cold. Melinda followed his gaze. He was looking toward the forest where Melinda had thought she'd seen Doran.

A shadow moved between two trees, just as it had before. She looked back at Kalek.

He was definitely staring at the shadow. The other two guys had their backs turned, so neither of them noticed when Kalek dropped to his knees and put his face in his hands. He slid his hands into his hair, pulling the curls from his face and turned toward Melinda. Even from a distance she could read the hate in those onyx eyes.

Melinda glanced over at Angel, who had lifted her head as if tuning her ears to hear something. Melinda looked back at Kalek. His mouth moved, but she couldn't hear him speak.

Angel stepped up in front of Melinda and just stared.

"What was he saying?" Melinda asked.

"He said, 'Let her rest.'"

"What does that mean?"

Angel didn't answer, her eyes no longer joyful from the music. She turned to Zack. "Come on, little man, let's go."

He took her other hand, and the three of them walked away from Melinda and onto the pathway. Melinda looked up at the Temple steps again. Kalek and the other two were gone. In their place stood Doran, holding something in his hand. He turned it sideways, and Melinda saw that it was a piece of paper. He set the paper on top of a broken pillar, then spun and ran into the forest on the other side of the clearing.

Melinda glanced over her shoulder. Angel and the boys were well out of sight. Melinda ran over to the pillar and grabbed the paper. It was stiff, and thick. As she crossed the clearing she looked at it. Not a piece of paper after all. It was a Tarot card.

The Magician.

It represented creativity, and gaining what one wants through will. *The magician means power to direct your own path. What's he trying to say by leaving that?* It only took a moment for her to answer her own question. *He wants me to come to the cave—he's figured out how to get his magic back.*

She smiled and tucked the card into her pocket.

Chapter Twenty-Six

Spooked

Angel walked into the loft to find Melinda still in bed.

"Hey, sleepy-head, get up!" She stepped over and knelt next to Melinda, gently shaking her. "Come on. I have to work today. I thought you wanted to go with me."

Melinda groaned, and blinked at the light. "You said this afternoon."

"It's almost noon."

Melinda stopped blinking and sat up. "Really?"

Angel laughed and stood up. "Yeah, really. You must have been wiped out."

"I didn't sleep well." Melinda climbed out from under her blanket. "I keep having this dream…" She rubbed her temples and then pulled her hair back from her face "It's the same dream I've been having every night since I got here."

Angel remembered Melinda saying something about a dream one morning…the morning she first found her mom's mirror in the guest room. "Tell me about it."

"It doesn't make any sense. I'm at the bottom of a hill in the beginning every time. I feel like I have to get to the top, but I don't know why. It's like…something's pulling me, from the inside. There's all these people everywhere. I think they're all trying to get to the top, too, 'cause some of them actually start walking up the hill, but most of 'em keep falling."

She stretched and sighed, and her eyes narrowed. "In the last one, I kept falling, too. I can see what's at the top of the hill at least. It's a light." She smiled, and turned toward the window. "A light, like sunlight, only…I don't know. Anyway, it's beautiful. I just want to get closer, but every time I try, I trip over my own feet and end up with my face in the dirt."

Melinda turned back to face Angel. "So, ya got any idea what it means? And why it keeps waking me up?"

Angel raked her bangs out of her face while she concentrated. "The only thing I can think is maybe there's something you want. Maybe something you don't even know you want. Like figuring out your Talent."

The smile on Melinda's face fell.

Great way to start the day, Angel. Get her mad before she even has a chance to pee.

She touched Melinda's arm. "I'm sorry. You'll find your Talent. I know you will."

Melinda brushed past Angel and headed down the stairs.

Melinda still wasn't speaking to Angel when they arrived at the bookstore. She muttered a half-hearted hello to Sir Benjamin and walked straight over to Niles.

Sir Benjamin crept up behind Angel as she started placing books on the shelf, and whispered, "What's bothering your friend?"

"She's mad at me. I opened my big mouth this morning. I was just trying to tell her she'd get her Talent eventually, but it came out all wrong."

"Well, give her time, Angel. She'll get past it."

Angel reached for another stack of books to work on the next section. She glanced over her shoulder and saw Sir Benjamin watching Melinda, who was playing fetch with Niles. "It's not just her being mad at me, Sir B. She and Kalek hate each other. We went to *Mori Zede* yesterday to hear him play. The music didn't reach her at all, but she said she's hearing it at night."

"Sounds less like hate and more like jealousy to me," Sir Benjamin said without taking his eyes off Melinda.

Angel paused, the book in her hand half-way on the shelf. Melinda wasn't angry-angry, she was pouty-angry. That definitely sounded more like jealousy.

"I can see that with her, yeah. She can't even master simple magic, while Zack is doing great. So great, my dad's working with him on some pretty advanced stuff today. She's probably mad that Kalek doesn't like her back."

Sir Benjamin's head swiveled sideways and he looked over his glasses. "I thought you said she hated him."

Angel smiled. "She does hate him, because she likes him and he doesn't like her back."

Sir Benjamin nodded. "Makes perfect sense." He looked back at the pair playing fetch. "But you say Kalek hates her. Why would that be?"

Angel stopped putting away books, and lowered her voice even more. "Well, actually, I was hoping to talk to you about that today." She glanced over to make sure Melinda wasn't paying attention to her. "I think he thinks she's up to something. She's met up with Doran Ashe a couple of times—"

Sir Benjamin's eyes seemed to overtake his glasses. He opened his mouth as if to speak and then shut it again.

Angel returned her attention to the bookshelf. "Don't worry, my parents know about it, and I've kept her away from him since then. Besides, I don't think that's what's making Kalek mad anymore. It's just so strange…Kalek was all freaked out about Doran at first—watching my house and stuff, but then he slacked off. He's acting like a spoiled little kid half the time, and the rest of the time he acts spooked."

"What, uh…what do you mean by 'spooked'?"

Sir Benjamin's quivering voice made Angel turn to look at him. One hand pinched his goatee while the other gripped his bent elbow. He seemed to be gazing *past* Melinda and Niles.

"Well…he keeps saying things, about Siophra. Not about her directly, but kind of *implying*." She measured her words, unable to think of a way to say it, except to just say it. "He acts as if he thinks she's haunting him."

Sir Benjamin continued to stare, unblinking, at the wall behind Melinda. Finally, a shaky whisper emerged.

"That's ludicrous. There's no such thing as ghosts." He blinked, and a tear glistened in the corner of his eye. "No such thing at all."

She reached out and touched his arm. "Sir B, you okay?"

He blinked again, and shook his head. His Santa cheeks pushed out with a smile. "Yes, of course I am. Now get those books on the shelf. I'm ready to finish up the puzzle." He glanced in Melinda's direction one more time, then walked over and poured a cup of tea with a trembling hand.

Chapter Twenty-Seven

Opportunity

The appearance of glowing butterflies at the loft window didn't surprise Melinda at all.

The day had dragged like a lead weight at the bookstore. Even playing with Niles got old quick. Especially with Angel and the old man watching her like that. Did they really think she couldn't tell they were talking about her? Whatever. Didn't matter now.

She stood at the top of the stairs and stared down at Zoe. The dog had taken to sleeping in the living room at the bottom of the stairs ever since Melinda moved up to the loft. It was almost as if the stupid thing was guarding her. She suspected the beetle had told Zoe to, as ridiculous as that sounded. Still, there was no way she'd get past Zoe without waking her up and alerting the whole house—the stairs creaked and Zoe had keener ears than Kalek. Jumping over the banister would make even more noise, and just wake Zoe faster. Still, Melinda might be able to make it to the door…

But then what? Everyone would just come after her.

Climbing out the window wasn't an option. It was too high, and there was a wicked looking bush directly below it. Even if she could jump, she couldn't get back up to the loft the same way.

She could have faked falling asleep on the couch, but Zoe would still have been an issue, probably curled up right next to her.

It was hopeless.

Melinda swung her gaze back to the hovering mass of butterflies outside the window. They rose and fell rhythmically, waiting for her. Her eyes stung, and she bit her lip to divert her attention from it. *It's not fair! I'm trapped in here.*

She had really thought she would've come up with an escape plan by now—being sneaky was the one thing she'd always been good at. She dug deeper into her lip, trying to stop her tears with the pain.

Her hand squeezed the banister as she worked to gain control of herself. After a moment, her grip started to slip. The banister tugged against her hand, trying to pull away. Melinda let her head drop slowly, blinking to clear her eyes as she gazed down at her feet.

She was floating.

Only a couple of inches off the floor, but she was doing it. She hesitated, and then let go of the banister and balanced. Her teeth threatened to draw blood if she bit any harder. She breathed through her nose as quietly as possible with her heart raging the way it was, and concentrated.

She moved forward and down.

Inch by inch, she floated. She held her hand over the banister so she could grab it if she lost her balance, but that didn't happen. If anything, she became steadier as she moved, and even rose off the ground a little more.

Holy crap, I'm flying!

Well, not exactly flying. More like hovering, but the rush sure had to compare. Halfway down the stairs she pushed a little harder and increased her speed. As she neared the bottom, she slowed down and concentrated on rising a little more.

Up she lifted, eased forward, and then moved around the end of the banister and over the sleeping dog. Once she cleared the living room, she lowered down again and sped up.

Seconds later she was at the kitchen door. She turned the knob slowly, expecting the slightest click to wake Zoe. But the door opened silently, and Melinda slipped through.

Closing the door behind her, she hovered as the butterflies descended and flitted toward the forest. Melinda followed, until she reached the fence. She couldn't quite get enough lift to go over it and cut the flow of energy so that she dropped to the ground. A twig snapped under her foot, and she tensed. A quick peek over her shoulder told her no one had heard.

The butterflies surged back and forth while Melinda climbed over the fence. She stepped toward them, a smile tugging her sore lip.

"Lead the way, ladies."

Melinda followed as closely as she could, but the butterflies were amazingly fast. She jogged most of the way, ducking low branches and jumping over tree roots. Everything around her blurred together in the silver moonlight, as she fixed her eyes on the path ahead.

The glow of the butterflies and the bright, full moon allowed her the occasional glimpse of color. A few times she dared to turn her head for a better view. The flowers on some of the trees were *enormous,* as were some of the toadstools poking up through the dense moss that coated parts of the forest floor.

Melinda burst into a clearing, and the butterflies zipped ahead so quickly she could barely keep up. She pumped her legs hard across the open ground, afraid the butterflies would slip into the trees on the other side and disappear from sight.

If only she could lift herself off the ground as she'd done on the staircase. She concentrated as she ran, imagining her feet gliding a few inches above the grass. Nothing happened, except for her slowing down. She almost didn't see the butterflies cut into an opening in the line of trees in front of her.

Melinda pushed harder, and lunged through the opening.

The forest on this side was much darker; and low, warbling animal sounds crept through the air like winged spiders. Rustling noises dropped from above her, and Melinda crouched as though the animals shaking the overhead leaves would be dropping at any moment as well.

The ground began to incline, and soon after, the trees spread out. Something familiar…She had to be getting close to the cave.

The butterflies darted to the left, and disappeared around the trunk of a huge tree. Melinda followed, but as she came around the other side, her foot snagged and she fell face-forward.

And stopped several inches before hitting the ground.

She gasped, and a dried leaf sucked into her mouth. She coughed to dislodge it, and landed smack on the pile of leaves. They didn't quite cushion well enough to keep the roots that laid beneath from jabbing into her knees and stomach.

With a huff, she stood and brushed the leaves from the front of her clothes.

"When'd ya learn to do that?"

Melinda lifted her head and turned to the side where Doran leaned against the rim of the cave. One eyebrow raised, he tilted his head and smiled.

"I told you I can do magic."

Doran shook his head, still smiling. "Tsk, tsk, Melinda. There is a difference between an accidental magical phenomenon and real magic." Now the other eyebrow rose. The eyes beneath shone ocean blue.

"Why do your eyes change color like that?"

The blue darkened. "Don't change the subject." He snorted a laugh. "Actually, I guess you didn't. I think you and I have that in common. Something of magic in both of us, but not quite coming out the way we want it to?"

He straightened and stepped toward her. The ocean blue was back. "I think things have gotten off wrong between us. I've made your friends mad, and made you mad. I didn't mean to." He stood less than a foot in front of her now, blue eyes turning green as Melinda gazed into them. "I had only one person to talk to for so long. I think I forgot what it was like to talk to anyone else."

His face moved forward, just a centimeter or so, and Melinda noticed tears in the corners of his eyes.

"I should have known I couldn't just go back to normal. Should have known people would think ill of me."

"Think ill of me?" Who says that? You're not kidding, dude—you've spent way too much time away from people.

Melinda's heart thumped against her ribs, but she wasn't sure if it was from nerves—was Doran dangerous?—or those eyes that were now the same shade of green they'd been the day they first met. The moonlight made his hair look almost golden.

Her fingers picked at her cell phone case. "I guess it's the same here as it is back home. Once you've got a record, no one sees you the same. It's like you're marked." She allowed her face to relax into a smile. "I don't see you that way, though. I'm willing to give you another chance, even if no one else will."

She straightened a little, as a vision of Caryn's face popped into her head. "But you're gonna have to be careful around Angel and Kalek and everyone. They don't trust you. I think they would, if you prove yourself some…"

His eyes swirled misty gray through the green. "I guess saving Angel from a falling rafter wasn't enough. Fine. I'll do what it takes. Whatever it takes."

He stepped back then and turned toward the cave. "First, I want to show you something."

"More glowing bugs?"

"Come on. You'll see."

The hordes of butterflies still clung to the wall. There was something different, though. She hadn't noticed with the pack that had led her here—she'd been too preoccupied with keeping up—but now, against the rocky walls, she could see that the butterflies' glow was slightly greenish rather than the metallic fire it was before. It reminded her of something…

She stopped walking and stared. The glow reminded her of those sticks kids wore on Halloween, with the liquid that reacts when the capsule inside is broken. The last time the butterflies had glowed like golden fireflies.

"Hey, come on," Doran called from ahead.

Melinda pulled her attention away from the pulsing walls. She scooted forward, her boots scraping along the rocky floor. As the ground declined, the air thickened with moisture. A drip of water hit her in the cheek and trickled down her neck. The mass of butterflies ended a few feet ahead, and beyond that Melinda saw only darkness.

"Where are you taking me?" She expected her voice to echo, but it disappeared in the pitch in front of her.

Doran moved past the last bit of fading light into the shadow before he answered.

"My home away from home."

"It's really dark over there. Why can't we stay out here?" She shuffled to the edge of the light and stopped.

His voice came from the shadow. "I told you. I want to show you something."

"In the dark? Bring it out here."

"Can't move it. Don't worry. It's not that dark. It just feels that way because you're standing in the light."

Or maybe you're just used to dark, enclosed spaces.

Melinda inhaled to clear her head of doubt. Those days were over for Doran. He wanted to prove himself. He *had* saved Angel from that rafter—why hadn't she pointed that out to Angel and her parents? It was as if they all conveniently forgot that fact when they talked about him.

She plunged into the unknown.

"They only grow in the dark," Doran said from Melinda's left. He knelt over lumps spreading across the cave floor.

She stepped closer and leaned forward for a closer look.

Her eyes adjusted even more to the dark, until she could make out the details. The lumps were plants, low to the ground and wide, with broad, flat leaves. In the dark, Melinda couldn't tell what color they were, although they had to have been close to white to show up the way they did against the cave floor. The roots stretched out beyond the reach of the leaves and burrowed into the rock below.

There was plenty of space between each plant for Melinda to walk, and she took a step forward with intent of wandering the maze.

Doran grabbed her arm.

"Don't step between them! Their roots aren't permanently attached, and they will grab at anything within reach. That's why they're spaced so far apart."

Melinda stared down at Doran's hand. Something about his grip felt odd, and she reached toward his hand with her free one.

He yanked his hand away.

"S-sorry," he said, and backed up.

"I'm not upset." Her voice quavered, but she wasn't frightened. Not exactly. Just curious. He'd never stood so close before. He'd always stayed just out of reach. And now—pulling away like that. Almost as if he was afraid of *her*. Not exactly the behavior of someone out to hurt people.

Neither was him stopping her from stepping into danger. Not that she could tell anyone about it—she wasn't exactly supposed to be here.

"What kind of plants are they?"

"Their common name is cave lettuce." He smiled, and even in the dim light Melinda could see his irises darken. "It's a stupid name, I know.

Especially for such a complex plant."

Doran squatted about two feet away from one of the larger plants in the front row. "I mean, other than the leaves being shaped like that, there's nothing similar between these plants and any kind of lettuce in the world. They're not even edible. Actually, they're quite toxic when ingested."

He grabbed something off the cave floor by his feet—a large stick—and reached toward one of the plants with it. "Watch this."

The end of the stick touched one of the leaves, and the leaf rolled up like a window shade. Where the leaf had just been, something whipped out and wrapped around the stick. A root. It didn't pull on the stick as Melinda had expected, instead it began to squeeze like a python, breaking the stick into several pieces.

The root withdrew back to its place under the plant, dragging splintered wood along with it, and the leaf unrolled.

Doran stood. "Keep watching."

Melinda stared at the plant. At first it seemed that nothing would happen, but then dark lines began to trail across the surface of the leaves.

She blinked, and then leaned forward a bit, squinting.

"That looks like wood grain."

"Yep. If you cut a board from the tree this branch came from, you'd see that exact pattern. It's Silver Spruce."

An image of Kalek's glaring face popped into Melinda's mind. She glanced over to the stick Doran held out. One end was splintered where the plant had broken it, but the other was blunt and smooth—it had been cut.

"But isn't that really rare?"

"Sure it's rare. But that doesn't matter now. These plants are incredibly prolific."

Melinda scrunched her brow.

"It means they reproduce easily," Doran said.

"I know what it means. I just don't understand—is the lettuce going to turn into a Silver Spruce now or something?"

"Not turn into. Hybridize. It means—"

"I know what that means, too! My father was a scientist. I understand hybridization. But is it normal for a plant to magically hybridize with a tree just from contact with a cut branch?"

"Your father?"

Melinda ignored the question. "Does it do that with any plant, or piece of plant, it touches?"

Doran's gaze intensified, and Melinda could have sworn his eyes changed to silver. "It will hybridize with *anything* it touches. And take on whatever magical power belongs to that plant, animal….human."

Melinda tensed, forcing herself to not gasp.

"Human? A plant that can hybridize with a human—you're serious?"

Doran tilted his head forward and grinned.

Melinda glanced back at the garden and shook her head. "You said you're doing this for that other guy. But what is *he* doing? Why does he want to hybridize this plant with…whatever? What's the point of a plant having special powers if it can only live in a dark cave?"

The sound of Doran's shoe grinding on the rocky floor pulled Melinda's attention back to him. He'd stepped even closer. His eyes most definitely looked silver now. Melinda swallowed as her gaze shifted to follow the movement of his hand. He reached up as if to stroke her cheek. She skipped a breath as she anticipated his touch, but he pulled his hand away.

"Don't you see? The plant is toxic, but if it wasn't it could be used to help someone regain their magic. The plant would just have to touch another person, and then it could be ground up and ingested." He smiled, and trailed his gaze down Melinda to the floor. "Instant magic. For me…and for you. For anyone who can't tap into their own powers."

"But I told you…I've got magic. It's happening for me. I just—"

"You can't control it, though, can you? With this, it would be instantaneous. No practicing, no frustration."

Melinda's throat burned. Was she that transparent? Still, the idea intrigued her. To not have to practice, to instantly be in control of her magic. Well, technically someone else's magic. Which meant their Talent as well. She could pick whatever Talent she wanted this way. Her left cheek tugged the corner of her mouth into a half smile.

"So, let me guess. The professor guy you were in jail with figured out a way around the whole toxic thing."

Doran's eyes flickered gold and he raised one eyebrow. "Yes, I believe he has."

"Okay, then, what do we do?"

Chapter Twenty-Eight

A Change of Strategy

Angel opened her eyes at the sound of her mom's voice coming from the hallway.

"Anna!"

Her mom appeared in the doorway of her bedroom. "She's not here."

"Who?" Angel scooted back on the mattress until she was sitting up.

"Melinda! She's gone." Her mom's voice tilted with panic and she rattled out her words. "She's not in the house, not in the yard. I went up to the loft to grab a sketchbook because I woke up early with an idea for a painting and couldn't get back to sleep. She wasn't up there, and she's not in the house—"

"You said that. Hang on. I'll Find her."

Her mom steepled her hands under her chin and nodded.

Angel closed her eyes and concentrated. An image of Melinda walking through dense trees popped into her head, and she sensed the distance and direction. She opened her eyes.

"In the forest, heading home. She's a ways away, but she's definitely moving this direction."

Her mom let out a breath.

Angel blinked and looked toward the window. She waved her hand and the curtain slid open. Day had just begun to break, and the faintest light filtered through the forest, behind the yard. She waved the curtain back in place and lay back down.

"Oh, no, you don't," her mom said.

Angel felt the sheets lift off her and fold back on the bed.

Her mom stood with her hand raised. "We need to talk. Up, up." She turned and left.

Angel climbed out of bed, stopped in the bathroom, then joined her parents in the living room. She tucked one leg under the other and leaned into the back of the couch. Her mom paced the living room floor, while her dad sat on the chair, his foot tapping.

"This has to stop," her mom said, scratching the tip of her nose with a paint-spattered hand.

"I know, Mom, but…." She clenched her jaw to stifle a yawn. "…but you can't lock her in or something."

"No, but we can lay down stricter rules."

Angel shook her head. "Melinda is the kind of person who pushes back when she feels pushed. That's why I didn't chase her down that first day when she ran out of the bookstore and met Doran. I figured if I didn't make a big deal out of it, she'd forget him."

"But she didn't," her father said.

"I know, but I promise, if we push her now it'll just make things worse."

"How can things get worse?" her mom asked.

"I don't know. I just know we can't jump on her when she gets here." Angel chewed her lip and tucked her other leg under her. "Besides, she was really different the other night, when I came back from the Temple. Like she's starting to see she belongs here. She might even have snuck off to tell Doran she's not going to see him anymore."

"Really, Anna?" Her mom shook her head. "That's a stretch."

"Maybe. But will y'all at least let me talk to her and try to find out?"

Her dad cleared his throat. "We've already let you talk to her. You promised—"

"I know what I promised. This is still *part* of that. If she really did go off to tell him she won't see him anymore, then my way worked. Just give me a chance."

Her mom sighed. "What if she tells you that's what she did, but she's lying again? Anna, we can't sit back and let her run around like this."

"What if you two talk to her and all she does is lie to *you*?"

"That's a possibility," her dad said. "But we'll handle it."

Handle it. That's exactly what they shouldn't do. Why wouldn't they listen to her? She bit down on her lip as her hand lingered near her bangs. She snatched her hand back down, wondering for the umpteenth time why Gregor's habit had transferred to her.

She *had* to get them to back off. And not just them. If Melinda really did have a crush on Kalek and was mad that he didn't like her back, Angel needed to get him to be nicer. Not pretend he's into her or anything, but if he'd at least be *civil*, it might take the edge off.

Her mom broke the silence. "Our top priority is keeping her safe."

Horatio buzzed into the room from the kitchen, chittering as he flew toward Angel. He hovered for a moment, then turned sharply, and landed on her father's shoulder.

She narrowed her eyes. "You're supposed to be keeping watch out there."

A shadow fell across Angel's eyes and something moved into the doorway.

"He *was* keeping watch."

"Kalek!" Her mother ran over and reached up as Kalek leaned down to hug her. Then she finally sat down, legs curled under her on the loveseat.

Angel jumped up and walked over to Kalek. "Hey, can I talk to you?"

He raised an eyebrow, but nodded.

Angel turned to her parents. "Be right back." She grabbed Kalek's arm and dragged him into the kitchen and across the room.

"I need you to do something," Angel said, still gripping his arm.

"What?"

"I'm worried about Melinda, and so are my mom and dad. She snuck off to see Doran last night. They won't listen to me, though. I told them we need to leave her alone, and give her time to get tired of Doran so she'll stop."

"Why should I care if she hangs out with him? It might keep him away from *you*."

"She's my friend, Kalek. I don't want her getting hurt, but I know she'll just sneak off even more if Mom and Dad harp on her."

He pulled his arm from her grasp. "What does this have to do with me?"

She inhaled. "I think if you were nicer to her she might not care so much about spending time with Doran."

His eyes narrowed and he tilted his head. "But why would…?" His eyes widened. "You mean she…? No." He shook his head. "No, no, no."

"Just be nice to her."

"So your bratty little friend can delude herself with the idea of us getting together?"

Angel huffed. "You may *hear* well, but you don't *listen.* I never said I want you to act like you want to be more than friends. Just be civil. In other words, stop being such a jerk to her."

He shook his head, shifting his tangled curls.

"Please, Kalek. If I can talk them into leaving her alone for just a little while longer, and you stop driving her off with your attitude, she might actually stay away from him. *Please.*"

He stared at her for a long moment. The light from the wall sconce flashed against his polished stone eyes. He blinked slowly and inhaled. "I will. But not for her. I'll do it for Siophra."

"Siophra?" Angel's voice was barely a whisper.

"*He's* doing something. Ever since he's been back, I see her everywhere. Whatever he's up to, I'm going to find out. And that means getting close to him. If I have to use your friend to do so, I will."

An icy chill gripped the back of Angel's neck. If Kalek was seeing Siophra, maybe she really was seeing Gregor. "What do you mean you're seeing Siophra?"

"I see her walking around, hiding in the shadows, watching me. I thought I was imagining it at first, but then last time at the Temple…" He shook is head again. "I know it sounds crazy, but with the way she died, maybe that old scientist Randall has a hold on her magic, and now her spirit can't move on."

"But you said Dor—"

A knock sounded behind Angel, and she turned to see her mother standing in the kitchen doorway. "Sorry, I didn't mean to interrupt. The early morning has caught up with us. Dad and I are heading back to bed. We'll discuss this again later."

"Okay, Mom."

Her mom nodded, but instead of leaving, she walked over to them and looked up at Kalek. "I'm sorry. I swear I wasn't eavesdropping, but I couldn't help overhearing what you said about Siophra." She gripped his arm. "You would have seen her before, if that was true. It's just your grief catching up with you."

He smiled, but it was a melancholy smile. "I hope so."

Her mom let go of his arm and gave him another hug, then touched Angel's cheek before leaving the room.

Angel looked at Kalek. Should she tell him she was seeing Gregor, too? Maybe it was what her mother said about Siophra—that it was her grief. Grief for both of them…triggered by…what? That's the part that didn't make sense.

Kalek cocked his head to the side. "She's coming. She's right behind the yard."

Angel sometimes wondered if Kalek exaggerated his hearing ability. How could he hear from inside the house that Melinda was still in the forest? She was about to give him a hard time about it, when Zoe dashed into the kitchen. Angel dove forward and grabbed Zoe's jaw just in time to stop her from barking.

"Let's go," Angel said.

They darted into and across the living room. Kalek headed for the front door. Angel grabbed Zoe's leash as Kalek opened the door. She squeezed through with Zoe before he had a chance to step into the doorway.

As soon as the door was shut behind them, Kalek turned to her. "What are you doing out here?" he said in the faintest whisper.

"We still need to talk. And Zoe could use a walk."

"Let's go then. She's opening the back door."

When they were in front of Ayden's house, Angel conjured her sneakers and knelt down to put them on. As she tied the laces she said, "I've been seeing Gregor, too."

Chapter Twenty-Nine

New Beginnings

Melinda's heart pounded against her ribs. It had taken her too long to return to Angel's house, and now it was almost full light. She hoped no one had woken up and found her gone. She twisted the doorknob as gently as possible and stepped into the kitchen.

Not a sound.

She reached the bottom of the stairs and grabbed the banister. Why was it so quiet? Where was the dog? Whatever. At least it wasn't here barking at her. She crept up the stairs, and without changing clothes, dropped onto her bed. Excitement fought with exhaustion as she stretched out.

She rolled to her side and in seconds exhaustion won.

The hilltop rose before her, higher than before. The clearing at the base felt even more crowded. She pushed against moving bodies, bringing her arms in close to protect herself from jutting elbows. It was hotter, too, and sweat rolled down her back. But this time, she tried to ignore the scenery and focus on the hilltop. That was her goal.

A trumpet blast.

She slapped her hands over her ears. Where had that come from? Everyone around her seemed to have not heard it, or were just ignoring it. She studied them to determine which was true, but couldn't tell by their faces. And as she stared more closely, their features began to blur.

She turned her gaze back toward the hilltop, tears burning her throat.

"What is this?" she cried. "What am I looking for?"

A glimmer of light appeared at the top. Just like last time…the purest of white. It pulsed like a heartbeat, and in moments Melinda's own heart beat in time with it. She moved toward it, her feet snagging on the rough terrain. But she didn't fall.

Until she heard the voice.

"I can help you, Melinda…turn back and I can help you…"

Her eyes popped open, and she scrambled backward at the sight of the face hovering above her.

"I'm sorry," Caryn said, stepping back as Melinda caught her breath. "You seemed like you were having a bad dream."

"No…not bad. Just strange."

"Well, you, um…you said something right before you woke up." Caryn tilted her head. "I think you said, 'Doran.'"

Melinda didn't move, didn't answer. Had she? All she remembered was the voice, and in the dream she hadn't recognized it.

Doran.

Her heart fluttered—but was it from excitement or fear?

"You really like him, don't you?" Caryn asked.

She could have held her silence, or lied, but Melinda nodded.

"I wish I could tell you I know how you feel. Liking someone who is so…misunderstood. But I've never loved anyone but William. He was a close family friend."

"Really? You've known him that long?"

"Feels like forever." Caryn slipped onto the edge of the mattress, legs crossed. "He's been there for me through everything. We were best friends for a long time, and our relationship grew slowly over the years."

Melinda had no idea what to say, what Caryn expected her to say. She pulled her knees to her chest and leaned back against the wall.

Caryn inhaled, as if getting ready for something, and then said, "I hope you know you can talk to us, Melinda. I may not have all the same experiences as you, but I promise that whatever you're going through I'll try to understand. And so will William.

"What I'm trying to say is, we're here for you. And we want you to be happy." She paused and looked out the window with her brow furrowed as if something pained her.

Melinda waited, her muscles tensing with each passing second. *What is she getting at?*

Finally, Caryn looked at her again. She smiled and reached a hand toward Melinda's face. She brushed Melinda's cheek tenderly. Her fingers were cold, and…sticky?

"Oh, sorry," Caryn said. "Paint." She laughed and pulled a rag from the pocket of her smock.

"Thanks." Melinda took the rag and rubbed at the paint on her cheek. "Where's Angel?"

Caryn glanced at the stair case, and then turned back with concern in her eyes. "Actually, I don't know. I came up here trying to find her."

Chapter Thirty

Me, Too

The neighborhood was washed with pale morning light. The only sounds in the air were a few faint bird songs and Zoe's tapping footsteps.

"You've seen Gregor?" Kalek's voice was tight and he stared straight ahead.

Angel didn't know where to begin. She only knew it was too coincidental.

"I'm not even sure, to be honest. I thought I saw him a couple of times, in the shadows at the edge of the forest. I figured my eyes were playing tricks on me. But now that you said that about Siophra…"

Zoe tugged at the leash, and Angel snapped it to get her back in line. The sudden movement sent Horatio tumbling from his perch on her shoulder. He chirped indignantly as he righted himself, and buzzed over to Kalek, where he clung to the musician's crossed forearms.

"She's appeared to me several times. At first, I thought the same thing. That she was an illusion. But this last time was during daylight." He turned to face her and stopped walking.

"She appeared as solid as you or me, Angel. I know it wasn't her body…that's buried…but what if it was her spirit, clinging to this world because that man has a hold on it?"

Angel's heart sank at the sight of torment in his eyes. She had no idea if what he suggested was even possible. Dr. Randall hadn't taken Gregor's life like he had Siophra, so how could it explain her seeing Gregor?

"He's in jail, though. Behind layers of electricity. His powers can't reach here."

"The same jail as Doran," Kalek said. "Funny how this all started when he got out, don't you think?"

Angel exhaled. "That's why you agreed to be nice to Melinda. You think Doran and Dr. Randall know each other from jail? Are working together or something? That makes no sense. Doran doesn't even have magic. It was completely stripped from him by—"

"Stripped!" Kalek's eyes burned with rage now. "I don't believe that for a minute. I still say he's lying. Thieving lowlife. No, he's just as capable…." His voice trailed off, and his mouth morphed into a wicked grin. "How did I not see this? I am such an idiot!" He laughed out loud.

"What?"

"Doran's Talent! It's Disguise. He's been disguising himself this whole time, skulking around, trying to drive us mad."

Angel wrapped Zoe's leash more tightly around her hand as she thought about what he was saying. Sir Benjamin had mentioned Doran using his Talent to disguise the tools he'd tried to steal. And possibly the notebooks. But he'd made it sound like it had to be small objects.

"He changed his own appearance? That sounds really complicated."

Kalek's expression fell, and his eyes narrowed. "I don't know. But I'd bet anything he lied about how strong his Talent was."

"Okay, so maybe he did lie. How do we know he can still do it?"

"Because we've seen it!"

"No, we only *think* we've seen it." Angel tugged on Zoe's leash with one hand and tapped Kalek's elbow with the other, nudging them to start walking again. "And if anything, being jailed would have made him weaker."

Kalek grunted, but kept walking.

"You think he's lying," she said, "that he didn't use magic to catch that falling beam, as part of an act. But that doesn't make sense. It all happened so suddenly. He didn't have time to think about whether or not to use magic—he just reacted.

"And if he wanted to hurt us, he could have just let the thing fall. But again, his first reaction was to knock me out of the way."

"No wonder Gregor complained about you driving him crazy. You're too logical."

Angel smiled with satisfaction, until he spoke again.

"It doesn't matter. One of them is doing it. Either Doran, Dr. Randall, or both of them working together."

Chapter Thirty-One

Decoys

Melinda sat forward on the pallet in her corner of the loft when Angel appeared at the top of the steps.

Caryn whipped her head toward Angel. "Where were you?"

Angel smiled, but her eyes were rimmed with red as if she were tired. "I took Zoe for a walk."

Caryn started to rise from her seat. "You know you're not to—."

"Kalek was with us."

Caryn sat back down.

Angel hung at the top step. "Mom, can you come down for a minute?"

"Sure." Caryn patted Melinda's knee. "William's probably about done cooking breakfast. Head on down and eat any time you're ready." She stood and followed Angel down the stairs.

Melinda rested her forehead against her knees. *What was that about?* The whole understanding mom thing. So weird. Her own mom never noticed when Melinda was home or not, much less if she talked in her sleep. But it didn't make a difference.

Caryn was still being freaky about Angel and Melinda going out unsupervised. No matter what she said about understanding, she still didn't trust Doran.

Or me.

Whatever, it was worth it. Eventually she'd have her full magic and could move out on her own. Or in with Doran. The corners of her mouth curled up at the thought. Those eyes really were amazing. He didn't quite have Kalek's cool factor, but if what he said was true, he could get it. He could actually get Kalek's Talent and *everything.*

An image popped into her head…the plant in the cave splintering the branch. Is that what had to happen to a person in order to get their magic into the plant?

No way.

Doran wouldn't do that just for magic, would he?

Melinda straightened out her legs and scooted to the edge of the bed. When she slid to her feet, something clanged on the floor beside her. Her heart thumped hard. She didn't have to look down to know what it was.

The mirror.

She bent over and picked it up. The handle was warm, as though someone had just been holding it. Could Caryn have slipped it under her pillow? The way it seemed to appear on its own meant either someone was leaving it where she would find it, or the mirror was somehow finding her.

She wasn't sure which she wanted to believe.

The glass glinted as she tilted the mirror toward the window. Light streamed in now that the sun had peaked the treetops. She twirled the mirror in her hands, wondering if she should try to pull any more images to its surface. If she'd even been the one to do it last time. Maybe the mirror just started up on its own.

She stopped twirling it, and stared. Her own face stared back at her from the crystalline glass. *What's up with you? What makes you turn on?* She was just about to tuck the mirror back under her pillow, when the glass fogged.

An image appeared, smeary and pale, and then darkened and sharpened into a familiar face. William couldn't have been more than seventeen. His glasses sat crooked on his nose, one blue iris framed by a metal oval, one nearly peeking over the top of the metal edge. A hand came into view, feminine and smeared with paint, and straightened the glasses.

William smiled. His gaze held such intensity. Melinda had to look at his cheek, his chin—anything but his eyes.

She wondered why this time Caryn wasn't visible. It had obviously been Caryn's hand that had straightened William's glasses.

The image faded, and was replaced by Melinda's face. She swallowed back tears at the sight of her own eyes, so empty and sad compared to William's sparkling blue. His had beamed of love and happiness. Would her eyes ever be capable of that?

Melinda tucked her hair behind her ears and sat at the table. Angel and Caryn were chatting about Zack as they ate Belgian waffles.

Angel turned to Melinda. "You want to go to the book store with me today?"

Melinda grabbed a waffle and plopped it on her plate. "I dunno. I might hang out here."

"You can join Zack and me," Caryn said.

Melinda shrugged. She'd have no need for more magic lessons if Doran helped her.

"Well, just let me know." Caryn took one more bite of waffle and carried her plate over to the sink.

Angel tilted her head. "Ayden's coming with me. I'm working for a little while and then we're going to hang out at the square. Come with us. It'll be fun."

Melinda shook her head. "Seriously, I just want to stay here."

Angel's lips pursed, and then she turned back to her waffles.

Melinda ate hers in silence. When she finished, Angel was at the sink washing dishes and Caryn had left to wake up Zack.

Melinda dumped her plate in the sink. "I'm going to go for a walk."

She heard Angel inhale and turned to face her.

Angel glanced nervously at the door to the hall. "Promise you'll be careful, okay?"

That's it? Be careful? Caryn had just nearly chewed out Angel for going for a walk, and Angel was going to sit back and let Melinda go? No lecture?

Melinda searched Angel's eyes for a moment. She couldn't read anything in them other than concern.

"Whatever." She turned away, and walked quickly to the front door. Out on the porch, she stared at the road. Dark Elm jutted off to the north, just east of Angel's house. She crossed the road at an angle and then turned on Dark Elm, pausing only when Doran's house came into view.

It looked strangely ordinary. She shook her head. *What'd you expect, girl? Black roof peaks and spider webs?*

She climbed the front steps and knocked. Her heart pounded unevenly, and she chewed the corner of her lip as her fingertip clicked against her cell phone case. She'd checked it over and over since that day at the Temple, and the battery had definitely died. She never figured out why that tiny bit of charge showed up, but it was gone now. Still, she found herself clipping it to her pocket every day.

The doorknob clicked, and turned. The door eased open a crack, and Doran's voice slid through. "Why are you here? This isn't any way to get them to earn my trust."

Melinda smiled and crossed her arms. "Does it matter?"

The door opened farther. Doran kept his grip on the handle. His black t-shirt blended in with the pitch dark of the room behind him. His hair hung down on one side and was hooked behind his ear on the other. He stared at her with violet eyes.

"Are you going to let me in, or what?"

His cheek pulled back into a half smile, and he opened the door all the way.

"You always keep the house this dark?" Melinda asked as he shut the door behind them. The room was cold.

"Only when I'm working."

"Working on what?"

Doran's presence was nothing more than a shadow in front of her, slightly darker than the rest of the room. She jumped when his hand grabbed hers, but allowed his fingers to mesh with hers.

"I'll show you."

She shuffled behind him in the darkness, until they reached a door at the end of a hallway. Doran let go of her hand. When he opened the door, Melinda's eyes widened.

The room looked like a homemade computer lab from before Melinda was born. Old electronics filled the metal shelves lining the walls. Wires ran along the corners of the room and across the ceiling like a colored spider web. An ancient desktop computer sat on top of a huge desk in the middle of the room. Its screen glowed beneath a fluorescent ceiling light.

"I—I thought you couldn't have electricity here," she said as they stood in the doorway.

Doran walked over to the desk. "I have no other way to get by right now, do I? I've got no magic, and I'm not going to live like a caveman."

"Where did you get all this stuff?"

"Oh, here and there." He beamed as if he were showing off a custom sports car. But the computer was nearly obsolete. "Not a bad set-up, eh?"

Melinda shook her head as she circled the desk. *These people need to get off the island more often.* She didn't have the heart to tell him his computer was a dinosaur. Her cell phone had more power than everything in the room combined.

She realized she was flicking the cell phone case again, and pulled her hand away. The case caught on her bracelet, and the clip slipped off the edge of her pocket. She caught it before it hit the floor, but the flap opened and the phone slid out.

The screen was lit.

She picked it up and stared. Full battery. "What the—?"

Doran stepped up next to her, and when she turned to him, his eyes were wide. He said nothing, though, and Melinda put the phone back in its case and clipped it on her pocket.

"So," she said. "What ya doin' with all this stuff?" She walked around, running her fingers along the edges of the shelves, acting as if she were impressed.

"Studying things. Following up on some research."

Melinda stopped when she saw a stack of leather books. "What are these?" She began to flip through the pages of the top one. Scratchy writing covered sheet after sheet—paragraphs and diagrams, with formulas scribbled into every available space.

"Those are just the manuals for the computer," Doran said as he stepped up behind her. He didn't touch her, but his breath warmed the back of her neck. "You wouldn't be interested."

Melinda closed the book. The cover, like all the books in the stack, was thick leather, with a strap that hung from the open side. The strap would have wrapped around and fit into a lock attached to the front. The spine had similar straps connected to the front with metal hinges. *Computer manual, not.*

She said nothing as she turned to face him.

He smiled. "So, seriously, how'd you manage to get away?"

Melinda shrugged. "I just said I was going for a walk."

He cocked an eyebrow.

"Okay, so technically, I told *Angel* I was going for a walk. But she didn't do anything to stop me. I'm not sure why....I mean, her parents won't let us out of the house without a freaking chaperone because they totally don't trust you. You should see the way Angel's dad looks when they talk about you. He's got this vein that sticks out on his forehead. He thinks you're a huge loser."

Doran's eyes darkened, the violet shifting to deep blue and then his pupils were swallowed by black. They shone like polished stone, but his eyebrows dipped.

"I'm sorry," Melinda said. "I shouldn't have said that. I mean...I don't agree with them."

"I'm not going to hurt you, Melinda."

"I know!" She straightened up and stepped toward him, and he matched with a step backwards. "I said I don't agree with them. It's just...they only see what you've done. They think you might be dangerous."

"And yet, Angel didn't stop you from coming here? Some friend."

"Hey, she's covering for me!"

He tilted his head. "She's lying to her parents for you? She doesn't seem like the type."

"She's not."

Doran stepped back again and sat against the corner of the desk. "Then why would she do it? Would she really risk getting into trouble for you?"

"I—"

"Or maybe it's only *her* they're worried about. You possibly getting hurt doesn't matter to them."

"But..."

"They think I'm dangerous, but no one has come after you. They're not exactly protecting *you*, are they? Don't they care what happens to you?"

"I didn't tell her *where* I was going. Just for a walk."

"She trusts you to stay away from me?"

Melinda bit her lip. *Does she?*

"I bet if their precious Angel wanted to *go for a walk* they wouldn't let her prance out the door."

Melinda's words scraped out, barely more than a whisper. "No, they wouldn't."

"Then why didn't she stop you?"

"Because..."

Melinda closed her mouth and swallowed. The look on Angel's face when Melinda had said she was going for a walk...the way she told Melinda to be careful... Did she know where Melinda was going?

It was one thing to cover for Melinda thinking she's just walking, but a whole different story if she *knew*. She would never risk getting into *that* kind of trouble.

Which meant, if Angel knew Melinda would go see him alone, they all knew. Her throat burned. *They're playing me! Using me as a decoy, so Doran messes with me and not Angel.* That was fine with her. She'd give them exactly what they wanted.

Chapter Thirty-Two

Double

Angel and Ayden arrived at *The Professor's Roost.* He slipped his arm from around her shoulder and stepped forward to open the door. Before Angel could enter, a man in a navy uniform appeared just inside the doorway. It was the same officer who had brought the notebooks to Sir Benjamin.

"Excuse me, miss," he said and tilted his hat to her. "I didn't see you. I thought the boy was holding the door for me." He stepped backwards, and motioned for Angel to pass through.

She thanked him, and he nodded then headed out the door. Ayden ducked inside behind Angel and wrapped his arms around her waist. Sir Benjamin looked up at them from behind his desk and smiled.

"Ah, the happy couple," he said, and winked.

Horatio twittered and zipped over to the corner where Niles was tugging on a sleeping Spike's tail.

Angel peeled Ayden's hands away. Fingers entwined, they walked over to his desk. Sir Benjamin twirled a pencil in his hand—something he only did when he was nervous.

"Everything all right, Sir B?"

"Yes and no." His chair creaked as he leaned back. "Officer Tolbert was telling me about some interesting things going on at the jail. I really shouldn't tell you this but..." He thumped the pencil against the desktop.

Angel squeezed Ayden's hand. "What is it?"

"Dr. Randall. He's...well he's got a bit of a problem. Not that he's aware of it, but still. It's kinda funny actually."

Angel clenched her jaw. She loved everything about Sir Benjamin, except the way he talked in circles when he was distracted.

"What's funny?" Ayden said. "What's going on?"

Sir Benjamin quit thumping the pencil and went back to twirling it. "Well, it seems the electricity in Randall's cell had an adverse effect. Rather than blocking all his magic, including his Talent, it funneled all his powers into it. His Talent, that is. He's...invisible, and apparently stuck that way."

Angel stifled a laugh. *Serves him right!*

"You said he wasn't aware. How can he not know that?" Ayden asked. The serious expression on his face made it even harder for Angel to stop herself from laughing.

"He's unconscious!" Sir Benjamin stopped moving the pencil altogether. "Has been for quite some time. Seems the constant use of his Talent has drained him."

The laughter Angel had been holding back disintegrated, and she shot a look at Ayden.

He slowly turned his face toward hers.

Angel tilted her head. *Sound familiar?*

"I know," he said.

She looked harder at him.

He narrowed his eyes. "Later."

"Anyway," Sir Benjamin said, glancing back and forth between them, "they need me to come down and help them out."

Angel opened her mouth to ask why they'd need him, but he stood and looked pointedly at Ayden.

"Your mom's meeting me there, actually."

Angel felt Ayden stiffen. Sir Benjamin must have noticed, because he said, "No worries. She'll be safe. He's heavily guarded, and they're strapping him down."

Ayden nodded.

Sir Benjamin walked over to a bookshelf and scanned a row of books. He snagged one and tucked it under his arm, then turned to Angel. "If I'm not back before you leave, go ahead and lock up. You don't have to stay till closing."

"Did Officer Tolbert say anything about the notebooks?" Angel asked.

"He said they'd do what they could."

"What does that mean?'

Sir Benjamin shrugged. "I suppose they'll look for them, but the ones they gave me are technically copies, made by one of the officers who can Replicate objects. They have the originals." He walked to the door and grabbed the handle, then turned around, looking over his glasses. "Oh, and Ayden, just because you come here with her doesn't mean I'm putting you on the payroll." His laughter mingled with the tinkle of the doorbell as he pulled the door open.

When the door banged shut, Angel spun to face Ayden.

"That could happen to you!"

Ayden's eyes scrunched. "What?"

Angel's hand moved toward her bangs, and she yanked it away and huffed. *Honestly!*

"Like Dr. Randall getting stuck invisible. Unconscious! You have to pick a Talent, and keep it, Ayden. Promise me. No more switching until you decide." Her throat suddenly burned and she swallowed hard.

Ayden shook his head. "So totally different, Angel. Dr. Randall is in that place, surrounded by electric current. Whatever happened to him is not going to happen to me." He stepped forward and put his hands on her waist. "But I promise anyway. I won't change Talents unless I really have to."

Angel pulled away from him and crossed her arms. "Not good enough. You have to promise, period. No exceptions."

"I can't do that."

"Why not?"

He reached for her again, but she took another step back. His eyes narrowed.

"Promise me," she said. "Now."

"Not if you could be in danger." He stuffed his hands into his jeans pockets.

This time when her hand reached for her bangs she didn't stop it. She let it stay there as she said, "How can you protect me from danger if you completely wear yourself out? If you end up blacked out like Dr. Randall. Or..."

"I told you that won't happen." Again, he moved toward her, but left his hands tucked in his pockets.

"There's no way to know that for sure."

"I feel *fine*."

She looked at his eyes, dark blue now. Shadows clung beneath them. His jaw twitched, and Angel noticed tiny creases at the corners of his mouth. *Fine, he says. Not.*

"I just don't want you to get sick, Ayden. Kalek can protect me."

The storm returned to his eyes and the creases by his mouth deepened. "*So can I.*" He grabbed her arms. "I *know* I have to make a choice. I *know* there are dangers, but I *can* protect you. I *will*."

Angel wanted to pull out of his grasp, but the *hurt* she saw in Ayden's eyes held her in place.

Her voice cracked as she whispered. "I just want you to be okay. I know you can protect me—I didn't mean anything when I said that about Kalek. I—" Tears pushed past her lids, and she closed her eyes.

The pressure released from her arms, and Ayden's warmth wrapped around her. She leaned into his chest. His breath tickled the hair on the top of her head.

The words *I'm sorry* were on the tip of her tongue, when—

"What's that?" Ayden asked.

Angel opened her eyes and shifted in Ayden's embrace. He was looking at the window in the front of the store, where a piece of paper clung to the outside of the glass.

The paper rolled up and pulled from the glass, then turned around, unrolled, and pressed back against the window. Big red letters spanned the top: Carnival.

They walked arm in arm across the room and read the flyer.

"A carnival, tomorrow!" Angel said. "Gregor told me about it. It actually came right after I came here, but Gregor didn't take me because I still had to stay hidden."

She searched her memory and found vague images from a time when her parents must have taken her as a young child. Riding on her father's shoulders, sticky cotton candy, and a carousel with real winged ponies.

Ayden put his hand on the glass and the flyer appeared on the inside of the window. He snatched it and smiled. "Perfect. I can finally take you on a proper date."

Angel found Melinda sitting on the couch when she got home. Shakespeare was curled up in her lap, eyes shut, tail flicking languidly as Melinda scratched his chin with one hand. With the other, she scribbled in a notebook perched on the arm of the couch.

"Where's lover boy?" she asked without looking up.

"Home." Angel shifted her weight to one foot and stared down at Melinda.

Melinda continued scrawling out what looked like a poem. The writing was big and loopy, something that had always struck Angel as odd. She caught a few of the words on the page…*pain*…*unfair...outcast*…and her stomach twisted.

"We're going to a carnival tomorrow. Wanna go?" The words slipped out before she had a chance to think.

So much for our proper date. Hopefully Ayden could deal with it.

Melinda scratched down a few more words, then looked up. *Smiling.* She propped her elbow on the couch arm and cupped her chin in her palm. "Sure. Sounds fun. I'll go ask Doran to come with us—we can double."

Chapter Thirty-Three

Taken

Melinda pressed her lips together so she wouldn't laugh. The look on Angel's face was too much. "What? Don't stand there like you have no idea where I went this morning."

Angel straightened her shoulders. "Uh…right. Sure. Go ahead. I'll…go with you." A tense smile curved her lips. The creepy beetle on her shoulder chirped and squeaked, but Angel ignored it.

"Really?" Melinda shrugged. *I'll believe it when I see it.* She pulled her hand away from Shakespeare, who had fallen asleep and now gurgled his complaint, and then closed her notebook. "Let me put this away and we'll go."

"Okay." Angel's voice was stiff, hesitant. "Meet you at the front door."

Melinda shook her head as she stood, notebook clutched in her hand. *Give it up, Witchie-poo.* She climbed to the loft and tucked the notebook under her pillow. Her hand brushed against cold metal.

The mirror.

She yanked her hand away. Hadn't she put it over by Caryn's painting stuff last time? *Hmph. Doesn't matter.* She was *not* going to look at it. Whatever happened to Caryn way back when had nothing to do with now. Nothing to do with *her*.

Melinda forced a smile back in place as she descended the stairs.

Angel stood by the front door. "Okay, let's go!" She still looked tense, but her voice was calmer.

Melinda stopped a couple of steps from the bottom of the stairs. "You're actually going with me? To Doran's?"

"Yep. Just, um, not for long. Dinner's almost ready."

No way. There had to be more to it than that. Maybe Angel knew something—like Doran wasn't home. Or she was going to try to talk Melinda out of it on the way over. Or…

Angel opened the door and Melinda followed her out. The sky was orange-gray, fringed in darkness. Why would Angel's parents let them go out at this hour? What were they hiding? The muscles in her hands clenched as anger swelled. She didn't like being played, and someone was definitely playing her. Either it was Angel and her parents, or…

Doran.

No, he had no reason to pit her against Angel. There was nothing he seemed to want from her, either. Nothing she had to *give* him. Even his attention so far wasn't like *that.* He never got close enough to touch her. Except to grab her hand and guide her to his computer room—and that had felt like being led across the street by her father.

The house stood in front of her. Melinda hadn't even realized they'd walked all the way. The windows were dark except one toward the back of the house. A lantern burned by the front door.

Angel hadn't said a word to try and talk her out of anything. She blinked as she watched Angel march to the front door and hold her hand up to knock.

Angel just stood there for a moment,then slapped her hand against her thigh like she was calling a dog. "Melinda, get over here."

Was this really happening?

Melinda took a step forward.

Angel looked like she was suffering from stage fright—eyes wide and scared.

Melinda finally noticed that the ever-present and annoying beetle wasn't there.

She stepped up beside Angel. "You didn't ask permission to come here, did you?"

Angel opened her mouth, but before she could say a word the door creaked open a few inches.

Melinda nudged Angel out of the way. "Hey, Doran."

The door opened a little wider, but instead of letting her in, Doran stepped forward so he filled the space. One arm pressed against the door jamb and the other wrapped the edge of the door.

"What are you doing here?" His voice was husky, as if he'd been sleeping. "What's *she* doing here?"

Melinda inched forward. "Let us in and we'll tell you."

He shook his head. His eyes swirled silver-gray. "You don't want to come in. I'm sick."

"You were fine this morning." Melinda sucked her bottom lip between her teeth and waited for Angel to react.

Angel said nothing. Neither did Doran.

Melinda inhaled. "Well...we came to ask you to the carnival tomorrow. Maybe you'll feel better?"

"I doubt it." He glanced past Melinda at Angel. "I'm not much for carnivals anyway."

"Oh..."

"Sorry." He pulled back.

The door shut.

Shut. Just like that.

Melinda spun on her heel.

Jerk.

She felt Angel's hand on her shoulder. "Mel—"

Melinda smacked Angel's hand away. "Don't even!"

Angel grabbed Melinda's arm and pulled her several feet away from the front door, into the shadow of a huge tree. "What's your issue?"

Melinda stopped and lowered her voice to a whispered growl. "Your parents would never let you near his place. You all think he's a freaking psycho. What did you tell them, huh?"

She didn't give Angel a chance to answer. Her nostrils flared as she inhaled. "Whatever. The point is, no one even tried to stop *me* earlier today. What am I, the expendable one?"

Angel's eyes widened again. The emotion in them shifted. She looked like a hurt puppy. And then her eyes narrowed. No longer puppy-sad. They became angry-wolf.

"First of all, you didn't *tell* anyone you were coming here this morning. I figured you would when you said you were going on that walk, but I was trying to *trust you*. If my dad had known, he probably would have followed you. Mom and Dad didn't even know you were *gone*. Mom thought you were helping Dad, and Dad thought Mom was painting you again. I just let them think that."

She crossed her arms. Her hair looked like copper in the setting sun. "Why don't you get it, Melinda? Why don't you see we *care*?"

Melinda crossed her own arms and mocked Angel's expression. "Why don't *you* get it? I don't have the same choices you have. I didn't get to pick between two perfect families—I got stuck with one crappy one. Now it's *half* a crappy one."

She glanced over to the house. "I don't want to talk about this here. He's probably listening through the door."

Angel raised her hand and her eyes fluttered shut for a moment. When she spoke again, her voice echoed strangely. "There, now he can't hear us."

"What?" Melinda's voice echoed the same way. "What did you do? Why do we sound like this?"

"I put a sound barrier around us." She glared. "Now tell me."

"Fine. You really want to know? Magic isn't coming to me like it did for you, or Zack. I'm not like you all…"

"Melinda, it's just taking longer. We *do* understand."

"No…no, you don't. Not really." She tipped her head toward the house. "But he *does*."

"Is that why he slammed the door in your face?" Angel's hand slapped over her mouth. "Oh, Melinda! I'm sorry!"

Melinda squeezed her jaw until a sharp pain shot through the muscle. She ground out her words. "If *you* hadn't been here, he would never have done that. You don't know what he's been through. You could *never* know, Little Miss Perfect. He really doesn't have magic. He showed me the room in the back. He's got computers and stuff because he *can't do magic anymore*." She left out the fact that the equipment looked like it would need magic just to turn on.

"Computers? Are you serious?" Angel's hand rose and hovered by her bangs for a moment.

"Yeah, in that back room." Melinda tipped her head to the lit window on the side wall near the back of Doran's house.

"Back room?"

"Where the light is on," Melinda said.

"What light? All the windows are dark."

"You seriously don't see the light?" Melinda pointed.

"Uh...there's not even a window where you're pointing."

"What?" Melinda stumbled back a step. The window flickered in and out of view. Why was it doing that? And why couldn't Angel see it? Was she hallucinating? She stared, willing Angel to see the window so she wouldn't feel like she was going crazy.

Angel gasped. "There's a window now!" She stepped forward. "Melinda, that looks like the lights I saw upstairs the other night. It's *electric* light."

"I know. That's what I was trying to tell you."

All emotion dropped from Angel's expression. No more fear, no more anger, no more hurt. Now her brow crinkled with confusion and her eyes lit with curiosity. "That window has no blinds. Why would he be working with computers and stuff here, with electric lights, and not have blinds?"

Melinda kept her mouth shut about the fact that Angel had only moments ago claimed not to see the window at all. She also pushed from her mind the question of *why?*

Angel grabbed Melinda's hand. "I want to see. Keep close, so the sound barrier stays around us and he doesn't hear us walking."

Even so, they stepped as softly as possible. When they reached the window, Angel whispered, "Whoa! How'd he get all that stuff?"

Melinda smirked. *Junk shop? Dumpster?* Why was Angel gaping like that?

Doran walked into the room and they ducked below the window sill.

Melinda's heart beat a rampage against her ribs. What would he do if he caught them out here? She swallowed hard and inched up just enough to see in again. He was flipping through one of the leather notebooks.

She turned her head and found Angel peeking as well.

"What's he looking at?" Angel asked. Then, "Oh, just some manual. I'm surprised a computer like that comes with a book. Isn't everything on CD now?"

Melinda's brown creased. That computer looked like something that wouldn't even have a CD drive. *Maybe* a floppy drive. And why did Angel not see how obviously *leather* the book was? She thought back to when she'd flipped it open. The handwritten words inside. And a memory bubbled...something she'd seen scribbled along the margin, in a very different handwriting.

Confusion and anger boiled inside of her.

"C'mon, let's go." Melinda dragged Angel away from the window. "Your parents are going to have a hissy if you don't get home."

They ran all the way back to Angel's house, but Angel stopped Melinda before she could open the front door.

"Hang on." Angel held out her hand and a book appeared in her palm. "I told Mom we were walking over to Ayden's so I could get this back."

"And was it *at* Ayden's?"

Angel smiled with her bottom lip between her teeth. "Um...not exactly. It was kinda in my closet."

"There may be hope for you yet," Melinda said, and shoved the door open.

When Melinda climbed into bed, she remembered the mirror under her pillow. She reached between the pillow and mattress, but instead of long, cool metal, her hand touched something blunt and warm. She lifted the pillow. No mirror.

A leather book with a lock and hinges sat on the sheet.

She picked it up and opened it, heart pounding. Why was it here?

The scratchy words were there, filling page after page. Mixed in on most of the pages was the other handwriting. Her fingers trembled as she turned the pages. It was writing she knew all too well.

With her throat tight and burning, and acid slithering around in her stomach, she stayed awake until she'd read every word.

Chapter Thirty-Four

Carnival

Angel held hands with Ayden on one side and Zack on the other. The sky was perfect—crystal blue and filled with enough clouds to temper the bright afternoon sunlight. Kalek walked on the other side of Ayden. She tried to follow the guys' conversation for a while as they headed to the carnival, but her attention kept shifting to Melinda.

Black hair hanging in her face, Melinda slunk along behind them. Pouting.

"Why don't you come walk with us?" Angel called over her shoulder.

Melinda shook her head.

Angel let go of Zack's and Ayden's hands and back-stepped to her. "C'mon. At least tell me what's wrong."

Melinda continued walking, head hung low, and muttered, "'Vainly I had sought to borrow from my books surcease of sorrow.'"

"Are you quoting *Poe*?"

Her only response was a muffled *hmph*.

Whatever. Let her sulk. Angel quickened her pace and grabbed Ayden's hand again. Zack was now riding piggy-back on Kalek.

They crossed the town square, and as they passed Sir B's shop Angel peeked through the window. Dark. Hopefully that meant he was at the carnival and not stuck at the prison still helping with Dr. Randall.

They turned the corner and walked along the road past Roger's feed store, past *The Dreg*, through what Angel thought of as the industrial end of town. There were only a few buildings, but they were large and stark compared to the quaint brick storefronts in the square.

At the end of the road a field spread out before them, swarming with people. Colorful flags waved on the tops of poles and pointed canopies. Color everywhere. Sunlight glinted off the metal hardware fastened to what had to be rides from what little Angel could see of the structures through the crowd and the balloons that bobbed and weaved above their heads. Music and the rumbling of voices filled the air.

Zack jumped down from Kalek's back. He let out a squeak and pointed. "Angel, I want to ride that! I want to ride that!"

As if she could tell what he was pointing at amongst the activity in front of her.

Angel felt a yank on her arm and found herself being dragged along by Zack. Ayden gripped her other hand tightly and followed as they pushed through the crowd. Angel had to dodge a huge blue puff of cotton candy being waved around by a little girl.

"Purple!" the girl shouted, and the cotton candy changed color. The girl giggled as she pinched off a piece and stuffed it into her mouth. "It's grape now, Daddy!"

They twisted through the labyrinth of people, and then Zack slammed to a stop. Angel looked around to make sure Melinda and Kalek were still close. Oddly, they were walking side-by-side a few feet away. They weren't talking, but they weren't fighting either.

"Angel, *pleasepleasepleasepleaseplease* this one!"

She looked up at the ride. Dragons just big enough to fit two people on their backs circled a thick metal pole to which they were tethered. Children sat in pairs, one in front of the other, in saddles on the dragons' backs. Delighted squeals rang through the air.

The dragons cruised, their wings moving just enough to keep them in flight. They eased up and down as they circled, reminding Angel of the Dumbo ride at Disney World. She went one time when she was about nine years old, and she'd begged to ride Dumbo at least five times. If the line hadn't been so long, she would have made it a dozen.

"Okay, little man, but I'm riding with you."

Ayden squeezed her hand. "What about me?"

She turned to him and smiled. "You…can ride with Kalek."

He curled one side of his lip and crinkled his nose as if he smelled something rank. "Uh, not even." He let go of her hand and slipped his arms around her waist, then said over her shoulder. "Sorry, Zack, *you* get Kalek."

Angel spied the moping Melinda in her periphery. She wriggled out of Ayden's embrace and looked at Zack. "Or you can ride with Melinda."

"I don't do kiddie rides," Melinda said, her words snarky-jagged.

Angel exhaled, trying not to let it sound like an irritated huff. "I'll stay with y—"

"I don't need a babysitter, either." Melinda narrowed her eyes and crossed her arms. "Just go ride your little ride and I'll be over *there*." She flicked her head to the left where rows of vendor tables lined the walkway.

"C'mon." Kalek put his hand on Zack's shoulder. "She'll be fine. She's a big girl." He guided Zack over to the line.

Melinda gaped at Kalek for a moment, then blinked and stiffened her shoulders. Her expression snapped into a smirk and she turned and stalked over to the row of vendors.

Angel looked at Ayden. He shrugged, smiled, and tugged her hand as he took a step toward Zack and Kalek. "Don't worry about her. Kalek's right. She'll be fine."

"I know. She's just pouty. I want her to at least try and have a good time."

"Maybe rides aren't her thing."

They joined Kalek and Zack in line. Kalek handed them the tickets he'd bought. When they reached the front, Angel's heart fluttered. Looking up, she felt like a little kid about to ride a roller coaster for the first time—scared and excited all rolled into one. The ride went way higher than Dumbo. *Kiddie ride…not.*

But riding a real dragon…

When Angel climbed on she was grateful to feel Ayden's arms around her waist as the dragon lifted. The dragons were held to the pole only by heavy leather straps. They were muzzled so they couldn't bite the straps or breathe fire on them, but still. She inhaled and squeezed her knees into the saddle.

Zack leaned way out to the side on the dragon in front of them to look around Kalek and waved. Kalek all but lounged, legs dangling and hands linked behind his head.

In moments they were far above the crowd. Twenty feet? Thirty? Angel clung to the dragon's neck. It snorted, and she snatched her hands away.

Ayden laughed in her ear.

"It's not funny!"

He laughed harder.

She reached for the saddle horn, which moved and acted as a lever guiding the dragon up and down. She pushed forward to tell the dragon to go lower, but Ayden reached around her and wrapped her hand in his. He pulled back, and she couldn't match his strength. They rose higher.

"You're so mean!"

Ayden tightened his grip on her waist, and Angel felt his breath, warm against her neck. She gripped the saddle horn harder but let Ayden take them even higher.

When the ride ended and Angel climbed down, her legs felt like noodles.

Zack jumped up and down, squealing, "Again! Again!"

Angel shook her head. "No way, little man."

A girl's laugh came from behind Angel. She turned around and found Gwen, the assistant at Dr. Kate's office, standing there with a huge grin on her face. "See, if ya'd let me take you up on Wyatt you'd've been ready for that." She slapped her hand over her mouth and her eyes glistened with mischief.

"Thanks a lot," Angel said. "Can't *someone* be a little sympathetic?"

Gwen lowered her hand and smiled genuinely. "I'm sorry, Angel, but one day I *will* get you up on Wyatt." She held her arms open. "Forgive me?"

Angel stepped forward and hugged her.

"Is Dr. Kate around?"

"Yeah, over there with the ride attendant." Gwen glanced over at where Dr. Kate and a stocky man with bright red hair knelt over a dragon like those from the ride. "She comes to these things to make sure the dragons are being cared for properly. Fortunately for *him*, he's doing everything right." She reached down and unclipped the leather gloves hanging from her belt. "Anyway, I better go in case she needs anything. I just wanted to say *hey*."

As Gwen walked away, Angel scanned the crowd for Melinda. She spied her looking at a vendor table covered in silver jewelry.

Ayden put his hand on her shoulder blade. "Go on…go check on her."

Angel stepped away, dodging people as she wove her way to Melinda. She reached an opening in the crowd, only to discover people were clearing a path for a guy on ridiculously high stilts. She was right in his way—she ducked as his leg lifted, but he bounded over her as if the stilts were made of springs and landed gracefully on the other side of her.

She pushed through the next mass of people and found Melinda trying on a clunky silver bracelet with an iridescent purplish stone in the middle. *No*…Angel looked closer…it was a dragon scale set like a stone.

"Cool, huh?" Melinda ran her finger along the edge of the bracelet. "I wanted to buy it, but the guy said I have the wrong kind of money."

Angel looked at the price tag. "Uh…more like not enough. This would cost like seventy bucks."

Melinda *hmphed* and shrugged. "That's nothin'. Loan me the money they take here and I'll pay ya back. You can go get it exchanged later."

"Melinda, I don't *have* seventy bucks."

"Oh." Melinda shrugged again. "Sorry." She took the bracelet off and laid it on the corner of the table. "Too bad."

"If I had it I would. You know that, right?"

"Yeah, whatever. No big deal." Melinda nudged Angel. "Let's go find the guys."

Angel stood still for a second waiting for a break in the crowd. When she finally stepped forward, she looked behind her to make sure Melinda followed.

Melinda's hand was deep in her jeans pocket. She yanked it out and pulled the bottom of her t-shirt down so it hung loosely around her hips.

"Whatcha waitin' on?"

Angel looked at the vendor table behind Melinda. The bracelet wasn't where Melinda had laid it. She scanned as much of the tabletop as she could see, but it wasn't there.

"Urgh, this was your idea." Melinda tromped past, and into the crowd.

Angel sighed and ducked in behind her.

Chapter Thirty-Five

Poser

Melinda plowed past the island freaks, sight set on Kalek's curls, which she could just see over the tops of everyone's heads. Angel called for her to wait up, but whatever. Her heart thumped and it felt like a ball of clay sat in her stomach.

Had Angel seen?

It didn't matter. She'd left the right amount of money—more than enough. The guy had seen her take the bracelet and not said a word. Maybe he just couldn't *officially* take her kind of cash. Maybe he'd never seen that much foreign money. Maybe he was just stupid. No matter what, it wasn't her problem.

But she wasn't going to tell Angel. Miss Goodie-two-shoes would still say she did something wrong.

Kalek looked up as she approached.

Man, those eyes. And the *hair*. Doran's was so straight. It was nice, but it just didn't do that wild storm thing that Kalek's did. And there was something about the way Kalek stood, so *cool,* like he was completely comfortable in his total Kalekness.

And he was being *nice* today.

She shoved the thought away. It was probably an act, something Angel put him up to so Melinda wouldn't take off.

She stepped over to join the guys and Angel came up beside her.

"Melinda, I was *calling* you!"

Melinda cocked one eyebrow at her. "Your point?"

Angel huffed and made that squinty face of hers, but then Ayden lunged over and wrapped his arms around her waist. Dude could not keep his hands off that girl. Yeah, it was always in a nice way—those hands *never* went anywhere close to forbidden territory, but seriously. Could anyone be more totally in love? The ball of clay in Melinda's stomach shifted and pressed lower.

Zack stood beside Kalek, licking an ice-cream cone. "I want to do the petting zoo next." Chocolate dripped on his chin.

Melinda's jaw twitched. "Petting zoo? Dare I even ask what kind of whacked-out animals would be in that?"

Angel, looking all gushy in Ayden's arms, said, "Let's go find out."

The petting zoo just *had* to be on the far side of the carnival. Melinda stifled the griping comments that pushed into her mind about walking so much. They'd walked to the carnival because of her. No way was she riding some smelly horse. Thumb flicking her cellphone case, she followed the others through more wandering freaks.

What was it around here? Bonnets and overalls, full-on cowboys, preppies, Victorian dresses…on everyone from little kids to old people. In some ways it was pretty cool, but it was so strange. At Melinda's school every kid dressed like trendy clones. In her neighborhood you could barely tell one fashionista mom from another. The men were all suits during the week and golfer-geek on weekends.

A few teens here and there looked like they'd fit in with Melinda's crowd, but most of them lacked the whole dark-and-dreary expressions of her friends. One girl tromped by in the coolest boots Melinda had ever seen—black, laced up to her knees with laces that slithered like skinny snakes through the eyelets.

Melinda stopped and watched the girl as she stepped up to a vendor table. More jewelry of various metals and stones. The girl picked up a copper piece. "Can I try it on?"

The stout woman behind the table smiled. Dangly earrings sparkled and swayed as she dipped her head in a single nod. "Sure, hon."

The girl held the piece close to the side of her head. It looked to

Melinda like a long, slinky dragon figurine standing on her palm.

How do you try on something like that?

Then it *moved.*

It climbed onto the girl's ear, wrapping around the curve, and settled into shape. Now it clung like a lizard to a branch, with its head at the top and its tail trailing off her earlobe. The woman held up a mirror for the girl to see.

"Awesome, I'll take it." The girl opened her purse and dug around in it.

Melinda felt for the bracelet in her pocket. Too bad she hadn't found the dragon earring first.

She looked up and realized the others were nowhere around. Good. Let them go do their little petting zoo thing on their own. There was way cooler stuff here.

Several tables were stacked with more jewelry, but Melinda walked past those. A few booths had clothing of all styles, including a blood-red Gothic dress Melinda would have killed for.

She pulled it off the rack and held it up. Totally the wrong size. She scowled.

The vendor, a rail of a girl, no more than twenty and wearing some sort of Goth fairy outfit complete with corset, walked up and put her hand on the dress. "Thinking it's not your size?"

"Yeah."

"Well, watch." She took it from Melinda and held it against herself. She was plenty thin enough to fit it, but the dress was far too short.

But as Melinda watched, the dress lengthened.

Too freakin' cool.

"See? Guaranteed to fit."

Melinda paid for the dress—the girl seemed not at all put off by her American money.

"No need for a bag, either," she said with a sly smile as she folded the dress. And folded. It got smaller and smaller until it fit into Melinda's palm. It still weighed the same, but now she could tuck it into her pocket.

At the next stall, blank canvases leaned in stands on top of a long table. A man walked toward them, and as he approached, a picture emerged on one. Tropical flowers suddenly rimmed the canvas with a bright sunset in the middle.

"Gorgeous," the man said to the girl perched on a stool behind the table, "but I've got nothing left." He patted the side pocket of his cargo pants where a wallet-shaped bulge showed, then stepped away. The picture disappeared.

Melinda stepped closer and another picture began to emerge. A figure in a tunic and leather pants, cradling a sleek black guitar. His head leaned forward and a swirl of wild curls obscured his face—curls with a pointed ear poking through on one side. Her stomach twisted around the lump of clay that seemed to have reformed.

"They show exactly what you want them to."

Melinda looked up at the girl behind the table.

"I don't think so." She walked off, swallowing against the gnarled feeling rising into her chest.

She moved from table to table, looking up every once in a while to scan the crowd for the others. Angel would totally have not gone this long without coming back to her. The guys must be making her stay away. Melinda smiled, picturing Angel all mussy and fussy with Kalek and Ayden telling her to chill.

As her thoughts dissipated, Melinda turned to the next table. It was covered in feathers. Long, short, narrow, wide…some beautiful but simple, others with vibrant colors and patterns like peacock or tropical bird feathers. Some had metallic flecks or looked as if they were made completely from bronze, silver or gold. The metallic ones felt just as soft as the others when Melinda ran her fingers lightly over a few.

She picked one up. Deep blue, with deeper purple swirls running through it. It was *gorgeous*. But what was it for? It wasn't a quill pen or anything. Just a feather. She looked at the sign that showed the prices. Judging by the numbers she'd seen on the bracelet and dress and what that had converted to, she figured these meant the feathers were maybe twenty dollars.

For a feather?

The guy behind the table was leaning over another table behind him, arms deep in a box. Long black hair hung down a back covered in brown suede. She was just about to clear her throat to get his attention when he straightened up and turned around.

The suede was just a vest, and he was shirtless underneath. Tattoos covered his thickly muscled chest, shoulders and arms. The standard fare was there: a Celtic cross on one side of his chest, a skull and crossbones on one bicep, a dragon breathing fire on one forearm, and a whole array of others.

In between, curled around and connecting some of the images were feather tattoos.

A smile appeared inside a pointed goatee. "See something you like?" His voice was smooth baritone.

"Are these…? I mean…" She pointed to the feather on his arm that curled around the dragon. It was bright red with loopy black markings.

"Yep. Looks totally real, right? But not at all permanent. You can move them from place to place."

He pinched the skin at the base of the red feather tattoo, and the tip between his thumb and finger became three-dimensional. He pulled gently. The rest of the feather filled out as it released and lifted bit by bit from one end to the other. Then he held it out for Melinda to see.

Without a word, he found another spot of unmarked skin, not that there was much to choose from. He reversed the process, pushing the fluffier end of the feather against his arm first. As he moved along, twisting it into an S-curve, it melded into his skin.

Melinda shoved her hand into her back pocket. She had exactly twenty bucks left.

She held the bill in front of him. "Will this work?"

He nodded and took the money. "Sure. I go to America a lot."

Really? It had never occurred to Melinda that these island people left their little magical bubble. It was something she'd have to ask Angel about later.

She twirled the blue feather around with her fingertips. "This one."

"Good choice. Want me to help you?"

She shrugged. "Sure. Can you do it like that?" She pointed to his other forearm, where a feather curled like a cobra about to strike.

She pulled her sleeve up and twisted her arm so he could put the feather on the underside of her forearm. His hands were warm and gentle as he pressed the feather against her exposed skin. The slightest tingle followed. The feather was longer than the one on his arm, and he wrapped the tail end around to the other side of her wrist and down the back of her hand.

She smiled. "I like that."

"It won't wash off," the guy said as he inspected at the feather tattoo. "And it won't come off until you move it." He reached out and pinched her skin at the tip to show her one more time, then smoothed it back down.

He let go of her arm. "Enjoy."

"Thanks."

The blue made her skin look even paler. She ran her fingers over the feather. She couldn't feel it at all.

She turned to leave the table and spied Angel, dragging Ayden with one hand and Zack with the other. Kalek slunk along behind them.

Melinda crossed her arms. "Where have y'all *been*?" she said with mock accusation. "It took you long enough to come find me."

Angel's eyes widened and she opened her mouth, but Melinda cut her off before she could say anything.

"Any five-year-old knows that when you get lost you're supposed to stay put. So *where were you*?"

"Lost? What…?" Angel's face relaxed and she rolled her eyes.

Melinda laughed. "Two points for catching on."

She turned from Angel as she caught a glimpse of Kalek heading to the feather tattoo table. He and the tattoo guy gripped each other's hands in a knight's handshake.

"Dude, you here suckering posers into your fake tats?"

Tattoo guy laughed. "You're such a loser, K. Just 'cos you insist on the real deal doesn't make these less cool. You just wish *you* had a Talent like this."

"Oh, right. So much better than mine, man."

They continued talking, but Melinda tuned them out. She pulled her sleeve down over her hand and crossed her arms, pretending to listen to whatever Angel was in the middle of chattering about.

"…got to pet a baby griffin. And you should have seen the giant aquarium tank they had set up over there. The fish were incredible." Angel stopped talking and narrowed her eyes. "Melinda, are you okay?"

Before Melinda could answer, Kalek stepped up beside them laughing and shaking his head.

Melinda tightened her arms around her as his words replayed in her head. *Poser. Whatever.* Anyone could get a tattoo the ordinary way. Half Melinda's friends had them, from single ones to ink covering most of their body. She'd never done it because she'd seen an old lady with tattoos up both legs, distorted from wrinkles and faded. It just wasn't worth it.

But the feather looked so real, and she could do all kinds of stuff with it.

It was freaking *magic.*

So why were tears stinging her eyes?

And why did she suddenly find herself slamming through the crowd away from them?

Chapter Thirty-Six

Pulling Away

"Melinda, wait!"

Angel pushed herself faster. Melinda was nearly in reach, but punched it up a notch before Angel could grab her shirt. Angel's hand closed around air. *How is she going so fast? I'm the one everyone wanted on the track team, not her. I've never even seen her run before.*

Just as Angel was about to give up, Melinda tripped and crashed face-first into the dirt, then let out a stream of curse words as she flipped over. Angel lunged forward, sank to her knees, and grabbed Melinda's arm before she could stand back up.

"Seriously, Melinda, I just want to talk. What's got you so upset?"

Melinda's legs were stretched out in front of her and she leaned on her arms, palms against the ground. She turned to Angel with tears streaking her dusty, scowling face, fire burning behind hurt-filled eyes. "Nothing! Leave me alone!" She yanked her arm free, but Angel immediately grabbed her shirt and sat down next to her.

They were under a tree on the outer edge of the fairgrounds. Sunlight fell through the treetop in shining specks. Melinda scooted back toward the trunk.

"I can hold you here with magic if I choose, Melinda. Please don't make me do that."

The fire in Melinda's eyes intensified. "Why not? You can do anything, can't you, Little Miss Perfect, so why don't you?"

"I'm hardly perfect. Tell me what's going on. *Please.*"

"Hmmph." Melinda stopped pulling away.

Angel released her grip, but kept her hand ready to grab her shirt again the second she moved. She really was prepared to use magic to subdue Melinda. The words had been an empty threat until she saw the desperation in Melinda's face.

"You wouldn't understand," Melinda said weakly. Anger hardened her gaze, but fear and confusion mingled with it in her eyes.

Angel held on to the one string she did have—the fact that Melinda hadn't pulled away again. "Let me try."

Tears welled in Melinda's eyes, but no more fell.

"I don't belong here. Magic isn't something I can control, and never will be. Even getting it embedded in my genes won't *really* make it work."

"What are you talking about? It can't be embedded in your genes at all. It's part of your soul."

Melinda's eyes turned to ice. "Here we go again. I'm outta here."

All she did was shift sideways.

"You know it's true," Angel said. She could read it in Melinda's eyes. Behind the ice, behind the pain—it was there. *Why is she being so stubborn?* "It's in you, Melinda. You just need practice."

"What I *know* is that my father spent his whole life trying to prove it's *not* true. And I think he did. He came here and got magic, and it certainly didn't come from *inside* him. Or *stay* with him either."

Angel felt her jaw drop. The earth tilted beneath her. "How…how did you know about that?"

"You think I don't know my own father's handwriting?"

Angel could only stare as Melinda shoved herself up onto her feet and took off running again toward the town square.

The notebooks.

Angel thought back to Melinda standing in front of the jewelry table, stuffing something into her pocket. Angel had only looked away for a second. She'd left Melinda alone in the back room of the bookstore with the notebooks sitting on the shelf for far longer than that several times.

Pressure on Angel's arm brought her back to her senses. She looked up into Ayden's blue eyes. They were the color of denim in the sunlight.

"Hey, you." He knelt down next to her.

His smile made Angel's heart jump, but she couldn't smile back. He pushed a loose strand of hair behind her ear and slipped his arm around her shoulders.

Angel sighed and leaned against him. "Well, I found out who stole the notebooks."

"I just don't get why I can't Find her," she said to Ayden, as she crushed his hand in her grip. She couldn't help it. All her attempts at Finding Melinda resulted in darkness. Nothing more. No sense of where Melinda was, no direction at all. Panic nearly drowned her.

"I think Kalek's right—your Talent is freaking out because *you're* freaking out."

Maybe, but she should have checked sooner. She'd only wanted to give Melinda time to burn off steam before following. Over an hour later, they were making their way toward the square with emptiness Angel's only guide.

Ayden tightened his grip on her hand and she focused on the strength there. He was still an Enhancer…but it wasn't helping at all.

"What if you try *him*?"

"Doran?"

"She might be with him…"

Angel heard Kalek *hmph* and she looked over at him. *Smug*. "He's right, Kalek. You don't have to look so happy about this! If she's with him, she could be in real danger!"

Kalek didn't answer, but he walked over and leaned against the outside wall of *The Dreg*. Angel stopped. Kalek flourished his hand in a *be my guest* motion and then crossed his arms.

Angel exhaled through flared nostrils, but she kept her mouth shut. She closed her eyes and concentrated on Doran.

Again, darkness. Different than what she'd sensed when she tried to Find Melinda. Deeper, colder.

She opened her eyes and shook her head. Ayden gripped her hand tightly.

Kalek shrugged. "Guess we'll have to do this the old fashioned way."

They split up when they reached the town square—Angel with Ayden and Zack with Kalek.

Angel walked over to *The Professor's Roost* and tried the door even though the windows were still dark. Locked. She shielded around her eyes as she peeked through the window. Of course there was nothing to see. How could Melinda get inside anyway?

She pulled away from the glass to find Ayden scanning around the next building. As Angel walked toward him, movement caught her eye between the buildings. Shadows from the trees behind Angel stretched to fill the area in cobbled darkness, but she could make out the form of a woman in a long dress.

"Melinda?"

The woman spun to face her, but she was still obscured by shadow. Then the form changed…

The long dress faded and the shoulders broadened. A hand moved toward the figure's head in a motion that sent Angel's mind reeling.

The figure turned and disappeared behind the next building.

"Ayden!"

Her legs shook as she fought to remain standing.

He appeared at her side before she could blink. His arms circled her waist and she grabbed his shoulders.

"Doran's here," she whispered. "We need to find her."

They reached Angel's front yard just as the first drop of rain hit the top of Angel's head. Clouds had come out of nowhere as they headed home. She stopped walking once they were inside the gate. "We should have kept searching in town."

"If she was there, she'd've been with him," Ayden said. "She's got to be here."

Her heart pounded and her stomach lurched as she stared at the front door. What if Melinda hadn't come home? The sky was already gray and darkening quickly. Rain drops spattered all around them.

Kalek walked past her. Zack sat on his shoulders, hands holding Kalek's ears like handles.

Angel forced herself forward. Melinda *had* to be here.

The moment she opened the door, Horatio zipped out and around

Angel's head. He chittered frantically and hovered, wings whirring, right in front of her face. She fought the urge to swat at him.

"Not now, Horatio! Is Melinda here?"

He chirped. *No.*

Angel had insisted he stay home. Just one day without him on her shoulder. Without him watching her every move. She'd convinced her parents Doran would be hiding out, staying as far from the crowds as possible. And both Kalek and Ayden were with her.

Her eyes stung. Why had she chosen today? If Horatio had been with them, she could've sent him to follow Melinda and make sure she made it home.

He buzzed closer, almost touching her nose.

"Enough already!" she snapped. "I get it. You're mad. This is more important."

He chirped one last time and zipped back into the house.

Angel followed, heart wrenching, with the guys behind her.

Melinda's not here….

She found her parents in the kitchen. Her mother was stirring something in a pan, and her father sat on a barstool holding a small object in his hand.

"Hey, Anna, check this out. I Transformed thi—"

"Has Melinda been here?"

"Not since this morning when she left with you."

Her mother turned around, sauce dripping from the spoon in her hand. "What happened?" She moved toward them, her worried gaze darting from Angel to each of the others. "Did you get separated at the carnival?"

"She ran away."

Angel barely had the words out when thunder cracked. Her father jumped up and looked out the window.

"Why didn't you Find her before coming home?" Angel's mother asked.

Acid burned the back of Angel's throat. "I tried!"

Her father spun around. "Tried?"

"I panicked, and I can't Find her." Her voice trembled.

Angel's mother moved the pan to the empty cutting board and snapped the stove off. "I'll stay here with Zack." She sent Zack off to take get ready for bed while she gathered raincoats for everyone else. In minutes they were heading into the forest behind Angel's house.

Angel stood by the fence and tried one last time to Find Melinda as

Horatio darted into the forest at top speed ahead of the group. All she got was a dreadful sense that Melinda was out in the middle of the forest. Alone? Injured?

She had no way of knowing.

Chapter Thirty-Seven

Darkness

Melinda slumped to the ground against a broad tree, its jagged bark scraping her back like claws. The forest surrounded her on all sides, thick and foreboding. Darkness stalked between twisted trees, filling in every space as the sun disappeared in the distance.

Rain dripped around her. The branches above her blocked much of it, but she was cold and damp.

And scared.

All sense of direction had fled.

She'd even resorted to calling for Angel and Ayden, but only her own voice echoed back among the somber cries of unidentified creatures.

Alone, alone, alone….

She slammed her elbows into the tree trunk behind her. Pain shot through her arms, to her fisted hands. Frustration burst out of her in a throat-searing scream.

Darker now. Nothing but shadows and sounds. Clicks, caws, screeches—all crawling through Melinda's mind. Her heart raced. She heard, heard, heard, but never saw anything.

Were they even real?

Then…a speck of light.

Faint, but brightening as it moved closer. As Melinda watched, the speck divided—two, four, twenty, fifty flecks of light continued to approach, spreading out….

Fluttering.

A mass of butterflies soon hovered in front of her. Pale greenish light reflected off tree trunks and wet leaves. They pulsed, beckoned. And moved away.

Melinda jumped to her feet and darted after them.

Electricity moved through her like the day she'd floated down the stairs and across the back yard. She wasn't floating, but she kept her balance even as her feet slid on the slick leaves. The same thing had happened when she'd run away from Angel. The power had slipped from her grasp before, but it felt more secure now and she pushed harder, faster.

The rain met her rhythm, pounding the ground around her. It fogged her vision, blurring the forest as she whipped past trees and through clearings, but the butterflies stayed in focus.

In minutes she reached the cave. Of course she'd known where the butterflies were leading her, but the sight of the gaping black opening slammed her to a stop. She gasped for breath as the energy drained from her, leaving her shaky and dizzy.

Rain pelted the rock around the cave entrance. Melinda shivered as it soaked further into her clothes and skin. The butterflies darted into the cave, their light reflecting off smooth, dry ground. Only one choice to make.

It was oddly warm inside. Even dripping wet, Melinda felt heat easing into her, soothing her tense muscles. She breathed more easily.

The front part of the cave was empty other than the horde of butterflies clinging to the walls. Most of them were still as leaves, and the group that had led her quickly settled in with the rest.

Was Doran in the back? Wouldn't he have come out or called by now?

Melinda walked slowly toward the back chamber. A curtain of shadow blocked the entrance. She pressed against the rock wall, which was clear of butterflies for a good two feet in front of the chamber entrance, and peeked through.

Cave lettuce still lined the floor. Some of it now glowed like the butterflies. Others sparkled with metallic veining. Some had darkened into shadow versions.

There was no sign of Doran.

Melinda exhaled, shivering—and surprised at how relieved she was.

What now?

She could possibly make her way back to Angel's, but even from deep within the cave she heard the roar of rain and crash of thunder. She *so* did not want to go back out into that. Her clothes felt drier, and her eyelids drooped as if weights were pulling down on them.

Sleeping on the ground would suck but she had no other choice. She lowered herself and curled up on the smoothest spot she could find. The cool ground felt good against her cheek. She was truly warm—almost too warm.

Grit rubbed her forearms as she tried to get comfortable and keep her face out of the dirt at the same time. The only sound was the rush of rain. Thunder drifted farther and farther away.

Melinda closed her eyes, shivering despite waves of heat, but her nerves calmed and her mind fogged...

Light glowed brighter than ever at the top of the hill. She remembered the voice that had called to her last time. Doran? Could it have been?

She turned from the light and searched the crowd for his face. She'd made it much farther than she'd realized.

People blanketed the hill below Melinda, stumbling and crawling over each other. Some walked past, eyes set on the hilltop, but most fought through the mass of bodies desperately.

It was impossible to tell if Doran was among them. She turned back toward the hilltop.

The voice called to her again. "Come this way...."

Definitely Doran.

"This way, Melinda..."

She faced the direction from which it came.

"This way..."

It came from beyond the crowd.

Her heart hammered as she recognized the spot where she'd been standing in her first dream. Should she go back?

She plunged forward, expecting to battle the crowd, but they moved out of her way with each step.

The bottom of the hill splayed out before her, and as she realized what lay beyond she scrambled to stop her progress. Dark forest walled the hill base. Gnarled trees and inky shadow.

Doran's voice called to her from within, but it no longer sounded sweet and yearning…it screeched and gurgled…

"This...way…"

She froze.

Fire shot through her arm.

Melinda was instantly awake, but her eyes were locked shut. She struggled and failed to open them as the air weighed on her from head to toe—she could move nothing, could barely breathe.

Shuffling noises came from close by, then something bumped her arm—the same one that had hurt so horribly in her dream. It no longer burned, but Melinda felt a pinch, like something poking into the skin at the crook of her elbow. She flexed the muscles there. Her arm wouldn't move, but the pinching increased. It was a familiar feeling.

When she was eight she'd been sick for months, battling fevers and mysterious pains that would leave one spot to show up days later in another. Innumerable doctor visits ended in several hospital stays, which meant a lot of I.V.s.

Was she in a hospital? *Please, no…*

She tensed her muscles again in effort to shift position, but only made the slightest movement. It was enough to tell the surface under her was rough and gritty.

"You're not waking, are you?"

Doran.

Pressure above and below her eye…and the blinding light of a flashlight. One eye, then the other. Then no more pressure, and darkness again as her eyelids snapped shut.

"Hm."

Shuffle.

Fire blossomed from her elbow and trailed to both her hand and shoulder. She tried to struggle again, but her muscles only loosened as if her body were unraveling. The air above her turned to sand.

The last thing she remembered was Doran's garbled voice mumbling what sounded like *your father…*

Melinda's stomach churned as the world around her shifted up, down, up, down...

How am I moving?

Other sensations filtered through the fog in her brain. Pressure across her back just below her shoulder blades, and under the backs of her knees. Warmth on her left side, but cool air on her right. Cotton material against her cheek. The smell of sweat, and behind that the earthy scent of damp forest. The *crunch-swoosh* of shoes sliding across a leaf-strewn ground.

Her eyelids fluttered, but she couldn't force them open completely. The forest was still deeply shadowed, but a hint of sunlight tinged the air.

How did I get here?

She remembered arguing with Angel, running away. Something glowing.

Butterflies?

And then nothing.

She inhaled deeply, and a voice whispered to *be still.*

"It's okay...shhhh...almost there."

The voice...

...your father...

Why did those words pop into her head?

Melinda tried to speak Doran's name, but only managed a moan.

"*Shhh.* It's okay, Melinda. We're here."

The sounds changed from *swoosh-crunch* to the grinding of gravel. And then up, up, up steps. She was shifted in his arms. *Tap, tap*—knuckles against wood.

A click. Silence. Doran's arms tensed.

"Melinda!"

Chapter Thirty-Eight

Rescuer

“Oh my God, Mom! Come here!”

Angel yanked the door open all the way and moved to the side so Doran could carry Melinda in. Her mom stepped into the room just as he set Melinda gently on the couch.

“What happened?” her mom asked, hands pressed to her cheeks. She stepped closer, eyes narrowing, and glanced at Angel. “She looks feverish.”

Doran moved behind the chair as her mom knelt next to Melinda and pressed the back of her hand against Melinda’s forehead.

Melinda moaned.

Angel swayed. She leaned against the stair rail and wrapped her arms tightly around herself, fighting the chill that slithered through her. The guys had brought her home only two hours into the search because she’d started shivering uncontrollably. Ever since, she’d been achy and weak. The soreness in her throat radiated down to her collarbones and up to her temples, but she couldn’t sleep. She’d spent the rest of the night pacing the living room or curled up on the couch.

“I found her out in the forest.” Doran stood behind the chair in the darkest corner of the room. His hair hung in gnarled strands around his face as he gazed downward.

"How far away?" Her mom covered Melinda with a blanket. "Was she already unconscious?"

"About twenty minutes' walk, and yes." He glanced up, eyes silver-gray in the shadows. "Will she be okay?"

Angel's stomach flipped. Twenty minutes...that sounded like a long time.

Her mom turned to face him, but said, "Anna, call Ayden's mother and ask her to come over please."

Angel nodded, but before she made a move, Doran stepped back from the chair and toward the door.

"I better go."

He scuffled his feet as he walked across the wood floor. The lantern light flickered and danced around him. Angel stared. There was something odd about way the light and shadows laid against him...

"*Now*, Anna." Her mother was rubbing Melinda's hand and examining her face. As Angel headed toward the kitchen to call Sarah, she heard her mother whisper, "Hang in there, sweetie." And then, "Oh, what has that boy done?"

She'd just hung up the phone and stepped out of the kitchen when she noticed Zack in the hallway.

"Back to bed, little man." The words rasped out against her sore throat.

He stood stock-still, blinking. "Was that that guy? The one everyone is so scared of?"

She nodded, trying to swallow what felt like a burning cactus in her throat.

Zack hadn't moved, but he stopped blinking and looked up at her, wide-eyed. "How did he do that?"

"What?"

"That pixelly thing."

"Pixie thing?"

His shoulders dropped and he half-rolled his eyes. "Not *pixie*. Pixelly. Like *pixels*, as in the dots that make up a picture on a computer screen."

Angel opened her mouth to ask what he meant when Sarah walked in. Her long blond hair was pulled back in a slick ponytail. She slipped her glasses from where they were folded over the neckline of her shirt and went straight to Melinda.

Her mom scooted over. She and Sarah immediately began talking in whispers.

Another chill slithered through Angel as she caught a couple of phrases…*maybe a puncture…spine from something poisonous*…and Sarah's voice raised enough for Angel to hear the tail of her last comment clearly:

"..take some blood and test it."

Angel turned around to shoo Zack back to bed, but he'd already gone.

Melinda groaned and shifted on the couch.

Her mom moved to the right, and Angel could finally see Melinda's face clearly. It was ghastly pale, and her cheeks were blotched red. Her eyes fluttered amid sunken shadows.

"Where am I?" She tried to push herself up, but flopped back against the pillow with a grunt. "Oh…I'm back."

Sarah readjusted the blanket. "You need to lie still. You've been through a lot." She reached up and stroked Melinda's cheek. "Can you tell me what you remember?"

Melinda blinked several times, then closed her eyes. "The carnival, then someone carrying me."

Angel stepped closer. "You ran away. Doran said he found you passed out in the forest."

Melinda shook her head, and then put her fingers to her temple and moaned. "Man, that hurt. No head-shaking." She paused and took a deep breath. "I kinda remember. Kalek got all snotty about something, as usual, and you backed him up, *as usual*." She inhaled deeply again.

What was Melinda talking about? Angel thought back to the moment Melinda took off. Kalek was talking to Gunther about his feathers, and hadn't said a word to Melinda, much less *about* Melinda. So why—

Melinda flipped her arm so it lay on the pillow above her head. An inky wisp peeked out of her sleeve and curled around her wrist. A feather tattoo?

Ah…

Angel kept her mouth shut.

Her mom glanced at Angel, concern filling her eyes, and then turned back to Melinda. "What about after that?"

"No…it's all blank. I remember a pain in my arm, I think. And then being carried, and now this."

Sarah looked down at Melinda's other arm and then leaned in, scrutinizing it. The sleeve was pulled up, and Angel could see lines running like a web away from a dark spot on the inside of her elbow. Sarah raised her finger and barely touched the edge of the area.

Melinda sucked air in through her teeth and jerked her head up from the pillow.

"Agh! What th—?"

Her eyes were wide and wild. She yanked out of Sarah's grasp. "That hurt!" Then she looked down at her arm and gasped. "What's wrong with me?"

Sarah took her hand. "I'm sorry. I just needed to feel the skin. I touched only the very edge." She started to stand. "I'm going to call the hospital and let them know we're bringing her in."

Melinda scrambled on the couch, and Sarah dropped back to her knees, grabbing Melinda's legs.

"Nooooooo…" Melinda eyes were wild. Terror twisted her face. "No hospitals! I won't go!"

Her mom placed her hands on Melinda's shoulders, but Melinda yanked away and sat up.

Sarah held tight to her legs. "Relax, Melinda. It'll be okay. You have to stay calm."

Melinda shook her head from side to side and pried at Sarah's arms. Her breathing was loud and ragged.

"I won't go! No…I…can't…not another…hospital."

Angel lunged forward and squeezed between her mom and Sarah.

Melinda, panting, locked her gaze on Angel. "Don't…let them…take me…"

Angel turned to her mom. "Remember what I said about her being sick when she was little? She's completely phobic of being in a hospital. Does she have to go? Can't we call a doctor to come here?"

Sarah's voice made Angel turn.

"Melinda, you have to stay calm. The harder your heart pumps, the faster the poison can spread."

"Then…let me stay…" She inhaled a rattling breath. "I'll stay still…just…don't make…me go…"

Sarah nodded. "I'd prefer a medical doctor have a look at you, but with my background in toxicology, I'd likely be consulted anyway."

Melinda sank back into the couch. Her breathing hitched once, then slowed.

Sarah turned to Angel and her mom. "I brought some equipment home the other day for a project. I can draw a blood sample and check it out there. I'll call the hospital and speak with a doctor on staff in the meantime. Keep her still. Keep her arm below her heart." She held her hand out, and a pen appeared in her palm. She put a few small marks just beyond the edges of the area on Melinda's arm. "If this moves and touches those marks, you call me and we are taking her right in."

After Sarah left, Angel stacked the largest throw pillows next to the couch and told Melinda to rest her arm on top.

Sarah returned with a glass syringe in one hand. The room filled with sunlight through the open front door. The needle glinted as Sarah walked past.

Angel stepped over to close the door, but glanced outside first. The guys had sent Horatio with updates every couple of hours through the night, and he was due back again any time.

As she clicked the lock shut, Angel heard twittering on the other side of the door. She opened it again, and Horatio darted inside. He buzzed around her face, his little bug eyes fixed on hers.

"I'm feeling fine," Angel said. "You need to go get the guys. Melinda's here."

Horatio let out a squeak and buzzed over to Melinda. He chittered and looped the air before he zipped back out the door.

Angel laughed, which flared the spiny pain in her throat, and she started coughing.

"Sit down," her mother said.

Angel obeyed, sinking into the chair adjacent to the couch. A weird tingling ran under her skin at the thought that Doran had been standing right behind that very chair just a short time ago. She'd watched him leave, but the door had not gotten closed after that. She fought the urge to look behind her and make sure he wasn't still there.

Don't be silly. Invisibility is Dr. Randall's thing. What's Doran going to do—disguise himself as a floor lamp? Blend into the curtains?

She laughed again to try and calm her nerves.

"What is so freaking funny?" Melinda lay stiffly as Sarah rubbed her forearm with a cotton ball and then pressed the needle into the skin. Melinda flinched. "Dang, girl, answer me and take my mind off this!"

Angel forced a smile. "It's just Horatio, the way he flipped through the air. I've never seen him do that…and it was because he was happy to see you." Her forced smile relaxed into a real one.

Melinda turned her head toward Angel. The grimace on her face shifted to surprise. "Seriously?"

Angel nodded.

Melinda settled back into the pillow. "Cool."

Chapter Thirty-Nine

Poisoned

Melinda's head throbbed in time with her heartbeat. Fire crackled in her arm, which again rested on a stack of pillows next to the couch. The burning fanned out. It had only been maybe fifteen minutes, but judging by the way it felt it had to be worse. She should check, or call Caryn in to check, but her stomach twisted at the thought of knowing.

She swallowed and looked around the empty room. Caryn and Angel's voices were a dull murmur coming from the kitchen. The only other sound was Zoe barking in the back yard.

A loud *slam* popped her eyes open. Ayden burst into the room, followed by William and Kalek. Horatio buzzed past them, swerved through the air, and hovered in front of Melinda, chittering. A sense of meaning settled over her. *Relief.*

Where did that come from?

William looked at Melinda and shoved his glasses into place. Worry creased his forehead and eyes, but a warm smile spread across his face as he strode toward her.

"How are you feeling?" He knelt beside her on one knee. His eyes creased further when he glanced down at her arm.

"I'm okay," she creaked.

Angel and Caryn appeared in the room, and Caryn joined William at Melinda's side.

Horatio darted over to Angel.

"Thank you," she said as he settled onto her shoulder.

A thought popped into Melinda's mind—Horatio perched on her own shoulder the way he always was on Angel's. Not *such* a creepy thing…

Ayden joined Angel, his arm encircling her waist as she leaned into him. He examined Angel's fever-flushed face, and his eyes narrowed. Then he softly pressed his lips to her forehead.

A pang of jealousy hit Melinda unbidden. Would anyone ever be so happy to see her?

She glanced at Kalek, who leaned against the stair railing, staring past everyone into the corner of the room. His angular face looked like stone, and the firelight danced eerily in his onyx eyes, which seemed to be barely shifting focus. She followed his gaze and found nothing. Yet a chill crept down her spine with the sensation of being watched.

Melinda turned back to Caryn and William, who were whispering next to her. William frowned at Caryn's description of the night's events at the house. The frown deepened when her words turned to the poison in the veins of Melinda's arm.

"You're sure it's poison?" Ayden's voice rang across the room.

Caryn shook her head as she looked over at him. "Not entirely. Your mom believes it's the puncture from a plant spine or an insect bite."

Ayden stepped forward. "Let me see."

Caryn moved closer to William and Ayden knelt beside her. He looked at Melinda's arm, and then glanced back at Angel, whose tired eyes blinked rapidly as she chewed her bottom lip.

Ayden lowered his head and closed his eyes. His face hardened with concentration. Melinda saw the muscles tensing under his skin, not just in his face, but in his arms, all the way to his hands, which dug into the jeans covering his thighs.

What is he doing?

His breathing seemed to stop for a moment, and Caryn grabbed his shoulder, but he didn't move. Not even a flinch. His eyes stayed clamped shut.

"Ayden!" Angel shot forward and dropped down on her knees beside him.

Still nothing. He was like a statue. Angel tried to grip his hand, but couldn't move even one finger. Panic flashed across her face—wide eyes and a trembling lip—and then Ayden exhaled and Angel threw her arms around his shoulders.

He whispered something in Angel's ear and she backed away, confusion and…something else…making her eyes dart back and forth between Ayden and Melinda. Caryn and William stared, and Caryn looked as if she was about to speak when Ayden placed his hands on Melinda's arm.

One hand gripped above the burning area and one below. Melinda's arm jerked—his palms were like ice—but he didn't lose his hold.

Freezing cold flooded her arm. Melinda gasped, and an involuntary whimper bubbled through her throat. The burning seared hotter at her elbow, but coolness eased toward the center from where Ayden's hands squeezed her flesh. He tightened his grip even more, and Melinda gazed down at her arm, barely able to breathe.

Liquid oozed from a tiny spot on her elbow. Translucent green and glowing slightly like the butterflies in Doran's cave, it trailed down her arm and dripped onto the pillow beneath. The burning eased bit by bit as the liquid left her body.

When the last drop trickled out, Ayden let go of her arm and slumped to the floor.

Melinda hugged her knees as she curled up in the corner of the couch while Caryn and William hovered over Ayden. Angel, tears streaming down her face, sat cross-legged with his head cradled in her lap. Melinda's gut sank with emptiness. Her throat tightened. Ayden wasn't moving, but at least he was breathing.

"He's going to be okay." Zack's voice pulled Melinda's gaze to where he stood, curls sticking out every which way, in the hallway. Melinda wasn't sure if Zack was just trying his little-boy best to reassure everyone or if he could actually see something in Ayden the rest of them couldn't.

Melinda turned back toward the group on the floor, exhaling through flared nostrils as her gaze passed the empty staircase. Kalek had apparently bolted while Ayden was pulling the poison from Melinda's arm. How heartless could he be? He always talked as if the Kleidons were his real family because his dad was sick and his mom was a basket case, and of course his sister…

Angel had told Melinda all about Siophra and Gregor, and how Siophra was killed by some psycho professor. Kalek had been really close with his sister. Freaky close. Kalek was older than her, by barely a year, and Angel said most of the town referred to them as the Halvard twins because they spent so much time together. Melinda had never understood the appeal of siblings—her family was such a mess—but watching Angel and her parents, Zack, Ayden and Sarah, brought something to the surface, and the idea of just disappearing at a time like this suddenly felt terribly wrong.

Yet that's exactly what Kalek had done. So why?

She looked down at Ayden. Angel stroked his forehead with trembling fingers. His eyelids twitched.

"Did you see that?" Angel said.

Caryn nodded, and grasped Ayden's hand. "Come on. Your mom's on her way. Let's show her you're going to be fine."

His eyes popped open just as Sarah walked in the front door. She dashed to Caryn's side and gazed down at him.

He smiled weakly at his mom while she checked over him inch by inch, and then looked at Caryn. "Sorry about the pillow."

Caryn's shoulders visibly relaxed. "Don't think I won't make you buy me a new one." Her quavering voice betrayed the joke, but she managed a smile in return.

Sarah gripped Ayden's wrist with one hand and pressed the back of the other against his forehead. Angel, face tense and pale, shifted so Sarah had more room.

"You are so grounded for this," Sarah said sternly, and then stroked Ayden's cheek as her eyes shone with love and concern. "But as mad as I am at you, you need to know you saved Melinda's life." She lifted her gaze to Melinda. "You are one lucky girl."

Melinda swallowed and felt her eyes widen. "What…what was it?"

Sarah scooted toward her, eyes focused on Melinda's face. "Let me see your arm first."

Melinda stretched her arm out. Nothing but a small red dot remained near her elbow. The skin around it looked completely normal. Sarah ran her fingers over the underside of Melinda's forearm. It tickled, but wasn't at all painful.

Sarah looked up again. "I want to take more blood, just to be sure, but I think you're going to be completely fine now. If Ayden hadn't done what he did, though…" She inhaled and blinked slowly.

"What was it?" William asked. He and Caryn now stood arm in arm.

Ayden still lay on the floor, head in Angel's lap, as she ran her fingers through his sweat-damp hair. The relief on Angel's face lightened the empty weight in Melinda's chest.

"I honestly don't know," Sarah said. "There were cellular changes in her blood. I can't be sure, but I believe whatever toxin entered her bloodstream was altering her DNA cell by cell. I watched as cells transformed right before my eyes, but it was at a rather slow rate. Too bad it all soaked into the pillow. But a fresh blood test should tell me if Ayden got it all out." She smiled. "By the looks of things, I'm guessing he did."

Melinda laughed. "I guess I won't be turning into Spidergirl, then, huh?"

"We need to find the plant or insect that did that."

Everyone turned to Zack.

"Don't we?" he said. "I mean, we don't want this to happen to anyone else. If we get a specimen, maybe someone can make an antidote."

Sarah nodded. "Wise little guy you have there. Yes, I think that's definitely the next thing on the agenda." She turned to the rest of the group. "*After* these kids get some rest. I'm ordering bed rest for all of you, Melinda, Angel, and especially you, Ayden Teric Reese. And you will *not* change Talents again, you hear me?"

Melinda's eyes popped open and she gulped a breath. The crowd at the hilltop had filled her dreams again, and she clutched the sheet in her fist as she sat up and tried to blink away the image of Doran's face.

Only it wasn't Doran's face.

She focused on her heartbeat, and it slowed, but a flash of dizziness forced her to steady herself with her arms propped behind her on the mattress. Her hand slipped under the pillow and her fingers bumped the leather notebook that had come from Doran's. But before she could grab it, Caryn appeared at the top of the stairs.

"You're awake! How do you feel?"

Melinda scooted back until she was sitting straight up, but kept her hand under the edge of the pillow. The dizziness was gone. "Fine."

Caryn smiled but her eyes darted to the side of her loft where she painted. "Um…would it bother you if I worked? Angel's still sleeping and I can't seem to focus on anything right now."

"No, sure. Go ahead…I'm wide awake…" Melinda spied her writing journal on top of her backpack. She slipped Doran's notebook behind her back, then grabbed her journal and pressed the notebook between it and her stomach. "I'll just go downstairs and write."

Caryn took another step into the loft. "You don't have to leave…"

"No, it's okay—I like the couch for writing." She scooted past Caryn and headed down the stairs, calling over her shoulder, "Have fun painting!"

She dropped onto the end of the couch and tucked the leather notebook between the cushions. The dream surged forward in her mind—she needed to clear her head before she could handle looking at the notebook. She pulled her legs up, tucked them under her, and opened her journal on her lap.

I stand among them, the searchers. Light shines at the top of the hill, but my eyes focus on darkness below. Gnarled trees reach for me like skeletal hands. And his voice calls.

Why do I find it so hard to decide which direction to move?

The darkness has been my home for so long it has become comfort. And he…he resides there, too, the only one to understand.

The light beckons me with promises my soul (do I have one?) has yearned for so strongly. Could those promises be true? If so, I would be a fool to ignore them.

I am a fool.

She lifted the pencil and stuck it crossways between her teeth. The dream images played in her mind, but now that she'd written them down she was able to push them away and turn her thoughts to the notebook with her father's handwriting. She pulled it out from between the cushions and opened it with her journal behind it, then scooted to the other side of the couch with her legs drawn up in front of her.

The scribbling described cellular changes in animals that crazy Dr. Randall had been experimenting on. Her father's handwriting filled the margins with comments regarding the results and suggestions for new experiments. Everything focused on integrating magic into DNA.

Sarah had said her cells were changing, that the toxin was altering her DNA. Doran had shown her the cave lettuce, which took on the magic of other organisms. Did the lettuce give some of its magic out in the process? She thought of the glowing butterflies. They were harmless, but what if some insect fed on the lettuce, or the butterflies—could it have bitten her and transferred the toxin to her?

She continued reading, but found nothing to connect the notes with what had happened to her. Plus, everything in the notes made it sound like they'd been unsuccessful with all their experiments.

There was at least one other notebook, though, with who-knows-what inside. Doran said Dr. Randall told him he'd figured some things out while he was in jail. Maybe her father had, too. They'd never found a body. Was he not dead at all, and really off hiding in some Empowered town with magic of his own? He definitely wasn't here—he wasn't the type to hermit-hole and if he lived in this town, everyone would know him. Maybe somewhere else?

The question that scraped the back of her skull... *Why didn't he come get me and Mom?*

Melinda slammed the notebook shut and then closed her journal around it. She hugged the books against her as she stood and walked to Angel's room.

Angel sat on her bed, propped against frilly pillows, a corded phone tucked between her ear and shoulder. The sappy look on her face told Melinda she was listening to Ayden.

Melinda cleared her throat and Angel glanced up.

"I know loverboy saved my life and all, and you're all *swoony* over his heroics, but call him back later. I need to talk to you." She leaned against the doorframe and pulled the notebook out of her journal. "About my dad."

Chapter Forty

Daddy Dawric

"Ayden, I gotta go."

Angel gaped at Melinda. In all the chaos with Melinda's arm and Ayden's Talent switching, she'd forgotten about the whole reason Melinda had run off—the notebook with her dad's writing in it.

She shushed Ayden's protests. "I'll tell you later."

"Promise?" He sounded hurt.

"Yes, I promise. Now go rest."

There was silence on the phone for a moment and then, "Angel, I..."

His voice made Angel's heart thrum—the way he hesitated as if he wanted to say something important. She swallowed and whispered, "What?"

"I...um...just promise to call me later." Then a soft click.

Angel hung up the phone. She closed her eyes and cleared her thoughts, then looked up at Melinda, who still stood in the doorway with the notebook clutched in her hand.

"Close the door." Angel smoothed the bedspread as she stretched her legs out.

Melinda sat down on the foot of the bed, one leg pulled up beside her and the other hanging over the edge. Her black hair was sleep-rumpled and her oversized gray t-shirt hung off-kilter on her shoulders. Black cotton pants flowed around her legs. She set the notebook on the bed between them.

"You knew all this time, didn't you? My dad was here, working with that kook you hate so much. I want to know the truth—what happened to him?"

Angel's hand dug into her bangs. For a moment, she thought about not telling Melinda the truth. Wouldn't it cause her more pain to know her dad wasn't just self-absorbed, but truly evil? That *he* was the one who'd tried to kill Angel?

If she lied now, it would only make things more complicated. She took a deep breath.

"He's dead, Melinda. Not missing, like the papers say."

Melinda's eyes narrowed and her head shook slightly side-to-side. "The notebook says they were trying to figure out a way to transfer magic by splicing it into the genome of someone without it. Maybe he did it, and moved to another magic place like this. Maybe—"

"No…" Angel sat forward and put her hand on Melinda's knee. "He died. Here. I saw it myself."

Melinda's face tensed. She blinked as if fighting tears, but her eyes stayed ice. "Tell me. All of it."

Angel nodded. She told Melinda the entire story of Dawric—Melinda's father—and Dr. Randall's experiments, and how they'd used Kalek's dagger, and how her father had killed Dr. Damian. Melinda only nodded now and then, and twisted the edge of her t-shirt with one hand. The other hand was clenched around the bedspread.

Finally, Angel got to the part with *Mori Zede*, and how Gregor made the Gate in the door. She'd told Melinda some of the details of the story before, but had left out anything that pointed to her father. Now, as Angel described the way he'd been sucked into the burning ground, relief flooded her at finally telling Melinda everything. But her heart ached at the pain glossing Melinda's eyes.

Angel reached for Melinda's hand, the knuckles of which had turned white from clenching the bedspread.

Melinda snatched her hand away, grabbed her writing journal, and stood up.

"*He deserved it.*"

She marched to the door, wrenched it open, and left the room, leaving the notebook on the bed.

Angel didn't follow. She stared at her open bedroom door and listened to Melinda's clomping footsteps on the wood floor in the hallway, then seconds of quiet, followed by the *tha-thunk* of the back door opening and closing. It took all her strength to stay put.

Give her some space…

Shakespeare appeared in her doorway and padded into the room. He hopped up on the bed.

Angel realized she hadn't seen him since before they left for the carnival the day before. "Where've you been hiding?" she asked as she scratched his chin.

He closed his eyes and purred, then curled up on the bed next to her.

A shadow from a passing cloud dimmed the sunlight coming through the window and Angel turned to peek outside. She waved her hand and the curtain slid across the rod, opening up a view of the back yard. Melinda stood by the fence, gazing out into the forest. Angel's heartbeat quickened. Was she planning on running off again?

Before the fear could set in, Melinda turned and walked back toward the house. Angel relaxed when she heard the door open and close again, and then Melinda's footsteps on the stairs.

She leaned back into the pillow propped against her headboard. The exhaustion of the night before had been only softened by a few hours' sleep. Her fever, chills, and sore throat were gone, but she felt like a rag doll.

The phone rang, and she snatched it up.

"Ayden?"

"Can I speak with your mom?" It was Sarah.

"Is everything okay? Ayden…"

"He's fine. Just tired." Sarah sighed. "We all are, I'm guessing. But no rest for the weary today. I have to go to the University…some kind of minor emergency. Miss Crick said she'd explain when I go there. I don't want Ayden staying home alone, though."

"He can come here! I'm sure Mom and Dad will be fine with it."

"Well, ask your mom first, okay?"

Angel rolled her eyes. *Seriously?* "Okay, hang on."

She jumped out of bed and ran to the living room, up the stairs, and into the loft. Melinda was perched on a stool, still in her pajamas, watching Angel's mom paint. Angel stopped for a second, debating whether to say something, but Melinda's blank stare told her it would only make things worse.

No…better to give her time. Besides, Sarah was waiting.

Angel relayed what Sarah had said and got a muffled "*mm-hm, fine*" from around the paintbrush held between her mom's teeth, then she ran downstairs and told Sarah to send Ayden over.

The second she hung up the phone rang again.

"Hello?"

"Angel, I need to speak with your father." Sir Benjamin's voice sounded burdened. *What's he need Dad for?*

"Sir B, hey. Um, he's probably out working in his shop. I'll go get him."

"Thank you, Angel. How are you feeling? Sarah told me what happened. I'm glad to hear your friend is okay."

"Yeah, she's…well, she seems to be all healed from the sting or whatever. But there's a whole lot more to the story that I'm going to have to tell you."

His voice got even heavier. "There always is, isn't there?"

"Sir B, is everything all right?" Why did he sound like that? Was something up with Dr. Randall?

"I really can't go into it. Actually, that's why I called. Is your father around?"

Huh? He just asked that…

"Yeah, he's here." She bit her lip and shifted the phone against her ear. "I told you that, remember?"

She heard a deep sigh.

"I'm sorry…I'm so distracted here, Maggie."

Maggie? That was his late wife's name. In all the time Angel had known him, he'd never called her that. If what he was doing was that stressful, she hoped it was over soon.

"I'll go get Dad. You take care, okay, Sir B?"

"Thanks, sweetie."

Angel ran down the hall to the kitchen, then out the back door and around to the small workshop her dad had added to the end of the house. She knocked on the door as she opened it, and called for him to pick up the phone, then went back inside. When she reached her room, she picked up the receiver that she'd left lying on the bed, and put it to her ear to make sure her dad was on.

"Sure, Benjamin," she heard him say, "I can probably have one made by tomorrow morning. Is that soon enough?"

She was going to hang up the phone when Sir Benjamin said, "That's fine," and his voice hitched as he added, "just fine." And then he was crying.

Angel covered the mouthpiece.

"Benjamin?" her dad said.

"Yes, yes, William. I'm sorry." He inhaled. When he continued his voice was steadier, but still hung heavy. "Remember what I mentioned to you the other day? It's happened again. At first I thought it might be because of the stress, like you said before. But it was too real this time. She was so close, right there next to the shop. I saw her—it was Maggie plain as day. I'm not imagining it, Will. How he's doing it from here, I don't know, but it's got to be him."

Angel bit down hard on her lip and gently hung up the phone.

Was Kalek right? Was Dr. Randall somehow pulling people back from the dead? Gregor and Siophra…and Sir Benjamin's wife? Could that be why he's unconscious?

Angel thought back to the times she'd seen Sir Benjamin looking so strange, and Ayden's words: "He looks as if he's seen a ghost."

Could this be Dr. Randall's revenge?

Angel and Sir Benjamin were definitely people Dr. Randall hated. And anyone related to Aldrik Halvard, which explained why he'd terrorize Kalek, too. Maybe Aldrik's stroke had been caused by *him* seeing a ghost as well—and Kalek had talked about how his mom seemed to have suffered a breakdown. Had she seen something, too?

It made more sense than Kalek's hypothesis, although Angel liked that one much better. If Doran was just playing a prank, it was mean and spiteful. But if Dr. Randall was somehow drawing spirits back to Earth….

Angel shivered. She'd have to talk to Kalek about it. After she chewed him out for leaving last night, of course. She still couldn't believe he did that!

He hadn't even come back to check on Melinda or Ayden. Should she Find him? He hated when she did that, but it'd been so long.

Only for a second…

She concentrated, just enough to get a fix on him. An image formed of him standing in a hallway with dark walls reflecting the flicker of ornate sconces. He was at home. At least he was safe. *Why* hadn't he come back?

Nothing she could do anyway. At least not until after something to eat and then a shower.

She grabbed Dr. Randall's notebook off the bed and stashed it in her dresser, then headed into the hall. When she stepped into the living room and saw the clock, her heart began to pound.

Almost noon. Sarah had called twenty minutes ago and said Ayden was coming over right away. Angel had gotten so sidetracked by Sir Benjamin's call and being mad at Kalek, she hadn't realized how much time had gone by.

Why wasn't he here yet?

She went into the kitchen and called his house. Her heart thrummed faster after five rings…six…nine….

She hung up and walked back into the living room.

Melinda clomped down the stairs in black combat boots. Baggy jeans hung off her hips below a fitted black t-shirt. Her eyes still sad and dark, she turned to Angel as she reached the bottom of the stairs.

Angel twisted a strand of hair at her shoulder. "Hey, um, can you tell my mom I'm going over to check on Ayden? He was supposed to be here by now and he's not answering the phone."

Melinda's lip curled in a smirk. "He's probably showering or something. Maybe I should go with you and chaperone."

"Not funny. Please—I'll be right back."

The smirk dropped, and Melinda shrugged. "Hang on. I'll tell her while you get some clothes on, and I'll go with you for real."

The idea of not going over alone suddenly sounded really good. She nodded, and then dashed to her room and pulled on jeans and a t-shirt.

When Angel got back to the living room, Melinda stood by the front door, hand already on the knob.

They walked over to Ayden's house. Angel inhaled to calm her nerves as she knocked.

And knocked again.

No answer.

Melinda reached past her and pounded on the door with the side of her fist. "Yo, loverboy! Open up!"

Angel was too worried to get angry, and shifted from one foot to the other as she twisted her hair. Where was he?

The scraping of Melinda's boot grabbed Angel's attention. Melinda had turned around, and then she jumped off the front steps and headed around the side of the house.

Angel jumped down and followed.

They came around to the back yard. Melinda was already a few yards ahead, almost to the back door, which Angel couldn't yet see.

"Holy sh—" Melinda slammed to a stop.

Angel rushed forward to join her, and then dropped to her knees as fear constricted her throat.

The back door was wide open, and red smeared the concrete pad below it. Red streaked the edge of the door as well, as if a blood-covered hand had gripped it and then was pulled away.

A dual trail in the leaves, as though two feet were being dragged across the ground, led from the back stoop to the far side of the fence, where a small gate hung slightly ajar.

Chapter Forty-One

Taken

Melinda sank to her knees next to Angel and wrapped her arm around Angel's trembling shoulders.

"Come on, we need to get your parents."

Angel nodded, face ghost white and chin quivering.

Melinda helped her to her feet. She grabbed Angel's hand and they ran full-speed back to Angel's house.

Caryn was coming down the stairs when they burst through the front door. Her eyes widened as the dreamy expression she normally wore while painting dissipated.

"Anna, what's wrong?"

She scurried the rest of the way down and wrapped her arms around her daughter.

Angel dropped her head onto Caryn's shoulder and sobbed.

"It's Ayden," Melinda said, feeling as if she were disconnected from her body—her mind knew she should be panicking, but somehow she'd gone on autopilot. "Something's happened…He's…." She sucked in a breath. "Maybe I should just get William and show him."

Without waiting for an answer, Melinda dashed through the kitchen, out the back door, and straight to William's shop. She threw the door open without knocking.

William glanced up at her. She expected him to get angry, but he jumped up from his stool and moved around the table. When he reached her, he put his hands gently on her elbows.

"What's wrong?"

She told him what she and Angel had seen, and with nothing more than a nod, he was out the door and running toward Ayden's house. Melinda followed.

When they reached the back yard, William turned to her. "You stay out here. I'm going in to check out the house."

"But—"

"I mean it! If I'm not out in five minutes, go back home and call for help."

He ducked into the house.

Melinda couldn't stand still. She paced back and forth, peering into the door, but stayed a couple of yards away. Soft clanking and shuffling noises came from inside, but nothing alarming. It just sounded like William was searching.

Finally, he appeared in the doorway again, where he stopped and inspected the blood smears.

He shook his head and then walked back over to her.

"The inside of the house looks fine. Nothing out of the ordinary. Whatever happened was right there at the back door." Enough sunlight filtered through the overcast sky and glinted off his glasses that Melinda couldn't see his eyes, but the rest of his face was grim. "Let's get back home and figure out our next move. We need to call the authorities if Caryn hasn't already."

They found Caryn and Angel in the living room, huddled on the couch. Both their heads lifted when Melinda and William walked in the door.

"We called the station," Caryn said. "They're sending someone out to investigate. I told them you'd gone over there and everything Anna told me. Sarah was already there, filing a report because her lab was broken into. They convinced her to stay because she's more of a help there." She closed her eyes and pressed her lips together. When her eyes opened, they were filled with as much anger as worry. "They seem to think Dr. Randall may actually have something to do with this, and if she can help him regain consciousness they can make him stop and find out where Ayden is. I don't understand. How can he be involved?"

William stepped over and sat next to Caryn, sliding his hand into hers. Melinda glanced at Angel, who stared at her parents with the strangest look.

What's up with her?

It was definitely more than just Ayden's disappearance. Angel sat forward as if hanging on her father's words as he told them about Sir Benjamin seeing visions of his late wife. Angel's head moved with the slightest nod, and she swiped her hand through her bangs in that weird way she did when she got nervous. It always made her scrunch her face or snatch her hand away as if she'd touched something hot, and Melinda could never figure out why Angel acted like it was such a bad habit.

Angel pushed her hands against her thighs and took a deep breath. Angel's parents looked curiously at her and waited.

Melinda found herself staring. Angel was jabbering something about seeing Gregor the same way Sir B had seen his wife—and then she said, as she glanced at Melinda, "And, Mom, remember what Kalek said about seeing Siophra?"

Caryn pressed her lips together. "I'd forgotten about that. I thought he was just grieving."

William's brow crinkled, but he nodded. "I told Benjamin the same thing about seeing Maggie. It makes sense. The anniversary of Siophra's death is coming up, and so is Benjamin's wedding anniversary." He sighed.

Melinda sat down on the edge of the chair. She'd thought Kalek was just always being arrogant, but if he was being tortured with visions of his sister, that was a whole different story.

"Hey, you okay?" Caryn's voice snapped Melinda back to attention.

"Uh, yeah," Melinda said. "Kinda mind-blowing though, huh? Some guy doing all that from so far away."

William pulled his glasses off and looked at Melinda, his eyebrows pinched. "I don't know about that hypothesis. It seems a bit far-fetched. Sir Benjamin has an emotional stake in this. He's got a lot of reasons to hate Dr. Randall."

"But he's helping the guy…"

"Not exactly," Caryn said. "He's helping to solve what's happened to him, yes. But it's because the jail is set up to withhold powers, and if it's failing for some reason, they have to figure out how. It's not just Sir Benjamin out there. There's a team of people working on this, to ensure no other prisoners start getting their powers back as well."

Melinda looked Caryn in the eye. "You think he's doing this, though, right?"

Caryn glanced nervously at William, and then back to Melinda. "Not exactly. I think he got his Talent back, but it malfunctioned. I'm not sure he'd be capable of projecting images from so far away."

"Then who's doing it?" Melinda had a feeling she knew what Caryn's answer would be.

"Listen, Melinda..." Caryn moved her arm from Angel's shoulders and put her hands in her lap, prayer-style around William's. "I know you like this guy, and we're trying very hard to trust him, but—"

"It's not Doran." Melinda said it as calmly as she could. At this point, she could not afford to come across as defensive. A thought bubbled in the back of her head, something that, if true, would change everything.

Her hand automatically moved toward the cellphone case she normally carried. It wasn't there, and her fingers twitched until she dug them into the chair arm. She swallowed and steeled herself.

"It can't be Doran. He really doesn't have magic."

William cleared his throat, and said softly. "He could be faking.""

Melinda nodded. "I know. But he's not. And the reason I know he's not is what makes me think he's the one who took Ayden."

Angel all but popped right off the couch.

"What? Melinda, are you serious?" Her voice cracked. "You think...oh my God, *are you serious*?"

"I...I don't know how he knows..." Melinda glanced back and forth between Angel and her parents. Three gazes bore into her and she shifted under their weight. "Doran must know about Ayden's Talent. If he does, it would totally explain why he took him." Her fingers dug deeper into the couch. "He's found a way to get his magic back but it has to come from someone else, and with Ayden he'd get all the Talents he wants."

Angel covered her mouth with her hand and shook her head. Her words came between gasps. "He's going to kill Ayden...Noooo...We can't let him...No, no, no, no...."

Melinda slid forward and dropped to her knees in front of Angel. "He won't kill him. He doesn't have to. That doesn't work anyway, not permanently. Dr. Randall's notes talk about a plant, though—something that can do it."

Angel's eyes widened and her hand lowered to her lap. "I remember…that night, your…your dad. He said something about a plant that has some amino acid or something…"

"Yes! Dr. Randall told Doran all about it. Doran's been working on his experiments, trying to finish them. So he can get magic…"—her head dropped—"…and so can I."

She felt Angel's hand touch her shoulder and she looked up. Angel stared down at her, eyes shifting ever so slightly as she smiled a quivering smile. "You *have* magic, Melinda. You don't need him."

Melinda nodded and inhaled, blinking back tears. "Whether I have magic or not, you're right. I don't need him. Not if he'd hurt Ayden." She turned to Caryn and William. "I know where he is."

"Are you sure?" Caryn asked. "Because we can have Angel—"

"No, I'm sure."

"I can't Find him anyway," Angel said with a quavering voice as she looked at her mom. "I've tried before, and it doesn't work—and I've been trying to Find Ayden this whole time, but it's not working either."

"You're upset, though," Caryn said.

"This is different. I think something from him being in jail interferes even with whoever he's with." She turned to Melinda, fear and hope mingling in her eyes. "Are you sure you know where he is?"

Melinda nodded.

"Then let's go," William said as he stood. He held out his hand to Melinda and she let him pull her to her feet.

Caryn and Angel jumped up as well just as Zack appeared in the hall entrance. "I'm going, too!"

"No, you're not, little man," Angel said.

He shook his head, sending his curls in a wild bounce. "I am going! I can help! I can Magnify the things we find out there, and maybe see what stung Melinda. Or—"

"I said *no*." Angel looked at Caryn. "Tell him *no*, Mom."

William shook his head. "I hate to say it, but he's right. If by some chance Melinda is wrong about where Doran is, Zack can look for signs of where they may have passed through. I don't want to waste time coming back for Zack if we need him."

Angel's head bobbed in a slight nod. She turned toward the hall. "Horatio! Zoe! Let's go!"

Chapter Forty-Two

Leading the Way

Zoe tugged the leash so hard Angel's sneakers slid on the leaves as she dashed through the forest behind Melinda. She dug her heels in and nearly lost her balance coming around the trunk of a sprawling tree with spiny bark and purple-tinted leaves. It was a species she'd never seen before.

Actually, a lot of the plants looked unfamiliar…

Where is she taking us?

The ground sloped upwards slightly. She glanced over her shoulder at her parents and Zack. Her mom's face was tense with the effort of running, but Angel could tell it was more than that—this place wasn't familiar to her either. She couldn't read her dad's expression, but the way he scanned the area told her he was cataloguing information. Zack's eyes were wide and focused.

Horatio looped around Angel and the others, zipping between them in a blur. His chittering jangled Angel's already stretched nerves, but she held her tongue. She was pretty sure he was calling out to creatures in the forest, but nothing called back. Why were there no animals around here?

Angel pushed forward and caught up to Melinda.

"Are you sure we're going the right way?"

"Yeah," she huffed. Her face was flushed and sweat glistened on her skin. Black hair clung to the rim of her face and neck. "Not too much farther, I don't think. I came from a different way last time, but..." She glanced around and then cocked her head to the right. "More that way."

They shifted direction. The trees were less dense here. Tall and spindly, with bronze leaves shaped like palms fronds. Vines snaked over all their trunks, deep red and vicious looking. Definitely someplace Angel had never been.

Another minute or two passed and a cramp stabbed Angel's side. She pushed on, digging the heel of her hand into her ribs as she adjusted her grip on Zoe's leash. She would *not* stop, no matter what. Every now and then she tried to Find Ayden and got the same odd darkness she'd gotten when she'd tried to Find Melinda after the carnival. She took it to mean Ayden was with Doran—and she clung to the idea that it must mean he was still alive.

Her throat burned, and she gulped air and pumped harder.

Zack's muffled voice called from behind.

Angel slammed to a stop, and Melinda skidded up next to her.

"Over here!" he called again, this time clearly. "I found something!"

Angel and Melinda glanced at each other and then took off toward Zack. Her parents stood beside him gazing into a huge bush. Its leaves fluttered as if a breeze swirled around the bush, but nothing else moved—not the scrubby ferns on either side or the low branches of the spruce a few feet away.

"Zack, you can't stop us for weird bushes," Angel snapped. She was about to turn and start running again when he grabbed her arm.

"Not the plant, Angel. That."

Angel squinted as she scanned the bush where he pointed. "What?"

Then she saw it. The silver ring Ayden always wore on his right hand was stuck over the leafless end of one of the branches.

She reached out, hand trembling.

Zack grabbed her wrist. "Those aren't leaves on there. They're some kind of leaf-mimicking insect."

Angel looked harder. She saw leaves, only leaves. But she trusted Zack's Talent.

He held his hand up. "I'll get it."

"Okay," she said. "But be careful."

He gave her a look that said, *duh*, and turned his gaze toward the bush, concentration hardening his little boy face. The ring wobbled slightly, then began to slide along the branch.

A wave of movement rippled through the insect-leaves, and a mass of them converged on the ring.

Angel and Zack stumbled back, but before they could get out of the way, thousands of green insects swarmed them.

Blocking her face with one arm, Angel grabbed Zack with the other. But he yanked out of her grasp and ran.

The insects swarmed after him.

A scream clawed its way out of Angel's throat as she watched Zack flailing in the mass of insects.

Horatio darted past her and into the swarm, hissing in a way Angel had never heard before.

The insects dispersed instantly. Angel, her parents and Melinda ducked as winged leaves fanned out over their heads.

Angel lunged forward and skidded to where Zack lay on the ground.

Welts already marred his smooth, fair skin. His eyes were swollen closed and he moaned softly but didn't move. She called his name, but he didn't respond.

Her dad's arm circled her shoulders.

She pressed her weight against him

The ground was slipping out from under her.

Zack...

"He's breathing fine but we need to get him out of here," her mom said as she leaned over Zack. She stroked his bangs back and pressed her fingers against his forehead. "He's already feeling warm, but this doesn't look at all like the reaction Melinda had. Let's pray that means it's something there's an antidote to."

"We still have to get to Ayden," Angel said as panic squeezed her. She couldn't leave Zack, but she couldn't stop searching for Ayden. Her heart pounded so hard her ribs ached, and fear-laced energy surged through her. With a burst of adrenaline, she squeezed her eyes shut and concentrated once again on Ayden–and finally got a hazy view of him, as though he were sitting in deep shadow. She could just make out the contours of his face, eyes closed, and a trail of blood like an oily stream from temple to chin.

Behind him was pitch black but for a spot of greenish glow.

Angel's eyes popped open. She turned to Melinda and told her the vague direction and distance she sensed Ayden's presence.

Melinda's eyes glazed as she stared at Zack, and Angel at first thought she hadn't heard.

Melinda turned to her. "Then I was right."

"He's alive," Angel said. "But he's hurt, and I can't tell *exactly* where he is. It's someplace dark…"

"It's a cave." Melinda's voice dropped. "What if I take William, and you and Caryn get Zack to town?"

Angel's dad squeezed her shoulders. "That sounds like a good plan. Horatio can go ahead of you and get Sir Benjamin. If anyone knows what those insects are it's him."

Angel hugged her dad as tightly as she could. "I love you," she whispered.

She let go and looked down at Zack—his sweet face distorted and so still. She bit her lip and blinked back angry tears. He was still breathing normally and the welting hadn't gotten any worse, but it had only been a minute or so. Angel shifted into a squat and slipped one arm under his shoulders and one under his knees. He moaned as she lifted him up, and his head lolled against her upper arm.

She inhaled a ragged breath and pressed her cheek against his hot forehead as she hugged him to her. "Little man, you gotta make it!"

"You remember the way out of here?" she asked her mom.

"Yes. Let's go."

Her mom turned to her dad and touched his cheek. "Be careful," she said, and then kissed him.

Angel headed back the way they'd come. Her mom moved ahead, calling out or kicking away anything that might be a tripping hazard so Angel could walk as fast as possible without having to look down.

"We'll get him there," her mom called over her shoulder. "Sir Benjamin will know exactly what to do. He's going to be fine. They're both going to be fine."

"I know," Angel said. And she did know. She'd seen something in Melinda's eyes that told her Doran didn't stand a chance.

Chapter Forty-Three

Shadows

They reached the cave in minutes. William grabbed Melinda's arm, forcing her to stop a few feet from the entrance. Clouds hid the sun above them, tingeing the rock around the entrance with a ghostly gray, as they stood in the shadow of a tall tree.

"Me first," William whispered. He stared straight ahead, eyes narrowed.

Melinda wanted to insist she should go first, but she couldn't think of anything William would buy. She couldn't control her magic. She knew how to fight, of course, but Doran was an ex-con who'd beat a cop to a pulp. No chance against that.

The thought sent shivers through her. She'd been so sure he wouldn't hurt her—partly convinced he *couldn't* hurt her. But he was a criminal, and a dangerous one. What had she been thinking?

She nodded at William, but her breath caught as she pictured him facing Doran. William was older and more experienced, with magic that Doran didn't have—but William didn't strike Melinda as a fighter.

He stepped in front of her, and she exhaled. He'd said he wanted to go first, but that didn't mean she had to stay outside. She followed close behind as he entered the cave. The air was damp and warm.

Glowing butterflies clung to the walls in scattered patches, but most of the rock was bare and dark. Where were the rest? She hadn't seen any in the forest.

Melinda's boot slid, just enough to tell her it wasn't rock beneath her.

She swallowed and looked down. Faded and lifeless butterflies carpeted the cave floor from wall to wall. They crunched softly under her feet as she crept forward behind William. *What the—?* Why would they all start dying at once?

The darkness thickened around them as they moved deeper in, away from the entrance. Several more butterflies dropped to the ground from the walls and ceiling, floating like flakes of ash until they landed soundlessly in the mass grave with the others.

They closed in on the opening to the next chamber. Melinda's hands tightened to fists at her sides. William glanced over his shoulder. The faint green glow of the remaining butterflies reflected in his glasses, obscuring his eyes, and the rest of his face was barely visible in the darkness. But Melinda read his meaning. She nodded.

Ayden and Doran had to be back there. Or—Melinda let a hopeful thought creep in—maybe just Ayden. Maybe Doran had gotten what he needed and left. Angel said Ayden was hurt but still alive…Doran might have bolted before Ayden could wake up and fight back.

For some reason, Melinda's thoughts shifted to her dreams and the light that had called her from the top of the hill. Something about it comforted her, and she found herself mouthing the words, *Please help us…*

She shook her head. What could a light from a dream do?

William stopped again. They were at the edge of the chamber entrance. She watched as his hand pressed against the rock lining the opening, waited for him to lean forward to peer into the room…

He jerked forward, the hand he'd pressed against the wall was no longer visible as his arm stretched through the opening. He opened his mouth as if to scream, but his voice gurgled from his throat and he slumped to the floor.

Melinda dropped down beside him. A syringe protruded from his arm. He was breathing deeply as if asleep.

She looked up, heart rattling, but no one was there. The opening had been dark but obviously empty…

"Doran?" she whispered.

No answer.

She checked William again—still breathing fine. No blood that she could see. Nor that she could feel as she gently ran her fingertips around the back of his head and along the ground. The lifeless butterflies crumbled under her touch, and she pulled her hand away.

Finally, she reached over and eased the syringe from his arm. It was empty, but it was better than nothing. If Doran got too close, maybe she could stab him in the eye, or…

Movement caught Melinda's attention. A shifting of shadow just on the other side of the chamber entry. She squinted, trying to get a better look. There was definitely something there, but she could see no more than a deeper darkening about the size of a person.

"I know you're there." She tightened her fist around the syringe, but held it behind her and stood. Nearly gagging as she forced sweetness into her voice, she said, "He's unconscious, so you can come out now."

The shadow rippled as Melinda stared, light patches streaking through and colors mingling with the dark. In a matter of seconds Doran stood where the human-shaped shadow had been.

"How did you do that?" Of course she knew—he'd somehow succeeded in getting magic. Was Ayden his source, though? She didn't let herself ask the question. Better to play dumb and hopefully he'd lead her right to Ayden and then…

And then what, she didn't know.

He smiled, catlike, and stepped toward her. "If you follow me, you'll be able to do it, too."

"You figured out how to get rid of the toxin?" Melinda cringed at the involuntary enthusiasm in her voice.

He nodded. "For sure this time."

"What do you mean, 'this time'?"

His eyes glowed silver-gray and twitched to the side. "I just mean…finally."

The tone of his voice told Melinda he meant much more. She leaned toward the entryway, trying to peer into the chamber beyond, but couldn't see far enough through the darkness to tell if Ayden was there.

"Come on. Follow me." Doran stepped into the chamber.

Melinda scanned the shadowed room as she entered, her eyes quickly adjusting, but there was no sign of Ayden. Why wasn't he here? The creepy plants looked the same. What was different? How had Doran gotten rid of the toxin? Too much seemed to not add up, and a wave of panic washed over her.

Doran walked to the wall on the left side of the chamber. He reached over and opened a box sitting on a small ledge that jutted out from the rock like a shelf. He pulled out another syringe and carried it over to her. The liquid inside gave off the same faint green tint that the butterflies had before they started dying.

"That's from the plants?"

His head tilted as he held the syringe at eye level and gently thumped the side. "Of course."

"Aaaand…where did the—" She inhaled and glanced around the room again. Swallowed. Her voice creaked. "Whose magic is it?"

"Does it matter?"

"Yes, it does."

He held the plunger of the syringe with his thumb but didn't move toward her. In the dark, she couldn't make out the color of his eyes, but his expression flashed with irritation, and she imagined his eyes swirling grey-black and stormy.

"Tell me, Doran." Her voice was stronger now, but her heart beat erratically. "Whose magic? And where is he? What did you do with him?"

Doran's hand twitched and he pointed the syringe at Melinda. "Why do you assume it's a *him*? Although I suppose I shouldn't be surprised you figured it out. Your father was a brilliant man, and you would have gotten at least some intelligence from him."

"My father? What would you know—?"

Doran leaned forward, still pointing the syringe at her. "I know who you are. It took a little while to figure it out, but I put the pieces together. I also put the pieces together about your friend's boyfriend. His ability to change Talents. The *perfect* magic to take, don't you think? You can do anything!"

Melinda's hand tightened on the syringe behind her back so hard she feared it might break. "Where is he?"

"Don't worry. He's fine. Just tucked away for now. Sleeping, like your friend's father over there." He glanced at the opening to the outside chamber where William must still be knocked out. "Why did you bring him, anyway? I thought you wanted away from that family."

"We were looking for Ayden. Did you think we'd all just sit around if he got kidnapped? That we'd let him get killed?"

"Kidnapped…" His head shook suddenly, like someone with palsy. "Killed…no. No, I wouldn't do that. I just needed—" His words slammed short with a hiccup.

Doran shifted from one foot to the other, his head shaking even more. He slapped his hands against his ears. "It wasn't supposed to happen this way…I thought I had it all worked out. I really thought it was going to work the first time, but then…"

He looked up at her, head jerking only slightly, and lowered one arm, then held it out where she could see it better. Several red welts ran across his forearm as if a rope had been tied too tightly around and then yanked off. "I wanted to surprise you. I used my own magic the first time…"

Melinda took a step back. "What do you mean the first time? An—and you told me you didn't have magic!"

"I *had* to tell you that." His tone bordered on whining, and he held his other arm out. "In a way it's true. My magic changed, and I don't know why, but I thought with us…*together*—with you not having any, it might purify it. I could fix you, and then you could fix me…" His arms dropped to his sides. "But it didn't work."

He stood in the faint glow from the plants on the ground, but Melinda shifted into the shadows. She knew they couldn't protect her, but she felt so exposed, vulnerable…

What was he saying? His words whipped around inside her skull, and she gulped the dank air as she tried to process everything. Her arm tingled in the spot she'd been stung, and then realization hit. Her head popped up.

"You poisoned me! It wasn't an insect or a plant! You injected me with…with what? That plant extract after you let it touch you?" Her hand twitched and she remembered the syringe she held. She raised her arm and flung it at him, but it flew past his shoulder. "You experimented on me like some lab rat!"

"No—it wasn't like that. I found you here. I thought you'd come because you wanted me to help you, but you were asleep, shivering and burning up…I thought if I gave you magic it would *help* you. But then your arm…" He reached up and cupped the back of his neck with his hand. "I took you back so they could help you while I figured out what went wrong. And then that boy changed, and healed you, and I realized what he could do—what *we* could do with that kind of Talent."

"So you *kidnapped* him? And thought I'd be okay with that?"

"I asked him to come, but he—it wasn't supposed to be this way! Not again!"

Melinda took another step back and her heel caught on something. She fell backwards, landing hard on her hip and tucking her arm against her head to avoid cracking her skull on the rock floor. She struggled to retrieve the breath that had slammed out of her.

As her head cleared, she pushed herself up and looked around. To her right another unnatural shadow clung to the floor. She reached forward and touched the darkness where she'd tripped.

It felt like denim, like jeans over someone's leg. She gasped and pulled her hand away, staring hard at the shadow.

Doran's angry curse sliced through the air, and in seconds the shadow flickered with color and Ayden was in its place.

Chapter Forty-Four

Revealing

Melinda scrambled toward him and knelt by his side. Blood trailed down Ayden's face in several places, but she saw none anywhere else.

Nasty welts like Doran's marred his arm.

His chest moved steadily up and down. "Only sleeping," Doran had said. Like William. He must have injected them both with some sort of anesthesia.

She glared up at Doran.

He stood a couple of yards away, still armed with the syringe, but his eyes were glazed. There was something strange about his appearance. As his hand lifted and ran through his hair, it struck her. The movements didn't line up quite right…

What am I not seeing?

A light appeared near the cave ceiling. Faintly at first, but increasing in intensity as it moved down and closer.

Huh?

Melinda blinked. It was still there.

Doran seemed completely unaware as it nearly engulfed the area around him. It pulsed as though alive, stretching from wall to wall, and filling the room with warmth. The rock walls glowed in response to the touch of the light, matching the beat of the pulse.

Melinda grabbed Ayden's hand, willing his eyes to open, as the realization hit her.

"It's here!"

"What's here?" Doran spun, head jerking as he looked around the room, terror streaked across his face. "There's no one here!"

"You don't see the light?" she asked.

He shook his head angrily, and grabbed a rock from the ground.

"What are you talking about? There's no light in here! It's getting *darker*!" He brandished the rock like a weapon, nervously glancing around and backing toward the far wall.

Why was he acting so terrified? Melinda squeezed her eyes shut. *Am I imagining it? Dreaming again?*

When she opened her eyes, the light was still there. It pushed through the room, swirled and coalesced, pulsing and condensing as it had in her dreams, into a glowing ball in front of her. The warmth permeated even more strongly. It caressed her cheek, sending a wave of comfort through her and calming her trembling limbs.

Please tell me I'm not crazy…

Melinda felt the light reaching out for her. A single word formed in her head, not spoken by a voice she could hear, but rather felt like music playing insider her.

"See."

"Who are you?" she asked.

Doran's voice cut through, harsh and painful to her ears. "You know who I am! Who are you talking to?" He stood still as a statue, seemingly glued to the floor, fear etched on his face, knuckles white as he gripped the rock and stared at Melinda. His mouth hung half-open, but he didn't speak again.

"I don't understand," she said.

The light pulsed and music played in her mind again, that somehow translated to words. *"You have known all along, but you refuse to see. Reveal him."* A pause—and Melinda felt the presence pulling away. *"I must go now. I'm being called."*

Melinda's heart raced and she shifted on her knees. "You can't leave yet! I don't know what you mean!"

As she moved forward, the light faded slightly. It reached into her mind again, but not with music-words this time. A vision formed, the one from her recurring dream, a light at the top of a hill, beckoning to her. At the bottom of the hill, Doran stood with the dark forest clawing the air behind him. His image wavered, flickering into darkness and then back again.

A cough burst through the vision in Melinda's mind, and she turned to see Ayden gasping and blinking. His eyes widened and he tried to sit up, but only fell back against the rock.

"Melinda, he's—"

"I know," she said as she turned toward Doran.

He hadn't moved, but his expression was no longer one of confusion. He glared with venom at them.

The light's words crept into Melinda's mind, *"You have known all along, but you refuse to see. Reveal him."*

Doran was not Doran. Or at least, not the Doran he appeared to be.

"Reveal him."

She understood what it meant, but she didn't know how to do it.

She thought about the odd things that had happened to her, the things no one else seemed to notice or understand. Caryn's mirror revealing the diary to her. Was it really meant for her, as Angel had said? Or had she somehow made it show itself?

The notebook with her father's writing. Doran had told her it was a computer manual, and Angel had said that's what she saw it as, too—but Melinda had seen it for what it really was.

She stared at Doran as she stood. Ayden grabbed her hand and tugged, protesting even as his grip weakened and his hand slid past her fingertips.

Doran gripped the rock in one hand and the syringe in the other. Melinda stared hard and concentrated, trying to look past his appearance to what she knew had to be hidden beneath.

Anger, hatred, vileness, ugliness, death…

She clutched her stomach and fought the desire to release her gaze from those awful, swirling gray eyes. Melinda recoiled as she saw his flesh shift, phasing in and out like a hologram flickering from power fluctuations.

Piece by piece, the image of Doran disappeared, his long, sandy hair replaced by thin, graying strands, broad shoulders sagging into a bony frame, and swirling gray eyes sinking into hollow sockets.

"That's the guy from the University—Dr. Randall!"

Ayden's voice snapped Melinda's attention, but the image stayed. In

Doran's place stood a haggard old man, with a tattered gray lab coat and pants crookedly hemmed above sockless ankles.

Melinda's skin crawled. *This is the real Doran? This pathetic old man?*

Dr. Randall looked down at his arms and then back up at Melinda. He growled, "How did you do this?"

He raised his arm and hurled the rock at her.

She ducked, and the rock glanced off the wall behind her. As she straightened up again, she yelled, "You freak! You sick old freak!" She lunged forward, but yanked to a stop as Ayden's hand grabbed her leg. She looked down at him.

Now kneeling, he shook his head, then and let go and pushed himself up. He stood, slightly wobbling, beside her.

Dr. Randall made no other move. When she looked back at him, he was staring down at his hands, his tattered clothes. His head shook side to side as if saying, *no, no no….*

When his head lifted, desperation emanated from his sunken eyes.

"It wasn't supposed to be like this. It wasn't…." He gasped in a breath and began to sob. "I only ever wanted to help. I only ever wanted to bring us together."

He reached up and pulled his hair back behind his ears.

What?

Melinda blinked and looked more closely. *They're pointed!*

She heard Ayden beside her, whispering under his breath, "He's Elven. He's freaking Elven."

Dr. Randall turned and faced an empty spot in front of him, staring blankly.

"We should all have magic…humans, Elven…all of us…" His head snapped to the side, and his gaze bore down on the rows of sickly glowing plants.

"Tell them—tell them I never meant to kill her. Siophra…" He inhaled again, and held the syringe up in front of himself as if he were going to stab the air. He gazed at the spot as if someone stood there, and his lip trembled. "She startled me. I didn't mean to…she was nothing like her father, nothing like him."

He dropped the syringe and looked directly at Melinda. "It all changed. I don't know why, and I can't change it back."

Before Melinda could respond to his words or the pity that suddenly sank into her, Dr. Randall dove at the plants on the cave floor. Their glow intensified as his body thudded in the middle of the insane garden, and tentacle-like roots snapped up from everywhere. The roots whipped toward him and wrapped around him, while the cabbage-like leaves unfurled, stretching up and out, covering his body.

A scream resounded and echoed through the room—ghastly, agonizing—and Melinda clamped her hands over her ears and curled forward. Her stomach twisted and lurched inside of her, as Dr. Randall's horrified cries resonated louder and louder. She felt Ayden's arms wrap around her.

Then another set of arms.

Breath heated her neck as William said sharply, "Melinda, let's go."

William pulled gently and Ayden pushed from the other side, but she refused to budge. She forced her eyes open again and looked at the ravenous garden in front of her. The broad, open leaves shuddered and danced where Dr. Randall struggled beneath. His screams died down, allowing a wet crunching sound to mingle in.

Melinda's legs quaked and she fought the urge to retch.

The garden went still momentarily. The leaves shuddered one last time, and then retracted, the plants tightening in on themselves. Tattered cloth and bloody clumps lay strewn between the plants. Melinda's stomach churned again, but she couldn't pull her gaze away.

Shadows oozed like black tar from where the remains of Dr. Randall lay. Up and over the plants, slinking into leaf and root. As they touched each plant, the glow disappeared and the leaves darkened and shriveled.

The stench of decay rose up, forcing Melinda to slide her hands from her ears to cover her mouth and nose. She finally let William and Ayden pull her from the chamber.

They dashed through the front part of the cave, where the walls were now bare of butterflies and the carpet of fading green wings had thickened. They burst out into the overcast forest. Melinda gulped in a breath of air and released it in a sob. Ayden tightened his arm around her shoulder. She gazed up at him.

Without thought, she focused. Tingling coursed under her skin and she sensed true concern coming from him. Friendship. Worry about Angel—and a love for her that out-shone all else.

Melinda smiled through her tears. *I'm so telling her she needs to hang on to this one.*

She pulled away from Ayden and turned to William. She was slammed with a feeling that nearly knocked the breath from her. Fatherly love. Tears flowed harder as she flung her arms around his chest.

"I'm so sorry, William."

His arms wrapped around her and she felt his head move side to side against the top of her own.

"No, *I'm sorry*, Melinda. I didn't do enough to protect you from Doran."

Ayden's voice came from their side. "It wasn't Doran. It was that creepy guy from the University. Dr. Randall."

William's eyes widened as he let go of Melinda and she stepped back. "I couldn't see who knocked me out, but I assumed it was Doran."

"It was, but it wasn't." Melinda looked back and forth between William and Ayden. "Let's go find everyone and make sure Zack is okay, and then I'll tell all of you the whole story."

William glanced at Ayden, and then narrowed his eyes as his gaze hit Ayden's arm. "We need to have that taken care of, too."

Ayden nodded. He held out his uninjured arm to Melinda. She took it, and looped her other arm through William's. Together they began the trek through the forest into town.

Chapter Forty-Five

Healing

Angel sat on a chair between Ayden's and Zack's hospital beds, holding hands with both of them. The welts were nearly gone from Zack's skin, and only the faintest pink flushed his cheeks. He smiled at her from the pillow where his head rested as they listened to Melinda, perched on a stool in the corner of the room, tell her tale. She'd already spoken to Officer Tolbert and told the story once, with just Angel and her parents present, giving the facts and answering questions with a maturity Angel had never seen in her before.

Now, with everyone's attention, she was the dramatic Melinda Angel knew, despite the hospital room setting, lowering her voice like someone telling a campfire ghost story.

Angel's parents sat in chairs next to Melinda, her dad with his arm around her mom. Sarah stood on the other side of Ayden's bed, chewing her lip, and caressing his shoulder above his injured arm with her fingertips. A Healer had done all he could for Ayden's arm—the injury from the plant was part physical and part magic, he'd said—and it would take time to heal completely. But the scarring would never go away.

Ayden tightened his grip on Angel's hand when Melinda came to the part where she Revealed that Doran was really Dr. Randall in disguise, and

Angel squeezed his hand in reply.

Sarah gasped. "That means the man in prison is Doran!" Her gaze moved from person to person as she said, "Dr. Randall must have turned him invisible so we wouldn't know it was him. This explains so much…"

"Not exactly," Angel said as a disheveled Sir Benjamin appeared in the doorway. She nodded at him, but continued, directing her question to Sarah. "How did Dr. Randall get Doran's Talent?"

Sir Benjamin stepped into the room, his cowboy boots clomping on the slick floor. "I can answer that."

Angel's mom patted the empty chair next to her as she scooted closer to her husband. Sir B tipped his head at her, and a sigh heaved out of him as he sat down.

"There was no exchanging of Talents," he said sullenly. "Dr. Randall made him invisible. Doran regained consciousness right after you left the prison, Sarah, at what must have been the moment of Dr. Randall's death. That was the first clue. We've done what we can so far to determine Doran's level of magic—it's very low, but it's his own. The doctors here are going to run more tests, though."

"You mean he's here?" Angel asked.

"A few doors down, actually." He straightened in his chair and shook his head. "That boy's been through a lot, and I'm telling you right now I believe every word he's said. He's changed. Really regrets what he's done. I may spend most of my time studying critters, but I know people, and that is one remorseful young man."

Angel's mom put her hand on his shoulder. "I suppose that's a good thing, but what does it mean? How did Dr. Randall use Doran's Talent?"

"He didn't," Sir Benjamin said. "Doran could never do more than Disguise small objects. His Talent was based on making someone *think* they're seeing something else—and mind-altering Talents like that are…" He cleared his throat and glanced nervously at her dad. "They're rather delicate. Doran knew his limits well."

He lifted his head again. "Dr. Randall just mimicked Doran's Talent. He somehow…ramped up his Invisibility to a new level and was able to physically alter the image reaching our eyes."

"The pixels!"

Angel turned to Zack, who was grinning triumphantly.

"When I used my Talent, he looked all pixelly, like a low-res image on a computer screen or something. I knew it!"

"You knew he was disguising himself? And you didn't say anything?" Angel tilted her head and narrowed her eyes at him.

"I didn't know he was disguising himself, but I knew he was doing *something.* And I *did* say something, remember? You just thought I said *pixies.*" He rolled his eyes.

Ayden laughed a laugh that ended in a snort. "Pixies? Really?"

Angel's eyes narrowed more as she slowly turned to him. "Not funny."

He smiled innocently, letting go of her hand to touch her cheek.

Sir Benjamin cleared his throat again and Angel pulled her gaze from Ayden. "Funny you should mention computers, Zack," he said. "It seems an investigation of Doran's house showed a room full of computer equipment and other electronics. A generator was running them—with a sound barrier around it so it couldn't be heard by the neighbors."

Angel glanced at Melinda, who was already looking at her with wide eyes. They both shifted in their seats, and Angel noticed Melinda's hand reach for the spot where her cell phone case normally clipped.

Melinda closed her eyes as if steeling herself. "He told me he had all that stuff for his experiments. For research, I guess."

"Why didn't you report that, Melinda?" Sarah asked.

"Honestly, I just didn't think about it. Officer whats-his-name kept asking me about the cave stuff and all. I told him about the notebook, but he said not to worry—that it was a temporary copy. Not sure what that means, but I'm thinking it's like those spy messages that say they're going to self-destruct."

"Something like that," Sir Benjamin said. "It'll just disappear after a certain amount of time. But the electronics were quite important. He was being a bit deceptive when he said he was using them for research. Those ancient things couldn't have gotten him anywhere in that sense, but that doesn't matter. It was the electricity he needed and older electronics use more energy. He sort of recreated the prison cell by running wires and having devices placed around the room. It seems he'd learned to feed off the electricity in his prison cell, fueling his…" Sir B shook his head again. "Not sure what to call it. What he had wasn't real magic anymore."

Again, Angel noticed Melinda's hand twitch nervously by her front jeans pocket.

"That's what he meant," Melinda finally said. She looked straight at Sir

Benjamin. "He said something about his magic changing, and right before he dove onto those freaky plants, he said, *'It all changed. I don't know why, and I can't change it back.'* I thought he was just babbling."

Sir Benjamin nodded.

The rest of the room stayed quiet. Even Zack hadn't said a word since the pixie comment. Angel looked over at Ayden again. He was still so pale, and his eyes were half-closed.

As if reading Angel's thoughts, her mom said, "Well, I think it's time we let these guys get some sleep. It's late for all of us, too." She turned to Sarah. "You'll stay with us tonight."

Sarah nodded.

Everyone gathered belongings and said teary but joyful good-byes.

Sir Benjamin stopped her dad as they descended the front stairs of the hospital. "I can rest easy now, knowing it was never Maggie out there." Her father gave Sir B a hug, clapping him on the back. "Me, too."

Relief washed over Angel as well, knowing she'd never again be haunted by images of Gregor. Tomorrow she would have to tell Kalek, although he already believed it wasn't really Siophra. She sighed. It meant telling him he was right all along.

They took carriages home, Sir B heading off in one and Angel, her parents, Melinda and Sarah in another. Sarah told them along the way about her lab being broken into.

"It must have been Dr. Randall. A few key pieces of equipment were stolen that would have helped him analyze the blood sample I took from you, Melinda. The sample was the only thing taken from the house. If you were right about him experimenting on you that night, it makes sense. He could have used that blood for further tests."

Sarah sighed and pulled her ponytail holder from her hair, loosening tangled blond tresses around her shoulders, then leaned back in the carriage seat. She turned and stared out at the darkness.

"I'm just so glad Ayden is all right." Her voice quivered, but then she turned back and faced Angel directly. "One good thing has come from this, though. Ayden told me he's finally picked a Talent."

Angel smiled. "Yeah, he told me."

"Well," Melinda said, elbowing Angel in the side. "What is it?"

Angel's parents both looked at her silently, expectancy in their tired eyes.

"He didn't tell me *what* it is, just that it's something he hasn't picked before."

Melinda scowled, and her parents gave each other their *here she goes again* looks. Sarah winked.

Had Ayden told Sarah what he'd chosen? A ping of jealousy ran through her. *Why would he tell her and not me?* She glanced at Sarah, who was still looking at her with a sly smile, and she relaxed. Knowing Ayden and Sarah, a surprise was coming…

They climbed out of the carriage in front of Angel's house. The clear night sky was lit by a bright moon and spattering of stars. Her dad paid the driver as the rest of them walked to the front porch. Angel heard Zoe's toenails dancing on the wood floor through the door. Zoe burst through the moment Angel got the knob turned all the way, and nearly barreled Angel over as her whole body wiggled.

Horatio zipped through the door seconds later, chittering as he looped around Angel's head and then settled on her shoulder.

"Hang on, hang on!" she said. "I'll tell you everything in a minute." She reached up and touched his wing gently. "And thanks for bringing Zoe back home for us."

He chittered again and Angel nodded. "Yes, very clever of you leading her to the back so she could come in through the doggie door. I'm sorry she let it swing shut on you, though. At least she opened it again."

He made a sound that resembled a *hmph*, and darted over to Melinda, where he hovered in front of her face. Angel expected Melinda to swat him away, or at least gripe about the "creepy bug," but she just stared at him. A smile crept onto her face and she held out her hand. Horatio fluttered and lowered himself onto her palm.

Okay…

As the group made their way through the door, Angel thought she heard Melinda say to Horatio, "I know it wasn't you, but you have the exact same light." Angel turned when Horatio chittered happily with sounds she didn't recognize—almost as if he were speaking a different language. Maybe she was just so tired she couldn't understand.

Her dad kissed her goodnight before heading straight to his room. Melinda tromped up the stairs to the loft after hugging everyone goodnight—something that left Angel struggling to keep her jaw from dropping. Then her mom led Sarah to Zack's room to make the bed with clean sheets so Sarah could spend the night.

After washing up and changing, Angel climbed into bed. Before she could even pull up the sheets, though, Melinda appeared in her doorway, still dressed in the day's clothes and with one arm behind her back.

"Hey," Angel said.

"Hey."

"Come on in." Angel scooted to make room for Melinda.

Melinda stepped over and sat on the edge of the bed, keeping her arm behind her back. Then she brought her arm around her side revealing the hand mirror. Angel frowned as Melinda held it out.

"Your mom just came to talk to me. She wanted to see what I'd done with this."

Angel kept quiet. What did Melinda expect her to say?

"Anyway, I showed her, and she explained." She inhaled and pushed the mirror toward Angel. "She wanted to tell you, but I asked if I could. It was my Talent that made the mirror work for me. It's supposed to be handed down from mother to daughter, but at the right time. Your mom thinks that might be now."

Angel looked up. Was she serious?

Melinda grabbed Angel's hand and put the mirror's handle into her palm. "See for yourself. I'll leave the room so you know it's not me."

With that, Melinda stood up and left, stopping only for a moment to glance over her shoulder as she stepped through the doorway. Her black hair hung loosely, and her skin looked porcelain in the moonlight that cast the room in pale glow. Melinda's eyes also shone, but it had nothing to do with moonlight.

Angel looked down at the mirror in her hand. Her heart beat harder, and her fingers tingled as she wrapped them around the handle. She bit down on her lip as the glass fogged, and an image formed of her mom as a girl, maybe thirteen years old.

Her dad stood behind her mom, the same age but so much taller already. Her mom reached toward a painting of a flower, eyes wide and hand trembling. Her fingertips touched the painting's surface, and then disappeared into the canvas. Her father smiled and spoke. There was no sound, but Angel could tell he was urging her mom on.

Her mom pulled her hand from the painting, her fingers gripping the flower. Angel could read her father's lips, but in her mind she heard Melinda's voice, as he said, "I told you, didn't I?"

Chapter Forty-Six

Kalek's Story

Melinda was the first one up, and she curled on the couch with her notebook.

Angel sat beside her. She leaned forward, reaching with long arms. "Please! Just let me read one poem. Just *one*…"

"No…not yet." Melinda hugged the notebook to her chest. "Besides, I'm not working on poems. I had an idea for a short story, and it's just a rough draft right now."

Angel crossed her arms and pouted, and Melinda laughed. She remembered that same expression on Angel's face when they were little girls. This morning felt more like those days than she could believe. It must have for Angel as well, because it only took a moment for Angel's pout to turn into the sappy, nostalgic smile she'd sported half the morning. This time, it continued into a giggle fit.

When their laughter finally quieted, Caryn's voice carried from the kitchen. "Breakfast is almost ready! Five minutes!"

Melinda's stomach growled on cue, and Angel giggled again. Melinda swatted her with the notebook.

"Hey, if you won't let me read it, you can at least not *hit* me with it." Angel rubbed her arm as if it hurt, but her smile belied it. She tilted her head and looked at Melinda. "Notebook…hm…I wonder if the other one disappeared yet like Sir B said it would."

Before Melinda could answer Angel jumped off the bed and dashed toward the hallway. Moments later she was back, shaking her head.

"It's gone."

"I guess that's actually pretty cool." Melinda realized as she said it that she was truly glad the notebook was gone. Seeing her dad's handwriting like that, knowing who he'd been….

Knowing *what* he'd been….

It was too much. Eventually she'd work on dealing with all that, but for now she just wanted to concentrate on figuring out her life. She'd thought about it half the night, and before falling asleep she decided she'd tell her mom she was ready to move out and stay on the island permanently. If her mom said *no*, she'd be eighteen soon enough. It'd be worth it to wait a few months and do it right.

A knock on the front door snapped her out of her thoughts. She glanced over at Angel, who shrugged, stood up and walked to the door.

Melinda shifted on the couch for a better view as the door eased open.

Kalek.

He stepped into the room and Angel closed the door behind him. Hard. Then she moved in front of him and crossed her arms. There was no trace of the playful pout she'd used with Melinda.

"We're about to have breakfast and then head to the hospital to see Zack and Ayden. They're fine, by the way. Thanks for asking." Angel's voice was stone.

Melinda blinked and then stared.

"I haven't had a chance to ask *anything*, Angel." Kalek's normally smooth voice ground out hoarse. He ran his hand through his curls, exposing the point of his ear. His dark eyes were sunken and glazed as if he hadn't slept all night.

Melinda jumped up from the couch. "Yeah, girl, what's your damage? He looks completely wiped out."

He craned his head, catlike, and looked at her curiously. "Uh, thanks…" Then he turned back to Angel. "He died last night."

Angel's jaw worked as if she was trying to speak, but nothing came out. Finally, voice squeaking, she said, "Your father?"

Kalek nodded.

"Oh, Kalek, I'm sorry!" Angel threw her arms around his shoulders and he slipped one arm around her waist, peeking over her shoulder at Melinda. The look he gave Melinda was like he was seeing her for the first time.

Energy surged through her, like the day at the Temple, like the moment in the cave when she'd Revealed Dr. Randall. She sensed nervousness in Kalek. And fear.

Of her?

She also sensed that he was somehow drawn to her…and something else…

Pity.

Melinda's heartbeat skipped. She looked down at the floor and forced herself to pull back her magic.

Angel let go and stepped back, then grabbed Kalek's arm. "I'm so, so sorry. I thought you just bailed on us last night, and so much…I had no idea…" She inhaled as tears welled in her eyes and spilled over her lids. "Kalek, what happened?"

Caryn appeared in the doorway and walked over to them. She put a gentle hand on Kalek's shoulder. "I'm sorry." She slid her arms around him and hugged him. "Come on. Sarah and William are already at the table. I'll set another place. You can tell us all at once, okay?"

Kalek smiled weakly and nodded, and then followed her into the kitchen. Angel and Melinda joined them at the table as Caryn dished out pancakes.

"The night Melinda was stung," Kalek said, "I sensed someone in the room. I heard little noises no one else would be able to hear. Tiny shifts of weight and the slightest movement. The front door had been left open, and I felt someone leave during all the chaos of Ayden doing his thing."

He sighed, eyes glazing as he poked his fork around his plate without taking a bite. "I ran out after him. When I got to the road in front of the house, there was a shadow, and then it shifted into Siophra."

"Kalek," William said, "there's something we need—"

Kalek held his hand up and shook his head. "I already know. It wasn't really her. It was Doran. He took off into the forest and I followed. He went straight to my house. I don't know how he stayed ahead of me. Only the Elven can move like that."

Melinda and Angel looked at each other, and noticed Caryn, William and Sarah doing the same. None of them said anything. There would be time to fill him in when he finished his story.

"We got to my house and he somehow got past everything, even the dogs. I was still at the edge of the yard when he opened the front door as if it were unlocked and waiting. When I made it all the way inside, he was already there—in my parents' room."

He inhaled and ran his hand through his hair again. Then he looked up, his eyes sharp and clear. "Mother completely lost it, and then fainted. Father started convulsing and trying to talk, but it came out all garbled. I'm pretty sure it was another stroke. I ran to his side as Doran took off. I wanted to go after him, but Father grabbed my arm."

Tears glistened in Kalek's eyes and Melinda held her breath.

"I stayed with him most of the night. I completely lost track of time as I talked to him, and he listened. I told him about *Mori Zede*. He even let me sing to him…"

Kalek's forearm tensed as he squeezed the fork in his hand.

"Finally, he said something I could understand, although he was speaking in the old language. He made me learn some as a child even though I told him I'd never need it." Kalek paused and one corner of his mouth lifted in a sad smile. "He said the words for *I believe*. Then he took a breath—and called out like he was calling someone's name. But the word he said wasn't a name, it was *Zorar*. And then his eyes widened, and he smiled…and then..." He exhaled.

Angel reached across the table and touched his hand. "What does *Zorar* mean?"

He turned to her, but his eyes were aimed at Melinda. "It's the Elven word for *Light*."

Melinda's fork slipped from her hand. Kalek's eyebrow arced. Without thinking, Melinda felt her Talent take hold. She sensed the same nervousness in him that she had before, and the same curiosity. She also sensed that he was holding something, back, something he didn't want the others to know about.

She heard Angel talking, something about being happy that Kalek's father finally believed, but it sounded muffled and far away. Then dishes clattered and Melinda looked up to find Angel, Caryn, and Sarah clearing the table. Melinda grabbed her plate and stood as William told Kalek about Doran really being Dr. Randall.

Melinda watched Angel, whose hands flittered like butterflies as she waved stacks of plates into the cabinets while Caryn swept the last corner of the floor and Sarah wiped down the kitchen counter. She concentrated on Angel. Love poured out from her friend—for Zack and, differently, for Ayden. The sensation exactly matched the vibes Ayden sent out. They were ridiculously perfect for each other.

Finally, William stood. "Guess it's time we all head off to visit the boys."

Angel all but *squee-ed* as she closed the cabinet doors with a final wave of her hand.

Melinda stifled a laugh and leaned against the counter to hang the dish towel on the hook over the sink.

She felt the warmth of someone standing next to her. She turned and nearly choked when she saw Kalek. Wasn't he just sitting on the other side of the room?

Voice barely a whisper, he leaned in. "Can you stay here while they go? Just for a while. I can take you later…"

She dug her nails into her palms when she realized she was gawking.

"Uh, um, yeah. I guess."

Kalek tipped his head once, then walked over and said something to William that Melinda couldn't hear. William looked over his glasses at her, then nodded.

Angel, Caryn and Sarah were already standing in the kitchen doorway. William joined them and shuffled them out. Melinda heard him say, "She'll be there later," as they walked away. Their footsteps sounded for a few more seconds, then the opening and closing of the front door.

Melinda looked at Kalek. The room felt incredibly empty, and yet suddenly too small. She hooked her fingers on the belt loops of her jeans.

Kalek stepped over to her and glanced down at her arm. He smiled.

"Nice tat."

Melinda took a step back, sudden rage throttling her heart. "Are you *serious*? You asked me to stay so you can tease me about my *poser* tattoo?"

"Whoa, whoa! No!" He held his hands up in surrender. "What are you talking about?"

Melinda crossed her arms and dug her boots into the floor. "I heard you, at the carnival."

Kalek laughed as he lowered his arms. "Ah. I see. No, no, no. I say that to him all the time." His smile softened. "The feather tats are wicked cool." He stepped forward. "You picked a particularly awesome one."

"For real?"

"Yes. I'm sorry if you thought—I didn't even know you got one 'til I saw it just now or I wouldn't have said that in front of you."

Melinda kept her arms crossed, but shifted her weight to one leg. "Why would that stop you? You haven't let anything else stop you from dissing me at every turn."

He bobbed his head and aimed a long finger at her. "You are right. One reason I asked you to stay here is so I can apologize for that."

A faint haze appeared around him as Melinda focused on his words. *He really means it.*

But he's still afraid of something.

He's still afraid of me.

"You didn't like me because I didn't have magic."

He shook his head. His eyes shadowed again. "No, not true. I think everyone has the potential for magic if they open their hearts to it. What I don't like is when someone shows total disrespect for it."

"You're still upset about the pine needles?"

She gave him no chance to reply, reaching into her pocket and pulling out the needles she'd picked the day she arrived on the island. "Here, take 'em back."

He glanced down at her hand and then lifted his eyes, looking into her with such an intensity she found herself taking a step back. The sunlight streaming into the window played in his curls and lit his face, highlighting perfectly formed features.

"You've been carrying that around this whole time?"

She nodded.

"Listen," he said as he stepped over and leaned against the counter, "I didn't know what to make of you when we first met. You looked at everything so hatefully, and all you did was complain."

Melinda fought the urge to say, "*Yeah, because all you did was complain about me.*"

He cleared his throat. "And knowing who…I mean your…"

"My father."

"Yeah. But then you levitated that mirror. And I thought, 'Wow, she does have magic!'"

"You still kept treating me like dirt after that."

"I know. But you didn't experience my music. And…I thought you took the notebooks, like Angel said. I thought maybe you were like him."

"I'm not." She shoved down the anger that surged in her and refused to say more. She would *not* get off on that tangent.

He said, barely more than a whisper, "I know that, too."

After a deep breath, she said, "So, now what? You find out I have magic—a Talent even—and we're all hunky-dory again?"

He straightened back up and stepped closer. Melinda's heart thudded against her ribs.

"I'm happy to hear you have magic. Really, I am. But it's a lot more than that. You've opened your heart. Now you need to lock it."

"What?"

"You've opened your heart, and let the magic in. Now you need to decide whether you want to keep it—lock it in your heart for good—or leave the door open and risk letting something else come in and take its place."

"I don't understand."

He gazed down and her, and then he lifted his hand. Slowly, he moved it toward her, and gently ran a finger along her jaw.

She barely felt his fingers there, but electricity shot through her and the floor shifted under her feet.

Then he seemed to realize what he'd done and dropped his hand to his side. His lower lip tucked under the edge of his teeth for a second. "I know you don't. But I can help you with that."

Melinda's cheek tingled where his fingers had touched. Was he for real? Was he *flirting*? Was she suddenly hot to him because she had magic and she was all new to everything and he figured she was a sure thing?

She narrowed her eyes and remembered the haze she'd seen and the sensations she picked up. They were powerful and sure. *No, this is something way different.*

"Okay, so tell me."

"First, answer a question for me. Did you see something last night? A light?"

Melinda swallowed, but her voice came out hoarse. "Yes."

"I didn't tell the others, because, well…I don't know. But my father said something else right before he died. Something about a dark girl who had seen the *Zorar*, the Light. When you dropped your fork, I knew he was talking about you. He told me I was supposed to take you 'back' to the

Temple."

"But I've been to the Temple."

"I know. I guess that's why he said 'back'—but it seemed like something more." He leaned toward her. "So, you ready?"

"To go to the Temple? Now? Don't you need to go back to your family?"

"There's time for that." He held out his hand. "Come on."

Melinda took his hand, and they walked, fingers entwined, out the back door and through the forest. She kept expecting him to drop her hand, but he held on. It reminded her of Doran guiding her back to his workroom, but that hadn't sent electricity running through her like Kalek's touch did.

Why is he doing this?

Kalek talked nonstop for the first half of the walk. He told her about his childhood and his first time picking up a guitar. He asked Melinda about her childhood. But the thought of those days twisted her stomach. Instead she told him what Angel was like when they were friends before she moved away.

"She hasn't changed much, eh?" Kalek said as they reached the clearing.

Melinda laughed. "Not really."

The Temple shone brilliant white in the sunlight, towering even taller than Melinda remembered. The colored glass sent jagged shapes dancing on the walls. The air brushed by in a soft breeze that rustled the flowers peppering the clearing.

Kalek released her hand, and her skin felt his absence almost painfully. How had they gone so quickly from borderline enemies to her feeling like their hands had been formed to hold each other?

She followed him up the Temple steps and somehow was not surprised to find Kalek's guitar at the top leaning against the stone wall where there had once been a door.

Kalek stared at the guitar as if it were a ghost.

"How did that get here?"

She stepped up next to him. "You didn't leave it here?"

"No…" He leaned over and picked it up, then traced the edge of the sleek, black curve. "It's Phoebe, alright." He shrugged the strap over his shoulder and ran his fingers over the strings as he looked at her. "I guess that means I'm supposed to play for you."

His eyes gleamed, and he gazed at her with a sideways grin.

"What?" She shifted her weight, but couldn't break her stare.

"I think I understand now. *Back* to the Temple. Yep."

Huh? She shrugged. "Whatever you say."

"You ready?"

"I guess so." The words slipped out easily, but her heart thudded against her ribs. *Ready for what?*

He nodded to the broken columns on the edge of the stairs. "Might want to sit for this. It's gonna be a ride."

Melinda stepped over and found a smooth, flat spot on a stump of a column. She sat and crossed her ankles, then rubbed her palms on her jeans. "Go for it."

Silence hung in the air as Kalek's eyes closed and his hands took position on the guitar. Then he spoke, his voice carrying on the breeze like a whisper.

"Okay…story time."

Acknowledgments

Again, I would not have gotten through this process without the support of my family and friends. I love you and thank you for putting up with me!

Writing *Seeking Unseen* was such a different experience from writing *Finding Angel*, and I'd like to thank my awesome editors, Diane Graham and Robynn Tolbert, for being ruthless. It is what I needed, and you knew it, and you loved me and my book enough to follow through.

Thank you to Keven and DeAnna Newsome for turning my cover art concept and drawings into even more than I imagined.

Thank you to my beta-readers who gave their valuable input: Heather Titus, Kessie Carroll, Zoe Rayne, Katie Patchell, Kaylee Williams, and Priscilla Graham.

And, of course, thank you to my dear Space Kiwi publisher, Grace Bridges, whose faith in my writing means so much.

Special thanks to the Mystery Poet who composed, in real life, the poem written by Melinda in this story. You kept your identity secret all those years ago when you asked my friend to give me the poem, so I cannot properly credit you other than this.

Kat Heckenbach spent her childhood with pencil and sketchbook in hand, knowing she wanted to be an artist when she grew up—so naturally she graduated college with a degree in biology, went on to teach math, and now homeschools her two children while writing. Her fiction ranges from light-hearted fantasy to dark and disturbing, with multiple stories published online and in print. *Seeking Unseen* is her second novel, and the sequel to *Finding Angel.*

www.katheckenbach.com

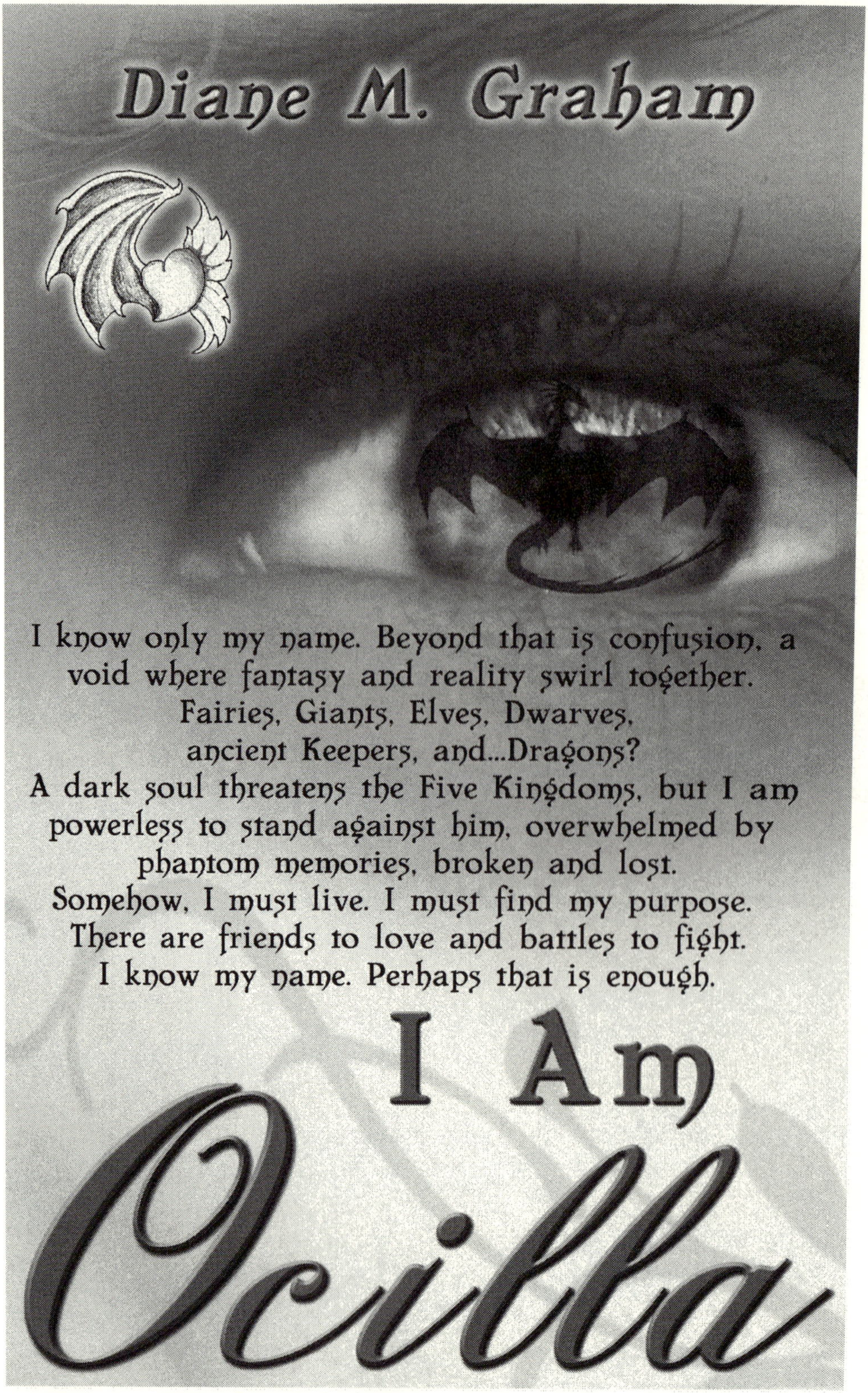
Diane M. Graham
I know only my name. Beyond that is confusion, a void where fantasy and reality swirl together.
Fairies, Giants, Elves, Dwarves, ancient Keepers, and...Dragons?
A dark soul threatens the Five Kingdoms, but I am powerless to stand against him, overwhelmed by phantom memories, broken and lost.
Somehow, I must live. I must find my purpose.
There are friends to love and battles to fight.
I know my name. Perhaps that is enough.
I Am
Ocilla

AVENIR ECLECTIA
VOLUME 1
Come with us on a journey to a planet the universe forgot.
Space stations...moon miners... undersea angels... an unstable home.
Multi-Author Mosaic Microfiction from the online shared-world project.
GRACE BRIDGES
JEFF CARTER
JEFF CHAPMAN
FRANK CREED
PAULINE CREEDEN
KARINA FABIAN
JOSEPH H. FICOR
KAT HECKENBACH
HOLLY HEISEY
GREG MITCHELL
KEVEN NEWSOME
TRAVIS PERRY
MARY RUTH PURSSELLEY
J. L. ROWAN
WALT STAPLES
H. A. TITUS
FRED WARREN
EDITED BY GRACE BRIDGES AND TRAVIS PERRY
Splashdown Books 2012

86646787R00171

Made in the USA
Columbia, SC
17 January 2018